DREAMER

BY
D.S. FISICHELLA

26   25   24   23   22   21   8   7   6   5   4   3   2   1

DREAMER
Copyright ©2021 D.S. Fisichella

All scripture taken from The ESV® Bible (The Holy Bible, English Standard Version®). ESV® Text Edition: 2016. Copyright © 2001 by Crossway, a publishing ministry of Good News Publishers. The ESV® text has been reproduced in cooperation with and by permission of Good News Publishers. Unauthorized reproduction of this publication is prohibited. All rights reserved.

All Rights Reserved. Except as permitted under the U.S. Copyright Act of 1976, no part of this publication may be reproduced, distributed, or transmitted in any form by any means, or stored in a database or retrieval system, without the prior written permission of the author and/or publisher.

Published by:
Barefoot Publishing

www.publishbarefoot.com

Cover Design by Nicholas Fisichella

Photography by Katherine Adcock Photography

Library of Congress Cataloging-in-Publication Data:

ISBN: 978-1-63972-657-8 Perfect Bound

Printed in the United States

Table of Contents

Acknowledgements vii
Chapter 1 1
Chapter 2 12
Chapter 3 20
Chapter 4 30
Chapter 5 35
Chapter 6 40
Chapter 7 47
Chapter 8 56
Chapter 9 65
Chapter 10 73
Chapter 11 86
Chapter 12 92
Chapter 13 105
Chapter 14 119
Chapter 15 131
Chapter 16 134
Chapter 17 144
Chapter 18 153
Chapter 19 162
Chapter 20 169
Chapter 21 178
Chapter 22 186
Chapter 23 196
Chapter 24 207
Chapter 25 215

To Jesus, the Author of Life who wrote my story and gave me this one to share.

For my husband Nick, for loving me at my worst, cheering me on at my best, and holding my hand every step in between.

For Agi, Soli and Selah:
Thanks for teaching me about unconditional love.

For the teens of Pinellas Park, FL and around the world:
May you never forget that no matter what life throws your way, God sees you, He loves You, and if you seek Him, He will never leave you.

In Memory of Monica Araya

2 Corinthians 5:17

FOREWORD

    I started doing podcasting as an outlet to tell my story. I knew I had many things I wanted to say about the modern church and the direction we, as the Body of Christ, were headed as we navigated this fallen world. The value of having a voice in a crowded field such as podcasting and blogging outweighed the drawbacks of being lost in that field. I firmly believe and passionately proclaim the value of sharing the Word of God with anyone who will listen by any means possible. So in early 2021, when my email inbox dinged with an interview request for the podcast I was currently hosting, I had no problem saying yes.

    In preparation for the show, I was advanced a first edition copy of Dreamer. As soon as I began reading, I knew I was in for a different type of interview than any I had done before.

    While emotion is certainly part of most creatives' output, there was an indescribable current of joy, bliss, and anguish all jumping off the pages I was reading. I knew that I had to dig deeper into the mind of the one who wrote the words I was taking in. I have to say I was not disappointed when the first interview occurred. Yes, I said first, because I believed in the material contained within these pages so much that when D.S. reached out to me again upon Dreamer's release to help with the promotion, I was more than happy to give her the platform of my show again - something I had never done before.

    You might ask what makes what you are about to read so powerful? We live in a world today where those who are in middle and high school are bombarded with one of two core philosophies.

    The first is that God is dead, God is not real, and God is unimportant. Schools aggressively continue to cast aside the notion of any moral center and instead are taking the place of both the family unit and the church. The second core philosophy is growing in churches across the nation and the world – the thought that we must shelter our young from the realities of sin and the world. It is the idea of simply putting our heads in the sand and pretending these evils of the world do not exist.

    Dreamer is an important work because it confronts both philosophies head on. D.S. is brave enough to challenge the church to look at real world issues that the youth of today are facing while at the same time making it be known the only real answer to facing these problems is through God's Word.

But understand that Dreamer is not just for those who are young. While it may be called a "young adult novel," it is anything but this. Personally, this book made me examine my life, both before I came to know Christ and after (I accepted Jesus as my Savior in September of 2013).

If you are someone more mature in age, this book will challenge you to look at the relationships you have and ask important questions like 'Is this person helping me grow in my walk with Christ?", "Can I look past the things this person may have done in their past?" and "Can I forgive myself for the wrongs I believe I have done to others?"

These are all heavy questions even the most learned theologians wrestle with, and here, in these pages, D.S. manages to bring a practical sensibility to these probing inquiries.

There is a unique talent at work in these pages. As you are about to embark on this journey to The Spot with Elleni, Julian and the rest of the crew in these pages, I want to encourage you to highlight, make notes and soak in the colorful narrative of Dreamer.

This is a book that is written to be returned to more than once. You will see many pieces of yourself in these characters, and that is what compelling literature does. It brings out both the best and the worst in us so that we can learn and grow, both in those relationships we have with each other, and most importantly in our relationship with our Savior.

"Finally, brothers, whatever is true, whatever is honorable, whatever is just, whatever is pure, whatever is lovely, whatever is commendable, if there is any excellence, if there is anything worthy of praise, think about these things."
Philippians 4:8

Patrick Lewis

www.patrickryanlewis.com

A Word From the Author

I remember a time when I said to God that if only five people would read DREAMER and be edified, I would be more than happy. We've come a long way. As an indie author, I didn't know how I would get the word out about my book, but through social media, the support of friends and lots of prayer, we managed to hit the Amazon Bestseller's List two times within a single year. Only God could do such a thing. The themes within these pages are dear to my heart. I am asked all the time if this story is based on my life. The short answer is no. The events, the backstory, and the specific struggles of each character are fictional, with that said, Elleni Salgado and I have a lot in common. I too was once a young Christian that doubted her freedom in Christ because of my strongholds, my mental health issues, and the trauma I endured. You'll learn also that Julian's character is loosely based on someone who is very dear to me. There are other characters that are inspired by real people but... well, enough lines have been blurred between fact and fiction to keep you guessing. **After all, fiction does not have to be fake.** It is my prayer, dear Dreamer, that you will find yourself in these pages. May this book inspire you to look outside of yourself and seek the face of the One who is but a whisper (or a dream) away.

Chapter 1

"For God speaks in one way, and in two, though man does not perceive it. In a dream, in a vision of the night, when deep sleep falls on men, while they slumber on their beds, then he opens the ears of men and terrifies them with warnings."
Job 33:14-16

4 Years Earlier

I'd never in my life felt the urge to run until the night of my thirteenth birthday. I reeked of vomit and alcohol, the stink threatening to choke me out if my sobs didn't do the job first.

The sun had dipped under the horizon, leaving a thick layer of humidity behind, but what I remember most was the way the pensive moon ruled the sky that night, like the eye of God reminding me I could never hide from Him.

Pain tore through my muscles but I ignored it, focusing instead on the rhythm of my bare feet across the pavement, my wedge heels thumping against each other as they swung back and forth in my grip. One more turn, three more houses, and I'd reached my destination.

I used a paint can as a stepping stool, and slid the window upward, letting my heels hit the carpet with a muted *thud* before hoisting myself through. A horde of stuffed animals scattered across my quilt as I tumbled clumsily onto my bed. There, in the darkness, it was easy to clench my eyes shut and pretend none of this was really happening, but eventually, I slid the window back down and closed the latch with trembling blood-stained hands.

A voice mocked from somewhere in my mind.

As if a little latch could keep out the mess you've left behind. My cheeks flushed as I hugged my knees to my chest, hot tears starting up fresh. *Elleni Salgado, what have you done?*

Present Day

God. Music. Exercise.

That was my formula for getting through those really hard days.

Exercise always seemed to help my mood. Daniel was the first to suggest I try it. It had been during a time when my family was willing to try anything to get me out of my room. I hated it, but Daniel started becoming somewhat of an exercise nut around that time, trying to build muscle for his martial arts training. I'd started to eat regularly again, but I wanted to take advantage of the weight I'd already lost and keep it off, only with healthier habits. Even with my lifestyle changes, nothing mattered until I met God.

When I fell apart, He was the one that put the pieces together. But something they don't tell you about being a Christian? It doesn't automatically make your problems go away. Jesus was a man of sorrows… At least I wasn't alone in that.

Shortly after meeting God for the first time, He gave me my second most effective way to cope. Through music. Most practically, music included a tempo, something that rarely changed and always made mathematical sense, constant and solid in a world full of so much uncertainty and chaos. Music was sound and emotion. It had a way of bringing out the true thoughts and intentions of my heart. At times I wouldn't even know what was keeping me down until I started writing a new melody or new lyrics, and then, *voila*, there it was. The root of the problem.

Every other time, I should say, except now.

"Focus, Elleni," I muttered to myself. "You can do this."

I gripped my pen tighter, closed my eyes and imagined a symphony trickling from somewhere in my mind. The chill of it was on my neck. The tension in my shoulders. The rush down my arm. The power in my fingertips.

Dreamer

If only the music could flow to my pen, through the ink.
Help me, Lord. The well is dry.
I put my pen down, slumped back against my pillows with a groan, and shook my charm bracelet in another attempt to clear my mind. The turquoise beads and single charm gleamed merrily in the sunlight coming through my curtains.
'Forever,' it read.
I looked up at my ceiling, tiny splatters of neon green still lingered around the trim. It had been three years since I'd convinced Daniel to switch bedrooms with me. Even after several coats of eggshell, there was no masking the memory of his pre-teen obsession with the *Ninja Turtles*.
The kick-start of a neighbor's leaf blower caused a little bird to abandon her perch near my open window. Spiky red Woodland Bromeliads swayed lazily in the breeze from our garden, more poetic and beautiful than anything I'd been able to come up with all afternoon.
Before I had music, I had Monica. She was my best friend. I owed my love of music to her. It was something inexplicable that we shared, even before we were even old enough to need a passion to drive us. We shared our birthday, July 7th, but she was older than me by a year — maybe that's why I followed in her footsteps. Or maybe, I would have found music on my own without her… that's something I would never know because as far back as I could remember, my friendship with Monica was synonymous with melody.
My obsession had always been with the piano, which, of course, Monica took to so naturally, but once she'd mastered sight-reading and could play well, she'd set her heart on the acoustic guitar. The first time she'd mentioned her desire to play guitar, I'd just been dropped over at her house to find her finishing up her daily practice. I let myself in through the back door that led to the kitchen, as was our common practice. Mrs. Josephs, Monica's mom, was stirring a pitcher of lemonade when she heard the jingle of the door and turned to find me standing there. She'd motioned with one finger to her lips before planting a kiss on my head and pouring me a glass. She knew I lived for her lemonade. I followed the sound of music to the Josephs' living room. Monica sat at the piano, her back straight as a ruler, her right foot on the sustain pedal, her eyes never leaving the page. Her blonde hair was styled in a fishtail braid. It had been a simple tune, but I was fascinated by the way her hands danced happily over the keys with

adult-like assurance and finesse, which was odd considering her fingernails were painted metallic blue and already starting to chip. She finished the piece perfectly. Mrs. Josephs and I clapped. Monica beamed widely, seeing me for the first time.

"I didn't hear you come in," she said. "How long have you been standing there?"

"I just got here," I said, taking a seat on the couch. "Mo, you keep getting better and better. I wish my parents could afford to put me in piano lessons."

Mrs. Josephs emerged from the kitchen, the second glass of lemonade in hand. "You should ask Brother Steve for lessons," she said to me, "he may do it for free." She handed the glass to her daughter who then turned to me excitedly.

"Yeah, Leni. You know Brother Steve, right? The church music director?"

"I think so," I said, looking down at my already half-empty glass. "But I'd feel weird asking him. We've never really talked before."

Monica took the seat next to me. "I'll go with you. I think I'm ready to start on a new instrument myself."

My eyebrows shot up. "A new one? But you love to play the piano!"

"I *do*, but what I want to play now is the guitar. Besides, guitars are way more portable. Can you imagine me trying to carry this huge thing on my back to a gig?"

I giggled.

Something flickered in her eyes as she turned back to me, a gentle firmness in her voice. "Elleni?"

"Yeah?" I asked, my smile fading.

"Please promise me that if you ever get a guitar you will learn how to play it. That way, even if I never learn, one of us will." She paused. "Please, for me."

The request seemed odd to me at the time, but I wrapped my pinkie finger around hers, a gesture of sealing the deal.

"Okay, Monica, I promise."

I was eleven, she was twelve.

Now, I strummed my fingers over the strings of my guitar, a lump in my throat because of the memory.

Strum, strum.

Did she know?

Dreamer

Strum, strum.
How could she?
Crash!
I jumped, startled by the ear-shattering sound.
"I'm okay!" Mami declared.

With my heart pounding, I left my blank notebook behind as I headed across the house to the racket. I stiffened when I found myself standing in a large puddle, my socks saturated as the mess came into view. My thoughts of Monica slowly slipped into the back of my mind, like so many other things.

My mother sported her usual tank top, shorts, and *'chancletas'* (flip-flops that double as a boomerang for Latina mothers), as she pranced around the chaos, sweeping up what was left of our fishbowl. Scattered about the sea of multicolored pebbles were plastic palm trees and a miniature treasure chest. I tried to keep judgment out of my voice.

"Mami, where is Betta Bob?"

She stopped sweeping long enough to shoot me a funny look. "Fish Heaven?" she offered with a mild accent. I groaned and headed for the hallway closet, reappearing a moment later with a mop and bucket in my hands. If only all of life was this simple: a quick sweep of the disarray and then something to soak up what's leftover. She plucked the little fish out of the dustpan and laid him on the counter using a square white napkin as his bed.

"What was the cause of death this time?" I asked, leaning down to examine Bob's tropical fins. His eyes were open wide, his mouth agape. I had a flashback to our time at the pet shop, how careful I'd been to pick out a plump-looking fellow, an older fish who, no matter how long he'd survive under our 'care' would be happy just to be out of that awful fluorescent environment and the tiny bowl they'd kept him in.

He seemed happy when we brought him home only a month ago.

"I changed his water while my avocado face mask dried. By the time I washed it off in the bathroom and came back into the kitchen, he was floating belly up. I think he died from shock."

"You always kill our fish when changing their water. The same thing happened to Betta Bella and Betta Bert. By now you could be tried for animal abuse."

My mother mimicked me wordlessly, splashing lemon-scented floor cleaner near my feet. I took a step back just as my brother came up beside me.

"Mom, another one?" he said incredulously. Daniel was my twin, but his complexion was lighter than mine, a fact that meant he burned more easily under the sun. I spotted the beginnings of a farmer's tan on his arm. We shared the same color of hair and eyes, but that's where our physical similarities ended. Still, we had the same sense of humor. "Do you realize that after three murders you're considered a serial killer?" he asked.

I nodded. "Death by water change can be her M.O."

Mami continued her task with unnecessary force, her knuckles turning white around the handle.

Daniel and I exchanged a smirk. He cleared his throat, resting his shoulder casually against the wall. "If PETA knew about the other Bettas I think they would dub her 'The Aquatic Assassin.'" He moved his hands in front of his face as if to frame the title in the air.

"It's catchy. They'll make documentaries about her." We pretended not to notice the daggers in her eyes.

"She's the cautionary tale fish tell their babies to keep them from wandering off too far," Daniel continued.

"Yep. Thanks to her, Nemo never got lost in the first place."

"*Ay, ya!*" Mami slammed the mop back into its bucket. "Two against one is not fair."

Without looking at each other, Daniel and I high-fived.

"Alright, to the bathroom," Mami said, all business-like. "Daniel, find something to carry him in. Elleni, you're in charge of the music."

I sighed. "Here we go again."

Mami wasn't a tree hugger, but she saw life as a miracle, and the loss of it, a result of the fall of man in the Garden of Eden.

"If we had not sinned," she told me when I was just a little girl sitting on her lap, my pigtails resting on my shoulders as I peered at the Bible picture book in her hands, "there would be no death and no suffering. The world would be perfect, just like our Heavenly Father intended." She kissed the top of my head. "But then we went and messed it up. *Tontos!*"

Back in my bedroom, I tossed my soggy socks into the laundry basket before helping myself to a fresh pair. I was almost out the door when I remembered I was in charge of the music. I doubled back to the bottom

Dreamer

drawer of my dresser, which had a sticky note on it labeled "Miscellaneous." From it, I produced a rosy recorder flute.

Once in the bathroom, I tried not to gawk at my twin who stood gravely under the showerhead having made a wardrobe change of his own. He'd replaced his tank with a tuxedo button-up, donned a pair of slacks and slicked his hair back with gel. In his hand lay an open box of matches, and inside, small and very dead, lay Betta Bob.

At the sight of me in my colorful stockings, Daniel shook his head in disgust. "Have you no *shame*?"

"Funny. I was getting ready to ask why you were standing in our bathtub wearing a *bowtie*."

"You know, dear sister, there's only a one letter difference between 'huh' and 'duh!'"

My mother cleared her throat from behind me, having changed into a black dress and heels. I'd missed the memo.

I stepped aside to let her through.

My brother exclaimed, "*Finally,* a woman with class. Mom, are you sure that this peasant girl and I hail from the same birth canal?"

"She had us through a C-section, you dope."

"Hush you two. It's time to get the ceremony started." I humored my mom with a solemn verse of "Amazing Grace." After a moment of silence, she spoke. "When explaining anything of great measure, we refer to it as an ocean," she began. "When a friend is broken-hearted, we say, 'There are plenty of fish in the sea.'"

I slapped the palm of my hand against my face.

"You, Betta Bob, were unique. Your blink-less eyes were open to the world around you. A small world. A plastic world. A fake world."

It was then that Papi walked through the front door, stomping out his shoes on the welcome mat. He sported a blue baseball cap and a sweaty grey shirt over cargo shorts. When he saw me peeking out of the bathroom and heard my mom's words of valediction, he joined us. I waited for his reaction to the ridiculous spectacle, but upon taking in the scene in front of him, he only arched an eyebrow, his lips a straight line.

"Does anybody else want to say a few words?" Mami asked.

"I would like to say something," Daniel said as he handed the little fish to my mother and produced a piece of paper from his slacks. It was typed up. They must have started funeral preparations right after the passing of Bert.

"Betta Robert, or, 'Bob' as he was known to his owners, was bred into captivity. He never tasted the open waters, and yet, ironically, it was that same liquid substance, that same lifeline, that brought his life to an end. Betta Bob, rest in your fishy paradise. Betta Bob, you will be missed."

Mami plucked the fish out of the matchbox, grimly placing him on the surface of the clean toilet water before producing a handful of glitter from somewhere in her dress.

"Where did you—"

"Shhh!" She sprinkled the glitter around Betta Bob with a flourish and finished the service with a *flush*.

My dad took one last look at the sparkly little voyager swirling down the porcelain portal, another look at my recorder, and finally, glanced past us to the kitchen, where the countertop now had space once occupied by the fishbowl.

"Not again," he said, shaking his head and moving toward his seat at the kitchen table.

I couldn't help it. I burst out laughing.

"Wow, you guys put A LOT of thought into that. I'm impressed."

"We've gotten better since Betta Bertrand, aka, Bert," Daniel said as he made the sign of the cross with his fingers. "May he rest in peace."

Mami washed her hands as I followed my dad into the kitchen area, only to find him rubbing his temples and talking to God in Spanish.

"Betta Bob's soul is the last soul we're sending to Fish Heaven, Lord. I won't allow another under this roof."

"Yeah, good luck with that!" called Daniel as he headed to his bedroom.

I ruffled Papi's sweaty salt-and-pepper hair on my way to the counter. The smell of Costa Rican coffee filled the kitchen over the gargle of the coffee maker. I pressed the button on the side to turn it off, reaching for his favorite mug.

Mami emerged from the bathroom. "Don't blame me, Marcos. God's the one that made me with two left feet. Plus, didn't He say we would have dominion over the beasts of the field and the fish of the sea?"

I poured dad's coffee, struggling to keep a straight face.

He replied, "*Si*, Marta. But not so that you can enslave them in a bowl and then kill them without eating them. You kill for sport, *Mujer*!"

Dreamer

"That little thing didn't have enough meat for a fish stick! Elleni, give your *padre* his coffee, he's going crazy."

"Here you go," I said, placing the mug in front of him.

Papi grumbled his thanks, touching the beverage to his lips. I watched as the drink took its effect, relaxing my grumpy dad at last.

Back in my bedroom I got tired of the barren college-ruled paper glaring at me and slammed the notebook cover shut before stepping into my pink *Converse* and grabbing my headphones off my desk on the way out the front door.

My favorite time during summers in Florida was when the afternoon slipped into early evening, the time when people walked their dogs or took to the tennis courts. During the school year, it was when you could hear Little League games going on at the stands down the street and the gargle of an announcer over the megaphone. Today, I decided to enjoy the sunset from *the Spot*.

The Spot was a grassy lookout over a man-made irrigation canal. The canal was made of cement walls that angled downward and held leftover rainwater in rainy and hurricane seasons to protect some neighborhoods from flooding. Out of sight from any major roads, the canal provided a sense of privacy from the bustle of everyday life, and because of the water, it had become home to several living creatures, especially cute families of Floridian fowl. From time to time, I would catch a glimpse of an alligator hatchling.

I'd settled into my usual place on the grass smelling of bug repellant and sweat and looked over the familiar setting. I'd memorized the dragonflies with their translucent wings and the animated quacks of the family of ducks that had made this place their home. Across the water was a white lanky crane with a long orange beak, digging in the ground for her dinner. Crickets chirped from the grass, and frogs croaked louder than Sister Bev during Sunday morning worship at my church. But my favorite of all was the rare butterfly or two.

Over the canal bridged an old railroad track, untouched except for early in the morning when I could hear the train horn from my bedroom a few blocks away. There was movement in the water under my feet, and I wondered if our poor Betta Bob had found his final resting place.

A *ding* sounded in my earbuds, and I looked down at my cell phone screen. A new notification from the *TuneTrapp app*.

D.S. Fisichella

User Beatz has uploaded a new mix! Take a listen.

I clicked on the link and waited a few seconds for the music to start. The moment the first notes struck, there were goosebumps down my arms.

Pinellas Park had a bustling urban hip hop and indie community which meant that a lot of young up-and-coming artists were often looking for ways to gain exposure as musicians and meet like-minded individuals to collaborate with.

One local artist had taken it upon himself to create the ultimate online musical hub for such transactions to take place. It was a genius idea. To become part of the *TuneTrapp* community you had to be a local musician willing to share your music free of charge for anyone to download and use in 'collaborations.' The app gave you the ability to upload, record and share original music and lyrics —chatting online with other creators was also possible on the platform.

Before joining, each individual had to agree to give credit to featured artists when sharing musical projects and collaborations on their personal social media profiles. In doing so, they were sure to gain more traction for fellow singers, lyricists, rappers, producers, and composers, like me. Already, the app was growing in local popularity and had even been responsible for several artists being discovered and signed to major labels. Out of all the creators on the music app, Beatz was my favorite.

I didn't know who he was in real life, and except for a brief contact page which listed him as "Male: ages 15-25," and his favorite genre as "90s RnB," there was not much I could gather from his profile. There was no photograph and no phone number. Only an email and an array of amazing original instrumentals. Every track he came up with was full of power and heart. In my mind, those characteristics made for the perfect song.

It wasn't like I lacked the know-how to create my own music, after all, I *did* play a couple of instruments, but I often opted to download Beatz's music and save it to my phone, writing lyrics to accompany it, but never daring to share my projects with anyone. Still, weirdly, putting lyrics to Beatz's music made me feel connected to him somehow.

As I thought about this, the roar of an engine blared from somewhere behind me. I turned to see a guy about my age peering into the open window of a flashy SUV. He wore a white tee that hugged his sculpted biceps and a backward black cap over jeans and sneakers.

Dreamer

From what I could see, there was an exchange taking place. The guy slipped something into the driver's hand, receiving a roll of bills in return. The SUV roared again as it disappeared down the street. I swallowed, finally registering that I'd just witnessed a drug deal. The young dealer must have sensed me looking at him because he turned in my direction. I diverted my eyes before he could see me looking at him, just as my ringtone came through the headphone still in my ear. I pulled my cell phone out of my pocket by the wire. It came unplugged and the ringtone echoed loudly off the walls of the canal.

In my haste to silence my phone, it slipped out of my hand and onto the edge of the canal. I reached for it, losing my balance and finding myself surfing the concrete downward. I panicked and landed halfway down on my butt with a painful *thunk.*

"Ouch."

"You okay?" A figure stood above me; it was the dealer.

"I slipped," I said, trying to get up to no avail. A whimper escaped my lips as I slipped further toward the dirty water. "I'm going to fall in!"

There was a shuffle of feet as he crawled down next to me, swinging one leg over both of mine so as not to let me slip any further down. His face was just inches from mine. "Turn around and climb up," he said in a low tone, his Adam's apple bobbing as he spoke. "I'll steady you from behind."

Flustered, I obeyed, shifting my body until my front was pressed up against the side of the slanted concrete wall. The only thing I felt now as I climbed up was the pressure of his hand on the small of my back. As I neared the edge he went on ahead of me.

"Here," he said, offering me his hand and hoisting me up. Before I pulled my hand away, he slipped something between my fingers. My phone. At what point he'd grabbed it, I had no clue.

"Thanks," I said, putting it back in my pocket. He nodded, and without a word, jogged back the way he came.

Chapter 2

"This is my commandment, that you love one another as I have loved you. Greater love has no one than this, that someone lay down his life for his friends."
John 15:12-13

When I first walked into the building of Agápē Baptist Church, I was met by a cold blast of air-conditioning in sharp contrast to the humidity outside. Everything was dark inside except for the sunlight coming in through the doors and the large windows facing the street. I walked down a side corridor, toward the counseling office, and knocked a beat. A voice better suited for the rodeo than an office rang from the other side of the door.

"Come on in, Elle Belle!"

When I came through the door, I was greeted by a pair of arms wrapping around me in a familiar embrace. Miss Josie took a step back, holding me at an arm's length. Wispy blonde hair embellished her sweet angular face, her fair skin was slightly tanned and her cobalt eyes sparkled in the light of her office behind plastic glasses. She wore a blush-colored T-shirt over jeans with white tennis shoes.

"Hi, sweetpea! Sit down," she said, her ruby lips turned up at the corners as she made her way to her office chair. "I don't know why in tarnation you ride that silly bike. It's hot as Hell out there."

Dreamer

"Miss Josie, I don't think you're supposed to say that in church."

"Girl, please. Hell's a place, ain't it?"

Miss Josie rented one of the church offices for her private practice. In all the years I'd been seeing Miss Josie, she never charged me a dime. When I asked her why, her response was: "I'll always have what I need so long as the Good Lord's willing and the creek don't rise."

With her crazy nicknames, her southern hospitality, and her unapologetic belly laughs, Miss Josie was never afraid to speak her mind. I once heard Pastor say that if God made most girls out of sugar and spice, he made Miss Josie out of sweet tea and gumption.

I sank into one of the large armchairs that faced her desk and slid out of my shoes, curling my legs beneath me before pulling a wooly blanket out of the wooden crate next to her desk. The smell of lavender filled the room from a corner table that held an essential oil air diffuser. Small twinkling white lights hung from the walls, giving the whole place a feel of tranquility.

"Spill the beans. How's your songwriting?" She took a sip of her coffee.

"It's going good, I guess."

"I still can't believe that old quack Steve, putting all that pressure on you to come up with new choir songs every month. Chris Tomlin doesn't even do that!"

"It's not so bad. I don't have a lot to do this summer. Besides, he's going to write me a college recommendation letter. He could help me get into a really good music program."

"His cornbread ain't done in the middle if you ask me."

"The Youth Group Band is improving," I said, changing the subject. Our youth pastor, Brother Todd, had practically forced me to join the band after catching wind that many of the choir songs were written by me.

"And how do you like being the new youth group worship leader?" asked Miss Josie with a smirk.

I rolled my eyes. "I still don't understand why they chose me," I murmured.

"You do too. That Jake Ferguson is stiffer than a stiff."

"He's a better guitarist than I am!"

"Maybe, but he's not as well-spoken as you."

"That's ridiculous. I'm the one that doesn't have any friends!"

"By choice."

"I'm *not* a people person."

D.S. Fisichella

"Let me stop you right there. Your humor tickles me pink. You are gifted with people skills… you've just avoided human interactions for so long that you've forgotten that."

I looked down at my hands. Maybe she was right. Maybe I just felt safer on my own. No friends meant no pain.

"What about that other song?" she asked, bringing me back to the present.

I cleared my throat. "I still have songwriter's block with that one."

She pulled a notepad out of her desk drawer and a pen out of one of the multiple mason jars adorning her rustic white desk. "You know what I'm gon' tell you, don't ya?" she said as she wrote something on the blank page. When I didn't answer, she put her pen down and fixed her gaze on me, leaning back in her seat. "Don't force it, Tooty Fruity. When the time is right, it will come to you. There must be something you still need to resolve."

I sighed, letting my chin rest on my chest. Miss Josie picked up on my mood, but she didn't pry.

"We had another fish funeral," I said, changing the subject.

"Don't tell me—"

"Yep. Mami again."

"Goodness Gracious," she said with a chuckle. "I wouldn't trust your mama with my chickens. It's a wonder she's kept you alive and well all these years."

I scoffed.

Miss Josie didn't miss a beat. "Now, you take that back, missy."

"I didn't say anything," I said innocently.

"I wasn't born yesterday."

I sighed. "I know it's not my mom's fault, but there's no way I'm *'well.'* Come on. I'm a sixteen-year-old with no life."

"That could change. You could hang out with someone for a change."

"I meet with the guys and Selah for band practice once a week." I thought about Selah, the pastor's eldest. She sang backup for the band and was the closest thing I had to a friend. She and her little sister Leah had always been sweet to me, but I'd never let them get too close.

What was *wrong* with me?

Miss Josie slid a box of tissues in my direction before I could feel the teardrop slide down my cheek.

Dreamer

"You've come such a long way," she was saying now, elbows on her desk. "Do you remember the first time you came through my door?" I felt a hollowness in my chest at the memory. She smiled sadly at me as if reading my mind. "I reckon you hadn't eaten in days. Bless your heart."

I wasn't sure what to expect when Pastor Tim led me to her office that first time. The nameplate on her door read, *Dr. Josephine Mae Abney: Family and Adolescent Counsellor*.

"She moved down here from Georgia just last week," he was saying. "You'll like her, Elleni. Doctor Abney is a sweet lady."

The door to her office swung open before Pastor Tim could knock, taking us both by surprise.

"For cryin' out loud, preacher. You're better off talking to a fence post than using that hoity-toity title on me!" She'd turned to me then, her expression softening. "Well, aren't you just cute as a button? Call me Josie, little chicken."

I loved her immediately.

"For your homework," she was saying now, bringing me back to the present, "I want you to find an opportunity to serve somebody else." I started to protest, but she put up a manicured fingernail, a warning in her eyes. "Stop that fussing, Elle Belle. You've gotten too comfortable feelin' sorry for yourself." I felt a pang at her words. She saw my expression and reached over to put her hand on my arm. "Now, now. Don't take that the wrong way, honey-pot. But all this doom and gloom you've got goin' on has kept you wrapped up in a little bubble. It holds you back from being used by the Lord to help others."

We finished our session with prayer, but I was still skeptical. Miss Josie had a way of bypassing my comfort zone with ease and without so much as a second thought. I knew she just wanted what was best for me. Still, it'd been so long since I'd been someone's friend that I didn't even know where to start.

Trust Me, Elleni.

There it was again. That little voice in my heart. Miss Josie told me it was the leading of the Holy Spirit. She told me how to tell the difference between God's leading and the devil's lies.

"When the Lord speaks directly to your heart," she'd said one morning from behind her desk, *"He never goes contrary to His word. He convicts you when you're headed the wrong way, and encourages you when you feel like you*

can't go on. But take care to always test the spirits, Elle Belle," she'd emphasized with a serious tone. *"Sometimes the enemy will try to sneak in some of his lies. You'll know it when he entices you to do what's evil or condemns you when you've messed up."*

Trust God. Okay.

I mounted my bike and scrolled through my phone until I found the Audio Bible and pressed 'Play.' I listened to the book of Jeremiah until I got home.

Be strong and courageous... Don't be afraid or dismayed... I will be with you.

When I got home everyone was already out working. I retreated to my bedroom with a snack and started to work on the song Brother Steve had tasked me with a week ago. *"I want you to write a chorus for the Hymn, 'O Sacred Head Now Wounded.'"* I opened my hymnal and scanned the notes with my finger. Key of A minor. Easy enough.

'O Sacred Head now wounded, with grief and shame weighed down, Now scornfully surrounded with thorns, Thine only crown... What language shall I borrow to thank Thee, dearest friend, For this Thy dying sorrow, Thy pity without end?'

Grief. Shame. Scorn. Sorrow. Jesus understood what it was like to feel like an outcast. Convicted, I bowed my head and asked for forgiveness. After everything He had done for me, couldn't I at least try to bless somebody else?

I spent all afternoon working on my new arrangement of the old hymn and stopped only when my stomach felt hungry enough to start eating itself. I emerged from my desk chair and stretched, eager to get my limbs moving again. I tossed a salad together and had a bowl before putting the rest in the refrigerator for my family to enjoy with dinner. With that done, I headed back out the door. It was my favorite time of day again.

The ground under my tires turned from gravel to grass as I pulled into the Spot, my childhood haven.

From time to time I might find some kids playing there or a couple holding hands and balancing on the train tracks that bridged over the water, but for the most part, I had the place all to myself. One time I found somebody fishing in the canal. Yuck! Sewage food for dinner? No, thank you. I noticed movement out of the corner of my eye. On the tracks, oblivious to my presence, stood the young drug dealer from the evening before.

It may have been the way he gripped the old rail, or the grief in his face as he looked down at the water, but whatever it was, I was drawn to a dark line that ran from his neck to the railing. That's when it hit me: the line was a rope.

My hands began to shake.

"Oh Jesus, Jesus, what do I do? I grabbed my cell phone out of my pocket and dialed 9-1-1.

"9-1-1. What's your emergency?"

"I'm on the corner of 84th Avenue and 63rd Way North in Pinellas Park. The railroad tracks. A teenage boy is standing on the edge of the bridge with a rope around his neck. It looks like he's going to hang himself."

"Dispatching the authorities to you now."

"I'm going to try to talk to him."

"Stay calm and keep me on the line."

I called out to the boy, "Hello?"

He looked up, startled, seeing me for the first time.

"Sorry to surprise you. Are you okay?" When he didn't answer me, I decided on a different approach. Taking a deep breath, I tore my eyes from him, moving my gaze across the sky while moving in his direction.

"It's a beautiful sky, isn't it?"

He scoffed.

"What's so funny?"

"You think I'm here for the view?" he asked.

"*I* am. I like to watch the ducks," I said, not even bothering to check if the ducks were out as I climbed onto the railroad tracks.

"You know, if you're trying to keep me from killing myself, you're doing a terrible job."

Less than six feet away from him, I noticed he was wearing jeans and a black jacket, the hood pulled over his baseball cap, and had a beer bottle in his hand. He noticed me looking at his drink.

"What, this?" he asked, raising it slightly. "You're scared I'll damage my liver?" he said, letting out a laugh.

"I'm scared you'll lose your balance."

He took a swig. "If anything, this is the only thing that's kept me from doing it already."

My knees started to knock together. "If what you're looking for is a way out, you're not going to find it on the other side of eternity," I said, a small tremor in my voice. "I promise you that."

"I don't believe in an afterlife."

"And *I* don't believe in coincidences," I said. "I think I was supposed to come here and find you."

"Find me? For what? Do you think I just woke up this morning and on a whim decided to kill myself? You have no idea how long I've been wanting to do this. You don't know what I've been through."

The voice in my earpiece spoke again, startling me. I'd nearly forgotten. "Ma'am, first responders will be there in three minutes."

I thought about diving toward his feet to keep him from jumping, but then I imagined falling with him. I could survive the fall with just a few broken bones, but there was still the issue of the rope. No doubt the boy would be strangled.

God, what am I supposed to do?

Tell him about Me.

"I know you said you don't believe in the afterlife, but the Bible talks about there being a Heaven, a Hell and a judgment. God will deal with the people that have hurt you, but the bad news is that He has to deal with your sin too," I said, trying to keep the panic out of my voice. "But there's still hope, and I'd be happy to help you find it, but you have to step away from that ledge. Please."

His gaze fell on my outstretched hand, and for a moment, I dared to hope, but then he raised his cryptic eyes toward me again, his chin determined.

"This is not a cry for help, sweetheart," he said. "It's the nail in the coffin. You can stand there, or you can walk away. It makes no difference to me."

A frigid chill ran the length of my spine as I watched the boy take a step off the bridge, his hands spread out to his sides as if to embrace the finality of it all.

Adrenaline shot through my body as I reached out to grab his jacket with both my hands and attempted to use all of my weight to propel us backward. My sneakers dug into the crevices between the metal and wood of the tracks. There was a moment of terror as I felt my knees giving away, but that's when I saw the flash of a hand and felt the pressure of its grip on my shoulder.

Before I could register what was happening, I was pulled backward with the violence of a cyclone. All of my focus was on my hands, which were locked on his jacket like iron shackles. I fell on my back. The wind was knocked out of me. The boy toppled over my legs. When I finally caught my breath, I turned to look behind me, but no one was there.

Chapter 3

"For he has not despised or abhorred the affliction of the afflicted, and he has not hidden his face from him, but has heard when he cried to him."
Psalm 22:24

The events that took place following the suicide attempt went by in a blur. The arrival of the ambulance, the questions fired at me, the jumble of uniforms carrying me and the boy to the hospital under flashing lights. Somewhere along the way, I learned the boy's name. Julian Rossi. I couldn't remember if I was the one who found the wallet, or if it was the police officer, but in passing, the name was presented to me and vaulted in my memory.

My parents met me at the hospital where I was seen by Dr. Patel, a thirty-something Indian man with bright eyes and a broad smile who had the task of relocating my shoulder. Whatever the cause — a hurricane-level gust of wind, a troll under the bridge, or a spiritual encounter — the evidence that something else had been present at that bridge was unmistakable the moment Dr. Patel popped my shoulder into place, my scream echoing through the hospital halls. With a sympathetic smile, he announced that I'd be kept overnight as a safety precaution. Mami stayed in the room to help me get ready for bed, but as my hospital gown fell around my ankles, she gasped.

Dreamer

"What?" I asked.

Wordlessly, she turned me toward the mirror and pointed to the massive finger-shaped bruises cupping my shoulder in the shape of a huge hand. I turned slightly to get a look at the backside and felt my mouth go dry. I hadn't imagined it at all.

"Did the doctor do that to you?" she asked dubiously, her hand still to her mouth. I shook my head. Her tone implied what we both knew. No doctor on this side of heaven could leave a handprint that size.

*

I'd spent all night tossing and turning in my bed. If the nightmares weren't enough, the hourly visits from the nurse on staff made it impossible for me to get a wink of sleep. Not to mention the blood pressure cuff that threatened to break my arm every half an hour. By the time the first rays of sunrise made it through my hospital room window, I was gathering my things in anticipation of receiving my discharge papers.

The bustle of nurses made me nervous, but not nearly as much as the dead-eyed look on some of the people sitting in the waiting room. I stood in line at the hospital gift shop, but from where I was, I had a clear view of those waiting to be admitted.

One man held a wad of gauze to his head, soaked in blood. A woman just a few seats away from him cried into a handkerchief, and a third person sneezed into his hands. I hated hospitals. They smelled like bleach, bodily fluids and death. I waited for my turn with one arm resting securely in a sling while my opposite hand held a stuffed teddy bear. The little creature had an ice pack on his furry head and a thermometer sticking out from under his snout. It held a balloon with the words, 'Get Well Soon!' written across it. After purchasing the little gift, I wrote on the small card attached. It contained my cell phone number and the note: *"Please call me anytime! Feel better. -Elleni Salgado"*

The sound of my footsteps echoed through the hallway as I searched for his room number. A heart monitor beeped to my left and I peered inside to find an old man hooked up to an oxygen mask, his eyes shut. I shuddered.

When I reached Julian's room number, at last, I looked down at my outfit — an oversized pink sweatshirt and black skinny jeans — hoping I looked okay. Mami had brought them from home when she visited last night. I'd told her the hospital was too cold for my usual denim shorts. I had a half-hour before my parents arrived to take me home, but I didn't want to leave before checking to see if Julian was alright. Of course, I chose this very moment to remember I hadn't ditched my black-framed glasses. My mom had brought them instead of my contact lenses. They barely balanced on my button nose and made my brown eyes look bigger than usual. Paired with the bun I'd thrown together on top of my head, I felt like a cartoon character.

Why should I care, anyway?

I was getting ready to knock when a female voice came through from the other side.

"Did something happen between you and Bianca? Did she break your heart?"

"Mom. Don't do this."

"Baby, please. I need to know why you would *do* something like this! Where did I go wrong?"

Julian swore. "Stop! I just wish…"

"You wish what?" the woman's voice cracked.

"I wish I could leave!"

"Leave and go where? Do you want to go on vacation? Study abroad? I'll talk to Joe. I'm sure money's no object."

"Mom. No. I want to disappear, okay? I'm tired of feeling like a burden."

"Am I making you feel that way?"

"NO!"

"Then I don't understand," she said, followed by the sound of muffled sobs.

I felt guilty for eavesdropping and started to turn back the way I'd come, telling myself I'd try giving his room a call later.

"Hi sweetie, can I help you?"

I jumped at the sight of pink scrubs just inches from my face. My eyes traveled upward to see a tall nurse in a blonde ponytail smiling uncertainly at me.

"I was coming to visit Julian but…"

"He's right in here," she said, reaching for the door before I could protest. Panicked, I took a step back. "Don't be shy! He'll be happy to see you."

Dreamer

"Um—I'm not sure about that."

"Hello?" Julian's mom spoke up. "It's okay. You can come in."

Not knowing what else to do, I stepped through the doorway. The nurse followed me into the dimly lit room. The curtains were only halfway open, and none of the lights were on except for a night light. Julian's mother seemed confused at the sight of me.

"How are you doing? Did you order lunch?" the nurse asked.

"He doesn't want to eat a thing," Julian's mother said, dabbing her eyes with a tissue. From his hospital bed, Julian ignored the nurse and gawked at me.

I shuffled my feet while the nurse finished checking Julian's vitals. I looked around and found a pair of stiletto heels aligned neatly against the wall.

"All looks well. Your blood pressure is still in the lower range. Be sure to get some food in you soon, okay? I'll see if lunch is ready." As she passed by me, I bit my tongue. I knew if I didn't, I might beg her to stay for moral support.

With the nurse out of the room, Julian and his mother had now turned their full attention on me.

"Hi," I said, with a big smile, hoping something halfway intelligible would follow. No such luck. As I stood, my mouth still halfway open, and a ridiculous grin on my face, I imagined an automated message playing from my empty head.

We're sorry, Elleni can't come to her senses. Please leave a message after the tone.

Beep.

Julian's mother looked from me to him, back to me. Julian's face had gone from disbelief to contempt. His mother picked up on the tension, piping in with feigned cheerfulness.

"I'm Melissa Heron, Julian's mom." Melissa Heron was a brunette with light brown eyes and a heart-shaped face. She was very pretty, even with the sleepless circles under her eyes, and seemed much too young to be Julian's mother.

"Are you a friend from school?" she asked.

"No, I'm—"

"Leaving." Julian finished the sentence for me.

His mom gave him a warning with her eyes before turning back to me. "He's joking, hon. Of course, you can stay."

Julian raised his voice, matching his mom's tone with sarcasm. "No, *hon. You* can go to Hell. You know, the one you were telling me all about? That one."

"Julian!" Melissa looked horrified.

He dropped the act, his voice returning to its previous gruffness. "If I'd wanted help, I would have called for it myself."

Mrs. Heron's eyes grew wide, and she turned to me with wonder. "It was *you?*" She sprung up from her chair and ran across the room to me. Once I got over the shock of being embraced by a stranger, I hugged her back with my good arm.

"Thank you. So much."

Over her shoulder, I watched how Julian rolled his eyes, turning his face away from us in disgust.

I finally got the words out. "Mrs. Heron, I'm serious. You—*ouch*—don't have to thank me."

Julian's mother straightened up. "I'm sorry for being so emotional," she said with a nervous laugh. She ran her hands over her white blazer and pencil skirt before taking a deep breath and stretching her hand toward me.

"What is your name?"

I returned the handshake. "I'm Elleni Salgado."

"It's *so* nice to meet you. I apologize for being a mess. I had a very stressful night, as you can probably imagine."

I nodded.

She made her way back to Julian, bending down to say something in his ear. She then picked up her belongings and walked towards the door, turning to me once more. "Thanks again, honey. I have to go pick up my husband from the airport, but I appreciate you coming by."

The door clicked shut. I stared at it, biting my lip. *God, help me.* I turned back to Julian. "How long has your dad been gone?"

"He's not my dad."

"Oh."

Julian moved his eyes to my hand. I followed his gaze. The little bear which seemed cute to me before now seemed childish. When I looked up, he was glaring at me.

"What are you doing here?"

Dreamer

Good question. "I came to see how you were."

"I don't need your help."

I don't need your attitude.

Elleni...

Ugh, okay, Lord.

"I know, but I thought you might need a friend." He seemed taken aback. "It might take some time," I continued, "but I'm willing to try."

Something in his expression changed, like a thrown switch had turned his blatant dislike into something else that I couldn't place. His face relaxed and he gave me a small smile.

"And, uh, how do you plan on being my friend, exactly?"

"A friend is someone who proves themselves trustworthy, right?"

He let out a humorless laugh. If there was any question as to his intentions before, there wasn't anymore after he turned his jeering eyes back to me "How would *you* know what a real friend is?"

"Excuse me?"

"All this stuff about friendship is a lie. As real as your imaginary friends."

"You don't know anything about me," I said quietly.

"I don't need to know anything more than what I know now. You talk to strangers about a magical being in the sky, and for what? To save their souls? Well, everyone else might be too nice to say it, but don't waste your time. You're not saving anyone. Everyone thinks you're a *joke.*"

I felt like I'd been slapped across the face. I hated the tears threatening to spill over. If he wanted to be left alone to live, die, or fly a kite, so be it.

"Hey, hey, hey What's all *this*?" The nurse had come back with a tray of food.

Not knowing what else to do, I threw the teddy across the room and bolted past her, out the door.

HOME

Knock, knock, knock.

"*Mi Amor*, you can't stay in there all week!"

Watch me.

D.S. Fisichella

"Elleni, I know it's summer vacation and you don't have a paying job, but you promised you would keep busy."

My mother was right. It had been two days since my encounter with Julian at the hospital. I'd spent the car ride with my face flushed and tears making salty trails down my cheeks. When we got home, I told my mother what happened. She held me on her bed until I'd sniffled myself to sleep. I awoke to her urging me to wash my face and go back to my bedroom. I did. I didn't come out again except to use the restroom.

I pulled the covers over my face in defiance, not that my mother could see me anyway.

Knock, knock.

"That's *it*. I'm calling Josie."

MISS JOSIE'S OFFICE AN HOUR LATER

The sound machine was supposed to relax Miss Josie's visitors, but I thought Miss Josie's favorite setting, the sound of running water, only worked to remind me when I had to use the restroom. I admitted this to Miss Josie one afternoon during a visit. From that moment forward, she switched her machine to play other sounds when I was coming by. Today, the setting she'd chosen, the sound of crickets, was very fitting.

Miss Josie peered at me from over her spectacles. "Your hour's almost up. You going to talk to me, or not?"

I wasn't done sulking.

After my mother phoned Miss Josie, she convinced my brother to rattle my bedroom door open with a butter knife. Against my protests, she ripped my bed covers off my body and dragged me into the shower, clothes and all, with my brother's help. She turned the water on without even bothering to let it warm up.

I'd changed into dry clothes, but as I sat across from Miss Josie, my arms crossed and damp hair still dripping onto my shirt, I became convinced that I might as well have kept my soaked clothes on. Needless to say, I was very unhappy.

Chirp-chirp. Chirp-chirp.

I shivered in my seat.

Dreamer

"Your mama says you've been holed up in your bedroom since Wednesday. Didn't even go to Youth Group. Whatever went down must've been pretty serious."

I threw my head back and stared at the ceiling, biting my lip.

"You know you can tell me, Bumble-Bee."

"I can't take your nicknames today, Miss Josie."

"Sour Sally."

"No."

"Debbie Downer."

"Stop!"

"Doo-Doo Doll."

I couldn't help it and cracked a smile.

"Ah! There she is, my Sunshine Gal. Now, won't you tell me what ails ya?"

I felt a tickle in my nose. I could still feel the shame of trying to reach out to Julian only to have him reject me and watch me leave, the disgust in his face burning against my back as I ran out the door. Miss Josie waited patiently for me to speak.

"I've never felt more humiliated in my life. Julian never gave me a chance. He called me a *joke*." I felt the hurt welling up in me all over again. "I would never treat somebody like he treated me."

Miss Josie stood up, circling to the front of her desk. She took the seat next to me, crossing one denim-clad leg over another. Today she wore boots and a plaid top.

"Hmm," she angled her face upward and started to nod as if hearing a voice from heaven. "I know, Lord, I know… no, I don't think she does." She paused then started to laugh. "You're too much, Lord!"

I stared, my mouth halfway open, but just as I started to wonder if my counselor had finally lost her mind, she looked at me with a pleased expression, leaning forward in the chair.

"What?" I asked.

"Oh, nothing. I was just having a little conversation with the Lord."

"Really."

"He wanted me to ask if this Julian has treated you as bad as you've treated His Son." She pointed upward as she emphasized *His*.

I was stunned.

Miss Josie reached for her mug and used it to hide her smile.

She placed the mug back down. "Seems time's run out, June Bug." I looked at the clock over the door frame. Our hour was over. I got up from my seat and, still a bit shaken, walked to the door. "Oh, and Elle Belle—"

I turned around, bracing for whatever came next.

"I'd be darned if you can think of a single person who needs a friend more than that boy. God answered your prayer. What you gon' do about it?"

THE HOSPITAL

I handed the receptionist my ID and stared into the camera before taking the elevator to the second floor, all the while determined that no matter what objections Julian would have to my being there, it was where I was supposed to be, whether he liked it or not… or should I say, whether *I* liked it or not.

After Miss Josie's correction, God flooded me with a wave of conviction. She was right. If it wasn't for the Lord, I'd be in worse shape than Julian, and I knew it. I *said* I believed in God, and I was all too happy to let Him comfort me, but what was faith *really* if it wasn't lived out? A scripture from the book of James came to mind:

"So also faith by itself, if it does not have works, is dead." James 2:17

With this thought, I marched to Julian's hospital room door. After a deep breath, I knocked and stepped through at the same time, but nothing could have prepared me for what would be waiting for me on the other side.

The tiny hairs on my arms and the back of my neck stood on end as my eyes fell on the array of needles and sharp objects that littered the floor near Julian's bed, but it was Julian himself who gave me the biggest shock. He sat motionless on the bed, a flash of something silver poised to his wrist as a steady stream of blood dripped onto the sheets. I understood then that the scene in front of me would forever be engraved in my mind.

Snapping out of it, I flung the door wide open and screamed out onto the hallway.

"Somebody help!"

I didn't wait for the nurses to get to the door, instead, I ran to snatch the object away from Julian. He didn't fight me as I grabbed it and threw it on the floor before clamping my hands over his wound, pressing down as hard as I could to stop the bleeding.

Dreamer

I barely noticed when someone lifted my hands off Julian's wrist to clean his wound because when I finally looked up to meet his eyes, they were distant, disconnected, looking through me as if I were made of air. His lips were chapped, his face tear-stricken and ashen, the beautiful honey-green of his irises lost in the darkness I recognized all too well.

"Sweetheart, you have to leave and let us do our job, okay? He's going to be fine."

I didn't move my attention away from his face as I felt the nurse pulling me off his bed and to my feet. She walked me out into the hallway, allowing the door to click shut in my face.

In the restroom down the hall, soap and blood swirled down the drain until all I could see was clear running water. My mind flickered with a memory.

Bloody fingerprints on a window latch.

As if a little latch could keep out the mess you've left behind.

I pushed the thought out of my mind and shut off the faucet. When I looked up at the mirror over the sink, the horror of what I had witnessed was written all over my pale complexion.

Chapter 4

"For you have delivered my soul from death, my eyes from tears, my feet from stumbling; I will walk before the Lord in the land of the living."
Psalm 116:8-9

I scrolled through the *TuneTrapp* application on my phone in hopes of finding new tracks to inspire me, but there were no new uploads from my favorite artist, Beatz, who'd been offline for nearly one week. A small icon appeared at the top of my screen. I clicked on it and was sent to my voicemail inbox.

"*Hello, Elleni. It's Melissa, Julian's mom. I found your number attached to a stuffed animal you got for my son. I want to thank you for being there for him yesterday. He's under close monitoring and will be transferred to a mental wellness facility tomorrow morning so if you want to pay him another visit, today will be his last day at the hospital. I know he can be a handful, but I am so grateful that he didn't scare you away. Hope you're doing well, and if this is the last we've seen of you, just know that I am forever thankful to you. This is my number should you ever need me. Please keep in touch!*"

As I lowered my cell phone from my ear, I overheard my mother's voice as she picked up a call of her own.

"Hello? Oh my goodness. Yes, how *are* you?"

Mami's voice turned from surprise to endearment, the way it only did when a certain person called. My hands began to shake, my heart hammering in my ears.

"I believe *so*. Yes, I'll try to get her to speak to you."

As her footsteps got closer, I looked around for a way of escape. My eyes landed on my window. I'd given up the bedroom with the easy-access window to Daniel, there was no way I would fit through this one.

"One moment, she's in her room." Mami opened the door, her smile fading as she caught a glimpse of my panicked expression. I shook my head at her, a finger to my lips, pleading. She went back to the phone call.

"I'm sorry. She must have already left for the day. Yes. Of course, I'll tell her."

I stared after Mami as she walked away. I couldn't avoid the phone calls forever, but still, I hoped one day they'd stop. Until then, I'd have to endure my mother's lectures as she promised she wouldn't lie for me another time. I always called her bluff, but still, that didn't mean I wanted to be guilt-tripped about it. Mami was getting off the phone when I made the split-second decision not to be present when she re-emerged from her bedroom. Good thing I had someplace to be.

The Hospital

I knocked quietly, but when there was no answer, I opened the door, bracing for what I might find. Julian slept peacefully on his bed, an IV bag pumping fluids into his arm. His forearm sported clean bandages that stopped right over his wrist.

As I came closer I noticed that his chestnut hair was longer on top than on the sides and naturally parted to one side. His eyebrows which were usually narrowed and guarded were now relaxed into their natural shape over his olive skin. I followed the curve of his lips, slightly parted, his chest moving up and down with each breath.

Father, what if I mess up? What if I can't help him?

The words of a familiar hymn came to mind.

'If we do His good will, He abides with us still, never fear, only trust and obey...'

It was a promise. I wasn't alone in this.

I pulled my Bible out of my tote bag and opened it to Psalm 116. With one final look at Julian's sleeping form, I cleared my throat and began to read aloud.

"I love the Lord because he has heard my voice and my pleas for mercy.
Because he inclined his ear to me, therefore I will call on him as long as I live.
The snares of death encompassed me; the pangs of Sheol laid hold on me; I suffered distress and anguish. Then I called on the name of the Lord: 'O Lord, I pray, deliver my soul!'
Gracious is the Lord, and righteous, our God is merciful.
The Lord preserves the simple; when I was brought low, he saved me. Return, O my soul, to your rest; for the Lord has dealt bountifully with you.
For you have delivered my soul from death, my eyes from tears,
my feet from stumbling; I will walk before the Lord in the land of the living." Psalm 116:1-9

My reading was interrupted by the sound of my stomach grumbling. I checked the time. It was past noon and I hadn't eaten all day. I left Julian's room in search of a vending machine, and upon finding one, devoured the cereal bar in a few bites before strolling through the halls, following familiar signs to my chosen destination. It didn't take long to find it.

Towards the main entrance of the first floor, tucked away against a large corner window facing the ocean, stood a majestic grand piano. I'd passed it on my way out the door during my stay, but this being my last visit, it was my last chance to play it.

I took off my sling and ran my hands over the ivory keys, ignoring the dull pain in my shoulder.

I looked out the window and began to play. There was one place untouched by my grief, it was the place music took me to, the Spot of my dreams. This was not some irrigation canal, it was a place like no other, a place full of trees and flowers. It was abundant with butterflies, and running spring water trickled clearly, sparkling with the light of the sun.

It was a place I hoped was out there, waiting for me.

I first started having visions of it at the age of thirteen, but even time didn't exist at this Spot where the rest of the world retreated into silence.

I breathed out the tension in my shoulders, breathed in the wind against my face. My fingers moved across the keys, spelling out the sounds of the water, the motion of the trees swaying overhead.

Here, I wasn't the girl without friends. I wasn't a loner hiding behind a hobby to not have to face the rest of the world. Here, I had no past. Nothing threatening to suck me back into who I used to be.

Here I was free.

I looked at the time on the face of my phone. I'd been at the piano for almost an hour. I looked around, half expecting to see people irritated by my playing, but nobody seemed to mind.

I returned to the second floor and knocked on the door, half-expecting Julian not to answer.

"Come in."

I was surprised to find him sitting upon his bed, looking out the window. He turned in my direction. "Hey."

"How are you feeling?"

He sighed, looking tired. "How do you think? That's twice now that you've interrupted me."

I made my way across the room. "I'm sorry you feel that way about it."

He turned back to the window. "I never asked you to save my life."

I sat on the recliner by his bed. I hardly knew anything about Julian, but even I understood that if he were gone, he would be missed a whole lot more than he realized. He put his bandaged arm over his face, leaning his head back against his pillow.

"I know you were probably just trying to do the right thing," he said. "But you don't know what it's like to be me."

"What about the people who love you?"

"What people? My girlfriend? She cheated on me. My best friend? He's the one she cheated with. My other friends? My mom tried calling them, but nobody ever bothered to visit. I hate all of them. I have no one."

My mind traveled to something Mami said shortly after I'd been admitted to the hospital. I'd recounted the events that took place at the railroad track when my mother, not thinking, had voiced the one question that always worked to bring me shame.

"Why in the world would a child want to take their own life?"

I swallowed and looked over at Julian again. When he didn't look at me, I pulled the blue sling over my head. I winced when I stretched my arm out and rolled up my sleeve.

He zeroed in on the long, deliberate lines running vertically down to my wrist. I had some scars which were more faded than others. Some were obvious, while others blended with my skin. All of them were healed, outwardly at least. Julian lowered his arm, looking up at me as if seeing me for the first time. My memory flickered with visions of blood, the sound of sirens. I tried to push the images out of my mind, but I wasn't strong enough. The darkness fell all around me, sucking me into oblivion.

I was thirteen again. My heart was pounding too hard.

Why can't I swallow anymore? My mouth tastes like metal. God! God, forgive me. I'm sorry, I'm sorry.

'Elleni! Mi Amor, stay with me.'

"Stay with me!" Julian's voice broke through my trance.

I blinked. My breathing was coming too fast. I patted myself down, but I couldn't find my headphones. Julian put his hands to either side of my face and commanded my attention.

"Elleni, are you looking for an inhaler? What do you need?" he asked.

"To slow. My breathing. Music. Helps."

Julian's expression went from one of concern to one of concentration. He closed his eyes and before I knew what was happening, I heard the sound of a bass drum, followed by high hats and a snare.

BTT-KTT-TBT-KTT

He was beatboxing.

My heartbeat started to slow down as I found the pattern and hung on for dear life. Slowly, my awareness increased. There was the sound of the air-conditioning blowing from the vent over our heads, the feeling of the afternoon sunlight through the window, and then, ever so softly, the feeling of Julian's fingertips tapping the rhythm on the sides of my face while simultaneously humming a melody.

I breathed to his tempo until I'd found myself in his song.

Chapter 5

"Blessed be the God and Father of our Lord Jesus Christ, the Father of mercies and God of all comfort, who comforts us in all our affliction, so that we may be able to comfort those who are in any affliction, with the comfort with which we ourselves are comforted by God."
2 Corinthians 1:3-4

I received word from Julian's mother when Julian was discharged from the hospital and transferred to an in-patient mental health clinic. It took me a few days to carve out the time to visit him, mainly because my parents were catching on to how often I wasn't home and were becoming increasingly curious about my whereabouts.

Although they knew about my initial encounter with Julian at the hospital, they assumed that after our unpleasant exchange, I'd given up on trying to reach out to this random troubled boy. I thought about filling them in on my other visits and his second suicide attempt, but although I knew I should, I was worried they wouldn't let me visit him anymore because I might get triggered (never mind the fact that I already had).

I often found myself pacing my room and praying Julian was getting the treatment he needed.

A couple of times I felt uneasy about how invested I'd become in his life, but I also couldn't stop thinking about how God had put me in very specific places at very specific times for the very purpose of helping him.

I waited impatiently in my room until everyone had left for the day before getting ready to catch the bus. Once I was in my seat, on the way to see Julian, I opened my Bible to Second Corinthians chapter one. I stopped on verses three and four.

"Blessed be the God and Father of our Lord Jesus Christ, the Father of mercies and God of all comfort, who comforts us in all our affliction, so that we may be able to comfort those who are in any affliction, with the comfort with which we ourselves are comforted by God."

Okay God, do you expect me to use my pain and experience to continue to comfort Julian?

I looked down at my arm again, reaching under my sleeve and running my thumb over my scars. I put my Bible back in my bag then closed my eyes.

It hurts too much, Lord. I don't want to go back there again.

Nothing ever gets healed being covered up, I felt Him say. *Won't you let Me heal you?*

I pondered this for a moment before realizing my stop was coming fast. I reached up to pull the cord. The bell rang, the bus stopped, and I got off, avoiding the question.

The in-patient clinic was in a small grey building surrounded by unoccupied graffiti-laden properties. The sounds of traffic permeated through the air, sirens in the distance.

I'd never taken the bus this far from home.

I clutched my purse close to my chest and walked briskly to the entrance. Behind the counter, a grim-faced woman instructed me to put my belongings in a plastic bag that I could retrieve once my visit was over. I signed in, spelling out Julian's name on the clipboard before walking through a metal detector on the way to the waiting area. The woman spoke into a walkie-talkie, announcing that Julian Rossi had a visitor.

Julian emerged from the back of the building in sweatpants and a T-shirt. His brown hair stuck up on one side as if he'd been sleeping on it too much. His shirt was wrinkled and he sported a five o'clock shadow. When he caught sight of me, he raised his hand in greeting, a white paper bracelet wrapped around his wrist. My chest tightened at the sight of him

Dreamer

being escorted by a man who looked more like a club bouncer than a healthcare worker.

I looked at his badge. "Rocco," it read. A perfectly suited name for the boulder of a man.

I giggled.

Rocco narrowed his eyes at me before ushering us into an office with two plastic chairs facing each other. When Julian and I sat down, I looked at Rocco, half-expecting him to give us some privacy, but instead of leaving us, Rocco sat on a chair in the entrance, his back against the open door. The sound of incoherent screaming carried from the back of the building.

"That would be Bobby," Julian said. "He sleeps in the recliner next to me. Poor guy's been through some things."

I looked around the room. A television encased in a plastic box. An electrical outlet under lock and key. Julian watched me as I took in my surroundings.

"What are you thinking?" he asked.

"You don't belong here," I said.

"Don't I? Weren't you the one trying to get me 'help'?"

The tone in which he said it made me wince, but I didn't try to defend myself.

He exhaled. "I'm sorry."

My head snapped up. "What?"

"I said," he cleared his throat. "I'm sorry. It's not your fault that I'm sick in the head."

"Oh." I folded my hands in my lap. "I forgive you."

Julian nodded. "Thanks."

Although he still seemed a bit paler than when we first met, the bags under his eyes were gone. "You look rested," I said. "Are you feeling better?"

"I've been catching up on sleep. There's not much else to do here."

"How's the food?" I asked.

He made a face. "I never thought I would miss hospital food."

"Yikes."

"What happened to your arm?" he asked, nodding toward my sling.

"My shoulder got dislocated at the Spot."

"The what?" he asked, leaning forward.

"The place where we first met. I call it the Spot."

"Oh," he said. "But how did you dislocate your shoulder?"

"I'd tell you, but I don't think you'd believe me."

"Come on," he encouraged. "Humor me."

I let out a breath. "We were seconds from falling over the edge when I saw *and felt* a hand grab my shoulder and pull me back hard. When I looked behind me, no one was there."

"Wait a minute," he said, straightening up in his chair. "Are you sure it wasn't a first responder?"

"I'm sure," I insisted. "The ambulance hadn't even arrived yet."

"And you didn't imagine it?" he asked with a raised eyebrow.

"I can feel you judging me but I have proof." I unbuttoned my plaid shirt, revealing a black tank top underneath. "See?" I said, gesturing toward my shoulder. "What are these bruises shaped like?"

"Sausages?"

"Or... really big fingers," I insisted.

He studied the bruises for a moment more before nodding his head in agreement. "I'll give you that. Pretty creepy."

"Yeah," I said, buttoning my shirt back up. "So, how much longer are you here for?"

"They said they wanted to keep me for a few days to make sure I'm stable."

"Is there anything I can do?"

"I just need something to keep my mind occupied. I promised my mom I would try harder to work through my problems."

"Can I bring you anything that might help?" I asked.

"Maybe. Did you drive here?"

"No, I rode the bus."

"You did *what?* Pinellas Park has to be at least an hour away from here on the city bus. Why would you make that trip to come to see me?"

"I wanted to see if you were okay."

His expression softened. "Look, I don't want you to come to visit me anymore." He must have seen my surprise because he started to backtrack. "I didn't mean it that way," he said. "I'm glad you visited, but this is a really bad part of town."

"I understand," I said. "But still, I wish there was something I could do to help."

"A book. I've read through all of the instruction manuals they have here."

"You're kidding," I said.

"I wish I was. If I ever have to replace a smoke detector or an AC Unit, I'll be set."

I threw my hands up. "That's *it*. Wait here."

I marched over to Rocco. "Give me one minute, okay? I'll be right back." He nodded his head and watched me curiously as I made my way to the reception desk.

"Are you through with your visit?" asked the grim-faced receptionist.

"No. I was wondering if I could get something out of my bag to take to my friend."

She scowled. "What is it?"

"A book."

"Is it a softcover or a hardcover?"

"Soft."

She rummaged through the bag for a second before pulling it out. She flipped through the pages, running her fingers over the binding before handing it to me. I thanked her and hurried back to the office where Julian sat, waiting.

"Here," I said, handing it to him. He took one look at the purple book with the faded words, 'Holy Bible' on the binding, before letting out a laugh.

"Don't laugh at it," I said.

"I'm not. I'm just laughing at the irony that I've always thought that the Bible was the last book in the world I'd want to read."

"One more thing," I said before opening the front cover to the first page. A small note was written there in my writing. He read it out loud.

"If lost, please return to Elleni Salgado. Tel: 555-0123."

"Call me if you want," I said. "I told you I wanted to be there for you. I intend to try."

Chapter 6

*"The thief comes only to steal and kill and destroy.
I came that they may have life and have it abundantly."*
John 10:10

I was in the kitchen struggling to cut flour tortillas in preparation for lunch, a task made unnecessarily difficult by the sling still cradling my shoulder. It was my last day wearing it, but after two weeks of discomfort and chaffing, I was eager to get it off.

"It smells good," Papi said in Spanish, looking up from his cup of coffee. "How did you learn to make *chilaquiles?*"

"*La amiga de Mami,*" I responded before digging through a cabinet for the frying pan. "Teresa, I think, is her name."

I placed the pan on the stove and reached for the blender.

"Would you mind putting in *los tomatillos?*" I slid the green tomatoes in his direction. Papi smiled one of his rare smiles.

I once asked him what he thought my dominant language was.

'Spanglish,' he replied. Right, as usual.

"Did I tell you about my dream?" he asked.

When I shook my head 'no,' he leaned forward in his seat and began to describe it to me. Even with the folds on his skin, and the bags under his eyes, his demeanor lit up any time he recalled a dream about Costa Rica or fantasized about our return there.

Dreamer

With the Central American economy on a downward spiral, Papi was left with few choices when his workplace started to lay people off. Although he had a college degree, most places of business were more interested in hiring hot shots straight out of business school, than middle-aged men with families to care for.

When Tia, Papi's sister, offered to help him pursue citizenship in the U.S.A., he couldn't turn her down. I knew it wasn't easy for him, going from working in an office in Central America to working on cars in the scorching Florida heat, but he never complained.

"That's beautiful, Papi," I remarked when he was through explaining what our 'welcome home' party had been like in his dream. "I'm sure that's exactly how it will be."

I liked it when it was just me and him like this. Without Daniel's chatter and Mami's busy energy around the house, Papi and I, both on the more introverted side of the social spectrum, maintained a calmer vibe when we were together. Although I knew he could come off as stoic, my dad was the original dreamer of our family.

When my cell phone rang, I picked it up with two fingers and used my nose to hit the answer button before wedging it between my shoulder and my ear. *"Alo?"*

"Elleni?"

I almost dropped the phone, surprised to hear Julian's tenor voice on the other line.

"Julian?"

My dad arched an eyebrow at the unfamiliar name as he sipped his coffee.

"*Hey.* You caught me by surprise."

"Is this a bad time?" he asked.

"No, it's fine. What's up?"

"I was wondering if you, uh, want to hang out or something."

I smiled. "Are you hungry?"

"A little."

"I'm making *chilaquiles*."

"I don't know what that is."

"It's Mexican food."

"I'll leave my house now."

I gave Julian my home address. Before I knew it, there was a knock at the front door. I wiped my hand on my mother's apron, walking towards it.

My dad asked in Spanish, "Were we expecting someone?"

Oops.

I shot him a cheesy smile, hoping he wouldn't be mad. He raised an eyebrow at me.

"Sorry, I forgot to tell you that I invited my friend over for lunch," I said.

When Papi didn't respond, I headed for the front door.

I peeked through the side window, my breath catching at the sight of Julian on my doorstep. He stood with his feet slightly apart, his hands in his pockets, wearing a backward baseball cap that matched his navy blue V-neck. The material of the fabric hugged his slim waist, his T-shirt slightly tucked into his jeans in the front.

He fumbled for something in his pocket. Whipping out his cell phone, his long fingers moved quickly over the screen. The sharp edges of his jaw glistened with a layer of perspiration as he moved his lips silently, his eyes narrowing.

My cell phone vibrated from the pocket of my jeans. A text from Julian.

"You home? I think I'm here."

I caught a glimpse of my reflection on the window: a messy bun, an apron and glasses. I scurried to the bathroom to run a brush through my hair and replace my glasses with contacts and then to my room to apply body spray. All the while, Papi put down his coffee mug to watch me. The ordeal took no longer than a minute. I took one last look at my reflection, squared my shoulders and opened the door as gracefully as I could muster.

"*Hey*," I said a little too eagerly. "Come on in."

I wasn't used to seeing Julian on his best behavior, but he hesitated before stepping into the house. As I closed the door behind him, I caught a glimpse of a black bicycle leaning against the neighbor's fence.

"How was the ride?" I asked.

"Hot," he responded. I could feel the heat radiating off of him from where I stood.

"I forgot to tell my dad you were coming until, like, five seconds ago."

Julian's hazel eyes flickered with concern. "Is it okay that I'm here?"

"Yes," I said quickly. "I just need to introduce you. Follow me."

I led him to the kitchen where my dad had fully situated himself to look directly at our guest, an unamused look on his face.

"A boy?" Papi asked suspiciously. I could hear Miss Josie's voice in my head, *"Lord, have mercy!"* I gulped.

"Papi, this is my friend Julian. I invited him to have some lunch." When my dad said nothing, I cleared my throat and turned to Julian. "This is my dad. His name is Marcos."

"Mucho gusto, Don Marcos," Julian said, offering his hand. I felt my jaw drop.

My father returned the handshake, his eyebrows raised. "You too, Julian."

I looked from Julian to Papi, shaking my head in disbelief.

"Um. What just happened?"

Julian shrugged.

I put up a finger. "No, no. Why didn't you tell me you spoke Spanish?"

"We just met, and you didn't ask. I took three years of it in middle school."

I retrieved a cold water bottle from the fridge and slid it in Julian's direction. He took it gratefully and downed it in less than a minute.

"That hit the spot," he said. "Thank you."

My dad cut in with a question of his own. *"Equipo favorito?"*

"Tampa Bay Rays for baseball, but I used to play soccer. I'm Italian, it's in my blood."

My dad nodded approvingly between bites. "Italia is a good team."

I piled the contents of the frying pan on a plate, still shaking my head in disbelief as Papi and Julian exchanged easy chatter. A thought occurred to me then.

"Papi, when's Daniel getting home?"

Papi chuckled as he picked up his plate. "I'm sorry, Julian," he said, before disappearing into his bedroom. Julian turned to me with a puzzled look.

"Did he mean to say 'excuse me'?"

I looked uneasily at the front door, making a split-second decision.

"Let's eat outside, shall we?"

Julian looked less than enthusiastic about going back out in the heat, but he followed me through the laundry room and out to the backyard. I walked a few more feet before I realized he was no longer at my side. I turned back to find him still standing just past the back door, holding his plate of food, his eyes wide.

D.S. Fisichella

"Woah."

I knew what he was thinking. My backyard was a little piece of home. Scattered all around were fruit trees — banana, papaya and even a small pineapple or two growing on bushes out of the ground.

The latest addition to the yard, a pergola, towered above us about ten feet off the ground. For a few weeks, my father had spent the better part of his Saturday mornings working on it with my brother. It was a simple structure: four pillars and wooden beams made up the roof. The framework was decorated with vines and hanging lights.

"This is incredible!" Julian said, finally coming over to join me.

"Thanks. It's my favorite place when the weather permits."

I led him under the pergola to a patio furniture set that a neighbor had sitting on his yard with a "Free" sign on it. The hammock in the back was a gift from my uncle in *Puntarenas*. Tia had brought it back with her after her Christmas trip to Costa Rica.

I put my plate down on the coffee table before removing two cans of soda from the pockets of my mom's apron.

"Your dad is funny," said Julian, taking a seat on a nearby wicker chair.

"I've heard people call him strict, intimidating and even scary. Never funny."

"He's just being a good dad and protecting his little girl," he said, his lopsided grin revealing his single dimple.

"He can be a bit overprotective," I mumbled as I undid the straps of the apron.

Julian reached into his backpack. "Before I forget, here's your Bible."

"Thanks," I said, taking it from his hands.

Julian took his first bite of *chilaquiles*, a look of serenity coming over his face. "This is good. What's it made of?"

"Fried tortilla, green tomatoes, spices and eggs."

"Teach me."

I laughed.

"I'm not joking," he said with a straight face.

"*Sure*, I'll add '*cooking lessons*' to our summer to-do list."

"Sounds good," he said as if we had just sealed a business deal.

"Wait," I said. "You're serious?"

"Sure. If you're up for it."

Dreamer

"I thought you would get tired of hanging out with me." I moved the food around my plate until I'd stabbed a little bit of everything onto my fork. The acidity of the green tomatoes, mixed with the peppers, produced just a little bit of heat on the roof of my mouth, exactly how I liked it.

"Why would you think that?" asked Julian.

"What?"

"Why would you think I wouldn't want to hang out with you?"

"I thought you'd have better things to do with your time than to hang out with a home-schooler. I don't know how to be anyone's friend anymore."

"That's not true," he said, taking another bite.

"Yes, it is."

"I meant the part where you said I had better things to do. I don't."

"Oh."

Julian grinned. "I'm messing with you. You're a good friend, Elleni. You showed up when nobody else did." He stopped talking and looked away. "What I *can't* figure out is why you did it. You could have called the cops and left it at that. Or you could have walked away. But you stayed."

"Yes, I stayed," I said, unsure of what he wanted to hear.

"But why?" he asked.

"Because," I paused, looking down at my feet, "no one should feel so alone."

His sneakers appeared in front of my own, his face just inches from mine. I held my breath as I studied his narrow nose, the soft pink of his lips and his breathtaking honey-green eyes under thick black lashes.

"If that's not friendship," he said quietly, "I don't know what is."

At the hospital, I felt out of control and small, as if I were falling through a vortex. But Julian had brought me back. He did so by speaking in a language I understood. At the time, all I heard was the music, but now, as we sat under the pergola, the scent of fruit trees permeating the air, I understood that the language we shared *wasn't* music. It was grief.

The back door slammed open, interrupting my thoughts and causing both Julian and me to jump. My twin stood at the doorway, his shoulders rigid, his hands made into fists.

"Leni, I need to speak with you."

I looked at Julian apologetically. "I'll be right back, okay?"

He nodded, making his way back to his seat, both curious and slightly alarmed at my brother's presence. I followed Daniel into the house and closed the door behind me. He tugged me by my wrist into his bedroom before turning to face me.

"Leni, I've seen that guy around town. He's bad news."

"You don't know him."

"Neither do you. Look, I'm glad you're wanting to make friends and all, but you *can't* change him, you *know* that, right?"

One part of me wanted to scream at my brother that he had no idea what he was talking about and that Julian was my friend, but another, much more rational and quiet voice inside me, whispered that I hadn't really known Julian for very long, and that, perhaps there *was* something I should be more cautious about. When I went back outside, I found Julian about to walk in with our dirty dishes.

"Hey," he said. "Is everything okay?"

I nodded, taking the dishes from him. "Yeah, I'm sorry about my brother, he's a little paranoid." I placed them in the sink.

"You didn't finish your lunch," Julian said. "Want to go back outside?"

"I'm not that hungry anymore."

Julian looked at me for a moment before nodding. "I should probably get going then." He slid his hands in his pockets. "I'm sorry if I caused any trouble."

"You didn't," I said, but even as the words left my mouth, I could tell he thought I was lying.

"Tell your dad I said goodbye."

"Let me walk you out."

"No thanks," he said, walking past me. "I know the way."

Chapter 7

"And we know that for those who love God all things work together for good, for those who are called according to his purpose."
Romans 8:28

"Ugh!" I threw my notebook across the room and fought the tears of frustration threatening to make their appearance.

"Drama Queen!"

"Shut up!"

Daniel poked his head through my bedroom door. "You're thinking so hard I can smell the smoke from my room. I just came to tell you that Mami left the chicken salad in the fridge. I'm going to make myself a sandwich. Want something?"

"Would quiet be too much to ask?"

"Sheesh! I stand by my earlier statement. I'll leave you to your misery."

He closed the door in time for a stuffed animal to miss his head, landing at the foot of the door instead.

Daniel had returned to his normal easy-going self the moment Julian left our house. I couldn't understand it, but for some reason, Daniel was even more overprotective than Papi, which was saying something. He didn't get it, though. All he saw is that since Julian left, I'd been immersed in my songwriting, trying to meet Brother Steve's deadline for the month. So, that meant everything was back to normal, right?

Wrong.

I'd zipped through my song quota in a couple of days, and put together the setlist for the Youth Band in a few hours, but ever since, I'd been trying and trying to write that stupid song that I could never write. And now, with Julian's cold shoulder in the back of my mind (he hadn't returned any of my texts for a week), I was at an even more unfavorable place to try to write about *her*.

I looked over at my sling, now folded neatly on my desk, and found my mind traveling to Julian and his unanswered texts. I had to do *something* to get my mind off him. The Spot? No. That's where we met. Take the city bus somewhere? Where? I pathetically had nowhere to go now that Julian was out of the hospital. Call up Miss Josie? Gee, what is more pathetic than hanging out at a hospital? Answer: Hanging out with your therapist.

"I have *got* to make some friends."

My cell phone buzzed from the bedside table. I snatched it up, hoping it was a text, but was met with a notification from the *TuneTrapp* music application instead.

Beatz has uploaded a new track! Click here to listen.

I clicked on the link. The title of the track was, *"Too Good 2 Be/R&B Soul Piano Instrumental."* I moved my head to the beat accompanied by the soulful piano loop.

When the song came to an end, I tapped on the comment box and wrote out a message.

Songirl7: "You've done it again, @Beatz. Thanks for this super inspirational track. You're the only artist I follow closely on here."

I hit, 'comment.' And was about to close the app when a notification appeared on the top right corner. I opened it to find a response.

Beatz: "Thanks @Songirl7, that means a lot. I'm glad you like my beats."

Before I could think of a response, the chat bubble opened up, a direct message from Beatz.

Beatz: "Hey, saw you were still online. Just curious as to your opinion on some of my other tracks. How many have you listened to so far?"

Songirl7: "Hi :) I've listened to probably all of them a couple of times to be honest. I like all of your stuff."

Beatz: "Cool! Do you have any favorites?"

Dreamer

Songirl7: "I'm a little biased towards the tracks that contain piano since I play piano myself, but I also like your upbeat stuff, too. Though it's been a while since you posted anything like that, I noticed."

Beatz: "Yeah, I've been feeling the ballads a bit more lately. I'm glad you like them, though. I see you've been on this platform for over a year, how come you don't have any uploads?"

Songirl7: "I'm pretty shy about my work. I've recorded voice tracks to some of your instrumentals but didn't feel brave enough to post them."

Beatz: "Please be brave. You'd make my day."

I drummed my fingernails nervously on the face of my phone and took a deep breath before hitting the 'attachment' icon and browsing through my Music Library. I opened the folder entitled "Beatz Collaborations" and scanned the list of songs. I tapped on the file entitled, "It's Alright," remembering how moved I'd been by the instrumental, and how excited I'd been with the final product once I'd recorded my vocals over the track. Before I could think myself out of it, I clicked on the link to upload it to the chat, and hit, 'send.'

It would take him about four minutes to listen to the track and formulate a response, so rather than wait impatiently for the minutes to tick on by, I got up, left my phone on the bed, and made myself a smoothie in the kitchen, all the while trying not to look at the clock.

I sipped the berry drink through a straw as I came back into the room, ignoring the feeling of my blood pressure rising. My phone lit up with a notification. I inhaled sharply, forgetting about the straw still in my mouth. The cold drink hit the back of my throat, the berry seeds sending me into a coughing fit all while the iciness turned my brain into an igloo.

"Ah! Brain freeze!"

"That's what you get for not making me a smoothie!" called Daniel from his bedroom.

I set the drink down and held both sides of my head in agony. Thank goodness the only Person who could see me was God. At least He was used to me.

You have a message from Beatz!

With my heart hammering in my chest, I opened the chat bubble and scanned the message, an involuntary smile making its way across my face.

D.S. Fisichella

    Beatz: "Let me just start by saying, thank you for conquering your fear and sending me your collaboration. I wasn't wrong when I said it would make my day. It has. You have an amazing voice and your lyrics are fire. The moment you started to sing, I kid you not, my heart stopped. It's been a long time since someone's raw talent moved me like that. I hope you'll consider sending me more in the future. The only critique I have is the quality of your recording device. It's not terrible, but if we're going to work together, I'd love to get you into my recording studio so we can do this right. Let me know what you think.
    All my best,
    Beatz."

    I threw myself back on my bed with a squeal of delight. Beatz liked my voice. Beatz wanted to work with me. Beatz wanted me to record in a professional setting!
    "Ahhh!"
    "What now!?" came my brother's muffled response.
    "This is the best day of my life!" I called back.
    Daniel stormed out of his bedroom and opened the front door. "Somebody *please* explain girls to me!" he bellowed.
    I didn't care. Something positive was finally happening to me.
    "Thank you, Lord!"

    Beatz and I spent the next two days exchanging messages. Early on, I asked for some background information on how he got started.
    Beatz: "I first became interested in making my music when I started listening to '90s and early 2000s Hip Hop and R&B. I didn't know how to start, but over time, by doing some research, I found out what kind of equipment I would need and I started saving up for it. It took me a few years to get what I have now, but I started pretty young, so I had plenty of time to learn. I was a scrawny boy when I first started rapping, so no one expected me to be good. I did a talent show one time and, since their expectations of me were already so low, I surprised everyone. I've thrived off the challenge ever since."
    When Beatz asked me about my lyrics, I responded:
    "I spent the first half of my life trying to figure out what I felt and why I felt that way. Some of the things I experienced made me feel like my voice didn't matter. Silence breeds chaos, so I started to say what I felt. At first, I only told my journals. After a while, I told a trusted professional, but now, I sing it."

Dreamer

Beatz: "I hear you, Song."

I sent him five more of my collaborations using his tracks, and he sent me beats he hadn't finished yet, asking for advice on how to make them better. I was flattered, of course, that he was asking for my opinion, but every time I offered suggestions, he would make the changes within a few hours and send me an updated version of the track.

Julian never texted back, and while that kind of disappointed me, my correspondence with Beatz softened the blow a bit. It was Wednesday, and I was getting ready for Youth Group after an entire day of messaging back and forth with Beatz.

Beatz: "It was nice talking to you today, Song. I wish we could continue this conversation, but I have to get going. Hope your evening is as awesome as you are. I'll message you tonight."

I smiled as I did my makeup and hair in the mirror, replaying our conversations in my head as I picked out my outfit, an airy coral dress paired with silver hoops in my ears. The fact that Beatz lived in my area, made the prospect of me leaving my house that much more exciting. He could be my next-door neighbor or the bag boy at the grocery store for all I knew.

Even if we agreed to meet, I told myself, *I would take somebody with me. It's just exciting that somebody besides my church music director believes in my talent.*

There was a honk outside and I hurried out of the bathroom just as Daniel was emerging from his bedroom. He took one look at my outfit and raised an eyebrow.

"Since when do you get all dolled up for band practice?" he asked.

"Trying something new."

Daniel shrugged and opened the door. I followed him outside and into my cousin Macho's car. I climbed into the front passenger seat and turned to him with a smile.

"Hi, Macho!"

Macho gave me the same surprised look Daniel had, minus the suspicion. "Hey, Leni. You look nice!"

"Thanks!"

Macho was our age, the son of my dad's sister. Macho and Daniel exchanged video game talk as I looked over my song selection for the evening. When we arrived at the church building, we bounded up the steps and into the Youth Room to get set up. Joshua, our media and sound tech, was already behind his laptop screen. He looked up as we came in and gave us a nod. He was a boy of few words, but we all liked him.

In the middle of soundcheck, Daniel's best friend, Jake, came in with his guitar case. Another man of few words. I opened my colorful folder and took out the sheet music I'd recently printed. The papers were still warm in my hands. I passed them out to the boys.

"Geez, Cuz. Another new song?" called Macho from behind his music stand. He played the bass guitar.

"Don't complain, it's your basic circle of fifths chord progression," I said. Macho held up his hands as if I'd made my point and didn't complain again. One old song and a new one. Our practice went by pretty quickly and we were getting ready to take our seats when our youth pastor's voice came through the doorway.

"It's simple. Not much to do in the Youth Room, it comes down to making yourself available. If you come Wednesday nights and Sundays, I'll count your attendance towards your community service."

I wasn't paying much attention to Todd's conversation until Daniel knocked over his stool from how quickly he got up from behind the drums. When I saw Daniel's facial expression, surprise, mixed with outrage, I looked over to see what had brought it on. Just past the door to the Youth Room, a few steps behind Todd, stood Julian Rossi.

"Hey, gang!" called Brother Todd. "Meet Julian, the newest member of our team. He's completing some community service hours here so he'll be around for a while. Julian, this is our Youth Band. Daniel is on drums, Macho on bass, Jake on guitar, and that young lady is our resident singer/songwriter, Elleni." Julian raised his hand in greeting, his face flushed. I felt rooted to the ground. Community Service? *Here?* What were the odds?

Oh Lord, you *would*.

I walked over to Daniel to do damage control.

"Dani, I didn't know he would be here, I promise." He still hadn't torn his eyes away from Julian.

"What *is it* with this guy?" he murmured.

"I don't know, Dani, but I'm going to talk to him and you need to keep your cool. Okay?"

"I don't like it."

Dreamer

"You don't have to. He met Papi and they got along fine. You don't have to like it, you just have to accept it. He's not so bad once you get to know him." Daniel snorted.

I clenched my teeth, "Daniel. He needs the Lord."

Finally, Daniel's gaze dropped to meet mine. I turned and made my way over to Julian who now sat awkwardly towards the back wearing jeans and a black T-shirt, no baseball cap in sight. I sat down next to him; it was crazy to think how effortless being this close to him had felt just days ago.

We exchanged pleasantries.

"How was your week after you came to my house?" I asked.

"It was good. I've been staying busy at home."

"What's all this about you doing community service?" I asked. His cheeks grew crimson.

"A while back I got caught shoplifting and was sentenced to community service, and then all the stuff happened that happened recently, so now I'm having to do my hours here."

"I see. So, you still don't believe in God?"

Julian turned to me with a puzzled expression. "What do you mean?"

"I mean, what are the odds you would end up doing your community service hours at *my* church?"

"Good point. But if there *is* a God, why would he sentence me to community service? Isn't He supposed to be loving?"

I laughed. "Sometimes God allows us to go through tough things to help us grow."

Julian nodded his head. "I'm sorry I didn't respond to your texts."

"Yeah, thanks for reminding me about that. Next time, could you just let me know you're okay before ghosting me?"

"That's fair."

In the time we spoke, the rest of the youth showed up. Brother Todd made his way over to us, a surprised smile on his face.

"Elleni, you seem to know Julian!"

"I do. We became acquainted a few weeks back," I said, sharing a funny look with Julian when Todd wasn't looking. Julian looked down to hide his smile.

"That's wonderful," Brother Todd said. "We're about to get started, do you mind introducing him?"

"Sure."

D.S. Fisichella

Julian's eyes grew wide as Brother Todd started to walk away. "What did he mean by that?"

"What he said."

From behind the pulpit, Brother Todd smiled in our direction before addressing the room.

"Alright, alright, everyone settle down. Elleni, why don't you introduce your guest?"

I felt Julian stiffen next to me. I wanted to pat his shoulder knowingly, I also hated being the new kid. "Everybody, this is Julian. Julian, everybody."

They responded in an AA meeting style. "Hiiii, Julian!"

He nodded and raised a hand in greeting.

After Todd made his announcements, I leaned over to whisper, "I'll be back soon," before taking my place at the front.

As Jake played the introduction, everyone stood. The lyrics that I'd handed to Joshua earlier now popped up on the screen beside me. I allowed my eyes to travel to where Julian was, hands in his pockets, his eyes on me.

I joined Jake's strumming with my playing, a soft beginning. I closed my eyes, asking God to take over the service. Moving my hands down the keys, I began to sing.

> Though the lights dim
> And our hands rise
> Lord, we know that's not worship
> And the music can play softly
> But we know that's not worship
> We can look up, and call on Your Name
> We can stand in silence
> But the truth is that You're worthy
> And Your Spirit reminds us

My soprano voice carried through the room — broken, deliberate and free. As I sang, I felt the day slip away, the last few weeks, the last few years. Unlike when I simply listened to music, when I sang it, I became bold.

Dreamer

Daniel played a beat on the drums as the rest of us ceased our playing, and then, one by one, we joined. First Macho with his bass, then Jake with his electric guitar, and finally, me with my voice.

> Our God reigns forever
> Our Savior Christ is Worthy
> We cannot count Your blessings,
> As many as the stars
> Our Father is unchanging
> His love is never-ending
> So vast it drowns the ocean
> So deep, it fills our hearts

I imagined what it might be like to get lost in the eyes of Christ. As I sang, I felt like a child again — loved, protected and untouched by the world.

After the music portion, I returned to my seat next to Julian. I'd almost forgotten he was there. He looked at me as he had in the hospital when I had shown him my scars, like he was seeing me for the first time. This time, however, his expression was coupled with admiration and something else I couldn't place.

I sat down next to him, and for a moment he didn't say anything, but when Todd started to preach, he leaned over to whisper, "I didn't know you could do that."

"It wasn't my idea to begin with, but I'm trying to be brave."

Julian smiled and turned back to Todd.

Chapter 8

"Why do you see the speck that is in your brother's eye, but do not notice the log that is in your own eye?"
Matthew 7:3

Beatz: "Hey, you up?"
Songirl7: "Yeah. Hi, how was your evening."
Beatz: "Better than I expected, honestly."
Songirl7: "That's nice! Mine too."
Beatz: "I've been trying to get up the nerve to ask you something."
Songirl7: "What's that?"
Beatz: "Do you want to meet?"

*

Text from Julian

Julian: "Let's hang out tomorrow."
Elleni: "Okay, but first, can you do me a favor?"

*

Dreamer

I was chuckling again. "I truly cannot believe that out of all the reckless things that you've probably done in your entire life, you spent your first night in juvie for stealing a bar of soap." I took a sip from the oversized slushie in my hand.

Julian threw his head back and groaned. "I am never going to live this down, am I?"

"Not a chance."

He swiped his baseball cap off long enough to wipe the sweat off his brow. It was ninety-five degrees and fifty percent humidity, which meant it felt like 107 degrees. The air was so stuffy, I felt I might choke on the heat.

"Walk me through this again," said Julian. "You met this guy on a music app and he wants you to be a feature on some of his tracks?"

"Yep."

"And you don't find any of this just a little bit alarming?"

"No, why should I?"

Julian groaned. "Elleni, this guy could be a creep."

I rolled my eyes. "That's why I asked you to come along."

"I guess. That's probably the only wise thing you've done concerning this situation. I don't have a problem beating somebody up."

I laughed.

We'd finally arrived at our destination. I checked the time on my cell phone. It was now noon, the time I was supposed to meet Beatz.

My heart was beating wildly in my chest as I anticipated what he would be like. What if Julian was right?

We mounted the back steps of the Bandshell and stepped onto the stage. In the middle of the stage lay a large bouquet of red roses with an envelope. As I walked closer to it, I saw it was addressed to "Song."

I couldn't help smiling giddily as I picked up the roses, opening the envelope carefully, so as not to rip it.

Dear Song,
You are the best thing that's happened to me in a long time.
Love,
Beatz

At that moment, my cell phone buzzed from my pocket.

Beatz: "Song, I'm sorry I couldn't be there to give you flowers in person, but I had to be somewhere important. Hope you can forgive me. I promise to make it up to you soon."

I didn't know how to feel. No one had ever given me flowers before, and while it was true that Beatz made me feel special, a part of me was terrified that he was just playing me.

"Is everything okay?" asked Julian.

I didn't turn around. "He's not coming."

I twirled my bracelet around my wrist as Julian walked up.

"Are *you* okay?"

I swallowed. "I guess so. Just… disappointed."

"He's a coward," Julian muttered.

"What if he saw us coming from a distance, got a good look at me, and decided to bail?"

"You're joking. You get stood up by this guy, and you're asking what's wrong with *you?*"

I stared down at my feet. It sounded so stupid when he said it that way, but what else was I supposed to think?

A thunderclap resounded throughout the field, and in an instant, a downpour came like I hadn't seen all summer. How did the sky get so dark without our noticing? I breathed in, closing my eyes while listening to the rain, nature's soundtrack.

"Elleni?" I opened my eyes. Julian watched as I continued to spin my bracelet around my wrist. "You never take it off, it must be important to you."

"It's part of a set. My friend Monica has the one that says, 'Best Friends.' Mine says, 'Forever.'"

"Your best friend? How come you never mentioned her before?"

I shrugged. "It's a long story."

"If you hadn't noticed, I think we have time." He sat down against the back wall of the bandshell and motioned for me to do the same.

I joined him.

"We had just moved to Florida from Costa Rica," I recalled. "It was November. I was eight years old and shivering in a lightweight jacket when this skinny blonde girl around my age came outside to play. She said something along the lines of, 'Hi, I'm Monica. Can I play with you?' But I

Dreamer

had no idea what she was saying. I mean, I didn't even know how to speak English at that point, so all I could do was stare."

Julian chuckled.

"But then she brought out a memory game and we spent the rest of the morning matching up the cards and saying the names of the items in English and Spanish. She helped me adjust and I learned English soon after." The thunder subsided, but the rain still fell freely. I made my way to the edge of the stage with my arm out, cupping a few raindrops in the palm of my hand. I glanced back to where Julian still sat, watching me. "The water is so warm!"

He got up to join me, mimicking my motion with his hand out. We stood quietly, side by side, watching the little puddles in our hands growing bigger until the water ran over our fingers and onto the ground. Julian smirked, let out a "Ha!" and splashed me in the face. I was stunned long enough to give him a running head-start. When I snapped out of it, I chased him across the stage, kicking off my shoes as I went. Julian did the same.

We hopped down into the soft wet grass on bare feet, running around in circles like children laughing under the torrential downpour.

I stretched my arms out to the sides, my face heavenward, embracing the storm. Julian ran around me, moving like a soccer player kicking an imaginary ball and shouting, "Goooooal!" as if his team had won the FIFA World Cup. That's when he slipped, falling on his back near my feet. I laughed.

"Oh, you think that's funny, huh?" Julian shouted.

"Duh!"

He grabbed my ankle and caused me to stumble. I shrieked and slopped on my back next to him, the wetness of the soil and grass seeping through my clothes and hair. I gasped.

"Jerk!" I shrieked, between giggles. Julian turned on his side to look at me, propping himself up on his elbow, his face just inches above mine, the color of his eyes standing out especially bright against the mud smeared on his face. I'd never seen him so happy. I reached up to pluck a blade of grass from his hair. He didn't turn away from my touch, instead, he held my gaze, and I caught a flicker of something in his expression.

His Adam's apple bobbed up and down in his throat as he cupped my face in the palm of his hand, his thumb tracing my cheekbone, but before I could decipher the meaning of his actions, he pulled his hand away and stood to his feet, leaving me with nothing but the memory of his touch and a trail of internal chaos.

A bit dumbfounded, I sat up. He stretched out his hand to help me off the ground. As he pulled me up, I had a quick mental flashback to the first time he took my hand like this, back at the tracks. I remembered the effect he'd had on me then. It paled to what I was feeling now.

"We should find a place to get cleaned up," I said, forcing a smile. "You're a mess."

I couldn't understand why he started to laugh until he reached his hand to my hair, pulling a large twig from it.

"You were saying?"

I couldn't believe I'd missed it. We erupted into another fit of laughter. I was reminded of a verse of scripture I'd heard many times:

"Why do you see the speck that is in your brother's eye, but do not notice the log that is in your own eye?" Matthew 7:3

I didn't think the verse could be applied quite so literally until today.

"My mom is going to kill me when she sees this in the laundry basket!" Julian chortled.

"Tell me about it. I'm beginning to think you're a bad influence," I said with a wink. Julian opened his mouth to say something but instead looked away.

We walked over to a small building nearby, a public restroom. I tried not to think about the germy floor as I waddled barefoot over to the sink. I gasped as I caught a glimpse of my mud-stained reflection and my hair, looking more like a bird's nest than anything else. I doubled back to the door, locking it, before stripping down to my underwear.

I ran my shirt and denim shorts under running water, careful to get out as much mud as I could. Once I got done with that, I got to work on my hair, trying my best to get as much dirt out of it as I could before wiping my arms and legs down with paper towels. There was a knock at the door.

"You still in there?" asked Julian.

"Just a minute!"

I gathered my hair to the top of my head and twisted it into a bun before shivering into my wetter-than-earlier clothes. With one final look at the mirror, I realized my wet shirt was showing just a bit too much detail, the design of my blue bra clear through the thin material. I groaned, and unlocked the bathroom door, poking my head out, my body still out of sight.

"Julian?" I called out.

"Yes?" he replied coolly from the other side of the door. I opened the door a little wider to peer around to the other side where he leaned against the wall, arms crossed.

"I'm in a bit of a predicament," I admitted.

"Oh?"

"My shirt is see-through."

Julian's face turned crimson, and for a moment he seemed at a loss for words before letting out a cough. "Right. Let's, uh… do something about that," he said before slipping his T-shirt over his head. Now it was *my* turn to blush. I hid my face behind the door before he could catch a glimpse of my expression. I reached an arm out where it was met by Julian's grey shirt. I pulled it over myself. It, too, was still damp but at least you couldn't see through it. It was long enough to also hide the faint brown mud marks that I hadn't managed to wash out of my shorts by hand. I stepped out to find Julian with his back to me. He turned at the sound of the door closing shut behind me.

"You look good in my shirt."

He looked good out of it.

*

Miss Josie's Office

"Ahem."

I looked up from my phone screen to find Miss Josie frowning at me.

"Sorry. Where were we?"

"You were telling me about Julian."

"Uh-huh," my eyes flickered back down to my vibrating phone.

"Girl, gimme that phone," she reached her hand over the desk, palm up.

Reluctantly, I handed it over. She put it on her desk, turning back to me. "I think it's time we talked about boyfriends."

"What?"

"*Boyfriends.*"

I shifted uneasily in my chair. "Why?"

"Because I can see it all over your face. From the shimmery lip gloss to the silly grin. You like him."

"No, I don't!"

We slumped back in our seats in unison. I huffed as Miss Josie threw her glasses on her desk, fingers to her temples. "Listen here, *Sassy Pants*. We are going to talk about boys, even if I have to do all the tongue flapping myself."

I sighed, knowing perfectly well that she wasn't going to let it go.

For a moment I saw an expression on her that I very seldom saw: reluctance. She reached into her desk drawer, pulling out a picture frame before handing it to me. It was facing down and heavier than I expected. I turned it over in my hands and gave a little gasp. It was the teenage version of Miss Josie, except she wasn't a Miss. She was a Mrs! She wore a beautiful white gown with a train that wrapped around her feet. Long brunette hair cascaded down her back, and the smile on her face said it all: she was in love.

"I didn't know you were married!" I handed the frame back to her. "What happened?"

She responded, her eyes not leaving the picture, "I'd just turned eighteen in this picture. Known the bloke most of my life. We were high school sweethearts." She sighed before putting the frame back in the drawer and sliding it shut. "It wasn't until I married him that I found out what a dog he really was. He'd cheated on me all through school."

"I'm so sorry."

"Don't be. Back then I had stars in my eyes and a spring in my step. Just a spring chicken who didn't know any better." I watched the light drain from her eyes as she recalled. "He was my whole world. Daddy never liked him, but that only made me like him more."

I tried to picture the younger version of Miss Josie, playful, radiant, and untouched by the world. "All the girls were green with jealousy when he asked me to homecoming my freshman year. He was a Junior, but d'you know what the problem was? I knew the Lord. I'd kept my vow of chastity and I assumed he would do the same. We lived smack-dab in the middle of the Bible belt, and everyone went to church on Sundays, including him. Didn't occur to me that he didn't give a rip about God."

"So he wasn't saved?"

"Far from it. Once he was married and out of his folks' house, his idea of worship on Sundays was football and the bottle. I never noticed it when I dated him." She frowned. "No, I take that back. I knew he drank but I thought I could change him."

I shifted forward in my seat.

"The real problems started once he went off to college. When he wasn't partying or womanizing, he was skipping class. That's how he lost his football scholarship. He had to quit school. He lied to me about it, of course. Said he'd taken a semester off to spend time with me, but he never went back. Instead, he spent his days wondering what might have been and his nights in bed with other women. I worked nights at a gas station. I came home early one morning, excited to make him breakfast in bed, but when I came in with his bacon, eggs, and coffee, I found him with our neighbor's wife, ten years his senior. She was the church pianist."

I gasped.

"Yeah. The only person that got breakfast that morning was 'Sister' Brigitte."

"You mean…"

"Dumped it on her."

"Even the hot coffee?"

"No. That little treasure I left to Jagat and his stupid blonde head."

I sneered. "Jagat? Seriously?"

Miss Josie chuckled. "I know, I know. I should've known the moment he introduced himself." We laughed. "You live and learn, Elle Belle. That's what I'm tryin' to tell ya. Smart people learn from their mistakes, but wise ones learn from the mistakes of others."

Once our session was over, I headed outside to where I'd chained my bicycle. The church was only a fifteen-minute ride from my house. I stuffed a yellow sticky note into my pocket. Miss Josie had written something down, handing it to me before I left her office.

"Look it up when you get home."

I rode to the rumbling of the pavement under my tires and the sound of seagulls overhead. They reminded me that a month of vacation had come and gone, and I'd yet to visit the beach. Once I got to my house, I let myself in, heading for my bedroom. I retrieved the note from my pocket.

D.S. Fisichella

"Proverbs 4:23 & 2 Corinthians 6:14," it said. I snatched the Bible from my desk, ruffling through the pages until I found the verses.

"Watch over your heart with all diligence, for from it flow the springs of life."

"Do not be bound together with unbelievers; for what partnership have righteousness and lawlessness, or what fellowship has light with darkness."

"We're just friends," I said to no one. Still, I couldn't help the undeniable tug of disappointment that clung to my heart.

Chapter 9

"For freedom Christ has set us free; stand firm therefore, and do not submit again to a yoke of slavery."
Galatians 5:1

In the days following our adventure at the Bandshell, Julian and I kept up constant communication, filling our days with easy chatter and mindless tasks.

Between bike rides to the public library or skateboarding lessons at the park, I kept him up to date on my songwriting and Daniel's day-to-day shenanigans. Julian noted how his mother, Melissa, seemed less stressed and had even cut back her hours at work to make family dinner every night. According to Julian, that was merely one of the many changes that had taken place since he got back home. The events leading up to his time there were now fading into nothing more than an unpleasant memory, one that neither one of us wanted to re-live.

When I first met Julian, he had put up a wall of anger and hate, keeping anyone from getting too close, especially me. It turned out, we had a lot of things in common, things we didn't feel we could share with anyone else, but somehow, our differences proved to be the one thing about our friendship that we grew to appreciate most.

I learned all he needed was someone to take an interest in who he was as a person, without prejudice. Someone who knew what it felt like to hurt.

Julian seemed to understand that all I needed was someone to listen, to be willing to walk alongside me as I faced each day.

My parents had noticed a change in me as well. On the days I hung out with Julian, I sometimes didn't get home until after my parents did. At first, my dad was worried I was spending too much alone time with Julian, but when I told him we were constantly in public and never in the house when no one was home, that seemed to calm his worries.

My mother was happy to see me spending time outside of the house, but her greatest relief came from a recent change in my sleeping habits. She was the first of my family to notice that I'd been waking up later than usual, not too much later, but later enough that it meant I'd dodged yet another night terror. Although I sometimes missed my sunrises at the Spot, I was just happy that when I woke up, it was on good terms.

So much had changed for the better that I'd even cut back on my meetings with Miss Josie. I missed spending time with her, but seeing less of her meant improvement, so I'd settled on the occasional text conversation. The only other times I saw her were for Sunday morning worship.

I hadn't seen Julian in a week, both of our schedules were filled with family endeavors and other summer activities, but now it was time for Youth Group again. I waited outside the church building, barely able to contain my jitters as the minutes slowly ticked closer to six-thirty.

I looked up from my cell phone to see a black Volvo pulling up. The front passenger door opened, and Julian stepped out. He wore a plaid green button-down with the top button undone, revealing the top of his smooth chest. His dark jeans looked crisp over his casual tan sneakers. Needless to say, he cleaned up well. He even styled his hair. No baseball cap in sight. At the sight of me waiting for him, Julian gave me a rare full smile, revealing his single dimple and a row of white teeth.

"Elleni, come here, would you? Mom wants to say hi." I went over to the car and bent my head down, peering through the open window to wave hello.

"Hi, Mrs. Heron!"

"Sweetheart, Melissa is fine. It's so nice to see you again. I just wanted to say how grateful I am that you two have been able to bond these past couple of weeks. You've been a really good influence on him."

I looked over at Julian, who tried not to laugh. "Mom."

"Thank you. It's been good for me too."

Dreamer

"I'm glad, honey. I'll leave you two to it. Have a nice time." We waved goodbye and started for the door as she drove away.

Julian turned to me. "Sorry about that. She likes you."

"I like her too." We fell in step together. "You look good by the way."

Julian gave me a flirtatious sideways look, setting my heart aflutter. "Yeah?"

I let out a nervous laugh. "Stop."

He started laughing. "What? You said it."

"I shouldn't have said anything."

He leaned down to my ear. "*Sei bellissima*, Elleni." Italian! Oh, he was good.

I reached down to smooth my hands over the lace, trying to clear the fog in my head.

We reached the one-way mirror glass doors and he opened them for me. Just as I wondered what could snap my senses out of its swarm of butterflies, we were met by the perfect cure: my brother.

"Hey, you two!" he boomed. Some elderly man shushed him from across the room.

I sighed. "We're already late for Youth Group."

Julian put a hand on my shoulder and turned to Daniel. "Look man, I know we didn't get off on the right foot, but Elleni is one of the best friends I've ever had. I think it would be a good thing if the two of us tried to get along. Maybe I can buy you a pizza and we can play some video games at my place?"

My brother stood up straight. "You don't have any good games."

"How would you know? I have shooter games, *FIFA, Madden, MLB*, and I think I have a *Dragon Ball Z* game somewhere in there."

Daniel's ears perked up. "Maybe I'll take you on, as long as you understand that you're going to lose."

Julian chuckled. "Yeah okay, we'll see about that."

Daniel nodded before heading up the stairs, taking them two at a time. We followed behind him.

"Wow, I think you managed to get my brother to stop hating you for a split second."

"Eh, guys are easy. There's nothing that can't be fixed for us by some food and friendly competition."

We followed the sound of laughter into the Youth Room.

"Heads up!" A football sailed through the air in front of us. Julian caught it, just inches from my nose. Brother Todd, our youth pastor, spoke up from behind a simple wooden pulpit. "Alright Mickey D., I warned you guys about throwing stuff indoors. Mark, Southeast. Kota, Northwest."

Dakota grumbled under his breath on his way to the front of the classroom. As he passed us, Julian handed him the ball. Dakota smirked, "Nice catch, pretty boy."

"Uh, thanks?"

My brother had already made his way to the back of the room, sitting beside cousin Macho, Jake, and Jake's girlfriend Selah, who was the head pastor's eldest. Leah, Selah's younger sister, waved me over.

"Settle down, everyone," Todd was saying as we sat down next to Leah. "As you all know, for the past ten years our church has been going to the Florida Baptist Encampment in Groveland."

Identical twins, Mark and Dakota (dubbed Mickey D. by Brother Todd), chanted in unison from opposite sides of the room: "GROVELAND! GROVELAND! GROVELAND!" Todd dropped his head, massaging the bridge of his nose until their cheer was over.

"This year, our Association of churches has completed the building of a brand new retreat in Georgia. This camp has been in the construction process for about three years. Joshua, hit it." Our youth tech, Joshua, hit a few buttons on his laptop, the light of the screen reflecting off his glasses.

The white screen behind Brother Todd came to life with footage of a large property complete with hills and a forest backdrop, as well as images of half-built cabins and young adults taking part in the construction of timber frames.

"Youth from all over the country have been to this property to aid in the building of the facilities themselves. I would have loved to send you all to give a hand as well, but unfortunately, we didn't have the funds. The good news is that for the first time, this retreat called 'Grace Place' will be open to outsiders, and I think it's about time we had a road trip."

"Alright!" Daniel and Macho high-fived.

"Due in large part to the number of fundraisers our church has been able to host for the youth, we have enough money to give each one of our teens a partial payment towards a visit to the campground. Ladies and gentlemen, it's time to start packing!"

Dreamer

Applause erupted across the room as the teens whooped their approval. Next to me, Leah did a little jig from her seat before whispering to me. "Yay!"

"Last but not least, I would like to announce that some very lucky people will have their entire trip paid for." Todd looked at his watch, determined to push on. "I have some requirements for those that want a full payment: First off, you must attend every night of Vacation Bible School as a volunteer. Secondly, your church service attendance is vital. From this Sunday on, every Wednesday and Sunday you must be here on time. Third, if you put in extra hours to help the church function, you will be at the top of the list. Lastly, your conduct outside of this church building ought to be exemplary. Don't think I don't find things out."

Some chuckled, some murmured seriously in agreement.

"Any questions?"

Next to me, Leah who'd started filing her nails, stopped long enough to raise her hand, "Brother Todd? Since I'm new to this whole camp thing, what do we wear?"

Todd turned to his wife Amanda, a water cup poised to his lips. "You want to answer that, honey?"

Amanda stood from her place on the front row. "Sure. We usually have a strict dress code, but for you, Little Leah, I'm willing to bend the rules."

"Oh, goody!" Leah clapped her hands together, her ponytail bobbing.

"Since I already know you're going to have a hard time keeping to the dress code, you can just bring a potato sack and call it a day!" Brother Todd did a spit-take into his cup, sending the whole room into a fit of laughter.

"Not cool!" Leah pouted.

I whispered, "Don't worry, girl. I'll help you out."

"Thanks," she whispered back.

A minute later, my phone was vibrating from my purse.

"Check your text messages," whispered Leah. I did.

"Lenicious, I know what I want to do with you."

I cringed at her wording but typed back.

"What's that?"

She winked sideways at me. My phone vibrated with one last message, a GIF depicting the slumber party scene in *Grease*.

"SLEEPOVER!" she squealed so loud that everyone around us turned to look at her.

D.S. Fisichella

"Care to share what you're so excited about?" asked Brother Todd.

Leah shook her head innocently.

As more hands shot up all around the room, I turned to Julian who sat with his eyebrows raised, looking around. "Would you consider going on the road trip with us?" I asked.

Julian leaned close to my ear. "To be honest, all of this is a little overwhelming."

"How so?"

He looked embarrassed. "This is the first time I've ever seen a bunch of teens having a good time without a beer or a joint in their hand. It's nice, but not what I'm used to."

I was stunned. This was my world. Every Wednesday and Sunday, I could count on a group of teens to be there with Todd, ready to open up Scripture, all of us learning and laughing together.

It was true, I had avoided letting any of them get too close to me the past few years, but they had always treated me kindly. I had never thought about what it might be like to be a part of a group of friends who, instead of building one another up, took joy in seeing each other's downfall.

I whispered to Julian, "I'm glad you're here."

Once Brother Todd finished taking questions about the road trip, I made my way to the keyboard at the front of the room, adjusting the mic. My brother took his place at the drums as Jake took up the guitar and Macho, the bass.

Once the music portion of the youth service was over, I made my way back to my seat to find Julian looking down at his hands. From my tote bag, I produced two Bibles; one was mine, but the second was a brand-new black leather Bible with the name 'Julian Rossi' engraved along the bottom in gold, matching the gold page lining. I presented it to him.

"What's this?" he asked, as I put it in his hands. His fingers traced the name at the bottom with reverence.

"I figured you should have your own," I whispered. "Especially if you're going to be around for a while."

He looked at me, seemingly speechless. I reached over to guide him to Galatians chapter five, where Todd had announced we would be reading.

"Elleni," he murmured, "thank you."

I squeezed his hand before turning my attention back to my own Bible and Todd.

Dreamer

"Stand fast therefore in the liberty by which Christ has made us free, and do not be entangled again with a yoke of bondage," he read out loud before looking up to address us. "Guys, if you are in Christ, you are a new creature. It says so in chapter two of this same book. But does that mean we become immune to this world? No. It does not. As children of God, we are going to be tested and tried. Sometimes we are going to have to make the same mistakes several times before we can get it through our heads that we can surrender ourselves over to God and not go down those same roads of sin and destruction over and over again. Take a look at John chapter eight, starting on verse thirty-four."

"Jesus answered them, 'Truly, truly, I say to you, everyone who practices sin is a slave to sin. The slave does not remain in the house forever; the son remains forever. So if the Son sets you free, you will be free indeed.'"

Todd looked up from his Bible. "My question tonight for you all is this: are you a slave to sin? Or has the Son set you free?"

Todd went on with his lesson until the clock hit eight, at which time we were dismissed. As people were filing out, Todd made his way over to us to welcome Julian with a handshake. "We are going to be great friends, Julian. There sure is a whole lot I've been wanting to do with this Youth Room before it's time for Vacation Bible School. This reminds me, all the community service you'll be doing will put you right in line for that full scholarship to go to Georgia with us this summer. Does that sound like something you'd like to do?"

"I've never been to church camp before, but it does sound like fun. I'll ask my mom."

"As long as you can stay out of trouble, I don't see why you shouldn't be able to get it. I hope you'll consider joining us." He then turned his attention toward my brother who'd put Macho in a headlock. "Daniel! We talked about this." He walked towards the small commotion. A karate cry was heard and then an "Ouch!" as Todd thumped my brother on the back of the head.

Julian turned to me with a docile expression. Gone was his playful air from earlier. "I wanted to ask you something."

"Go ahead."

"My mom still wants to thank you for everything you've done for me. She asked me to invite you to dinner tonight."

"Tonight? That's kind of short notice. I need to ask my parents."

"I thought you'd say that. You should know that I was late today because I had my mom swing over to your house before church. I met your mom and introduced her to mine. We asked permission to have you over tonight and they said yes."

"You did all that?"

He shrugged it off. "So, will you come to have dinner with me and my family?"

"No."

"Huh?"

"*Joking.* Of course!"

We made our way down the stairs. I dialed my mom's number and waited until I heard her voice on the other end before thanking her for allowing me to have dinner with Julian and his parents.

"You're welcome, *Preciosa*. Julián es *guapísimo!*" I heard my dad's warning tone in the background. "Oh, calm down, Marcos. What I meant to say is that he is very nice and his mom is sweet." I laughed. "Be home by curfew, okay?"

"Yes ma'am." We said our goodbyes, and I hung up the phone, smiling.

"Making sure I wasn't trying to kidnap you?" Julian asked with his hands in his pockets.

"Something like that."

Chapter 10

"How long must I take counsel in my soul and have sorrow in my heart all the day? How long shall my enemy be exalted over me?"
Psalm 13:2

Melissa Heron waited outside of her car, dangling keys out to Julian.

"You're going to let me drive your car?" he asked.

"Why not? You have your license, it'd be a pity to let it go to waste. Also, this is the first time you're bringing home a girl I like."

I interjected, "Mrs. Heron, I think you have the wrong idea."

She laughed. "You'll understand when you have kids of your own, honey. Embarrassing your child in front of his friends is the funniest thing you will ever have the pleasure of doing." This playful woman stood in stark contrast from the weary, sad lady I had met at the hospital. I liked her.

Julian groaned. "I'm glad you're having fun laughing at me, but can we please get going?"

Melissa motioned for me to ride shotgun, climbing into the back before I could protest. It was evening time; the sun had begun to dip under the horizon.

I looked out the window and watched as trees went by in my vision: oaks, pines, palms and everything in between. The houses that went by also caught my attention. Small homes, like where I lived, turned into larger homes with multiple-car garages and luscious yards. Julian was silent, his fingers tapping on the steering wheel and his eyes looking straight ahead.

Just as I started wondering what we were doing in one of the fanciest neighborhoods in the county, we pulled up to a small mansion, for lack of a better word. When I looked out the window, I was astonished.

Standing two stories high was a Mediterranean style villa overlooking a glistening waterfront. A veranda wrapped around the house's second-floor balcony, while a beautiful chandelier was framed in the largest window of the first floor, over a bright dining area.

Julian turned off the ignition and unbuckled his seatbelt. "We're here." His mom stepped out of the car, straightening her jacket before heading inside. I still hadn't moved.

"Elleni? Are you going to stay in the car?"

"You have a big house," I responded stupidly.

Julian got out of the car, coming around to open my door. "Come on. It's time for you to meet the man of the house."

I got out of the car and waited for Julian to lead the way.

"So, I knew your folks were well off, but this is a castle."

"I don't know. I mean, it's nice, but I can't wait to get my own place."

As we walked closer to the fountain, I admired how the water cascaded into the little pool beneath, a mosaic pattern making up its floor.

"Not sure what you mean," I admitted. "If I lived here, I would never want to leave."

When we reached the front door, he held it open for me. Somehow, I was still surprised by this gesture.

"Come on in, Elleni!" called Melissa.

I stepped into the beautiful home to find a hardwood-floor staircase leading upward. To the left of it, the marble foyer opened up into a gorgeous sitting room, a large fluffy area rug spread in the middle under a coffee table. Behind the coffee table was a French-style couch with some tufted ivory armchairs to either side. I imagined the furniture in this room alone would probably cover our rent for a year. I followed Melissa's voice to the dining area on the opposite side of the staircase.

"Hey, kids!" Julian and I turned to see who I could only assume was Julian's stepdad coming down the stairs. "Hey Joe," Julian said. "Meet Elleni."

Dreamer

Joe Heron was a handsome man, about six feet tall with grey eyes. He spoke with a deep tone, revealing flawless teeth — artificially whitened, no doubt. He wore a white button-down over jeans and loafers. His hair was silver. I tried not to stare. He looked like he came straight out of a movie screen.

I waved. "Hi."

"Well hello, Elleni. I've heard so much about you," he said with a confident air. "Julian, you didn't mention she was a beautiful Latina."

"Latinos are hardly uncommon in Florida," Julian muttered under his breath.

"He's right, you know," I said to Joe, "I'm getting more common around here every day."

Joe shook his head. "You are gorgeous, darling. Where were you born?"

"Costa Rica."

"Ah, see. That's it. You come from one of the most beautiful places on Earth." He leaned in to whisper in my ear as Julian moved past us to the table. "I'm glad you're finally here. Julian hasn't shut up about this dinner since he asked us to have it." I didn't say anything as he led me to the dining area. Why would Julian lie about whose idea it was?

I sat down in a cushioned ivory chair, looking over the exquisite table settings. A crystal flower vase held a fresh arrangement of cream-colored top-of-the-line flowers in the center of the table. I looked up at the chandelier that hovered over the table. It glistened merrily.

Melissa placed a bowl of salad in front of me, shortly followed by a plate of stuffed chicken marsala. I breathed in the aroma of spices and mozzarella cheese, my stomach rumbling loud enough for everyone to hear. Julian chuckled next to me as Melissa set down his plate and Joe's. I elbowed him. Joe mused over Melissa. "Honey, we'd better start. The children are getting fussy."

"Do you mind if I pray?" I asked.

"Of course we don't mind, do we, honey?" Joe said, looking over to his wife.

"We'd love that," Melissa reassured me. She reached for my hand, and I responded by taking Julian's. His hand felt warm wrapped around my cold fingers.

Over dinner, Julian talked about his day of community service and how nice everyone at the church had been. I mentioned camp in hopes that Julian's parents might retain that knowledge for a later conversation about whether or not Julian would be allowed to go. Dinner was followed by dessert — key lime pie and vanilla ice cream.

"You know why Julian hasn't got a car, don't you Elleni?" asked Melissa.

I looked at Julian who suddenly seemed to take a big interest in the way the bubbles in his glass of soda sat on top of his drink. I turned back to Melissa. "No idea."

Joe said, "He's stubborn, that's why."

Melissa smacked him playfully on the arm. "No, he just wants to *earn* it."

"Not a good enough reason to turn down a sports car."

I turned to Melissa. "He turned down a car?"

"On his sixteenth birthday too," Joe said. "Here is this brand-new red Mustang with black racing stripes, presented to him in front of all his closest friends, mind you, and he turns it down. I know sixteen-year-olds that would sell their soul for a car like that. I thought he would be thrilled."

"And he wasn't?" I asked, stealing a side glance at Julian, who looked ready to leave the table.

"His girlfriend was way more excited than he was. The worst part was when I went to give him the keys. The kid turned around and walked back into the house. Didn't come out of his room until everyone left."

Melissa cut in. "The way I see it, when you come from next to nothing as I and Julian did, those material things become less and less important. I don't think he was being ungrateful. Were you, sweetheart?"

Julian cleared his throat. "Can we change the subject?"

I looked over at the clock. I had an hour and a half before curfew. When I mentioned this to Melissa, she asked me if I would feel comfortable with Julian driving me home on his own since she'd had a little more wine than she probably should have had.

"What time do we need to get going?" asked Julian.

"My curfew is not until eleven."

"Would you like a tour?"

"Sounds good."

Dreamer

We left the table, Julian leading the way toward the back of the house. I wondered how Melissa managed to keep this huge place looking as great as it did. For me, keeping my bedroom neat was a hassle.

"Do you have a moat?" I asked as we walked away from the dining area and Julian's folks.

"Sorry to disappoint you," he said with a smirk.

"How about a secret passageway?" I asked intently.

He pursed his lips. "I can't say we do. But if we did, where do you think it would lead?"

"I don't know," I admitted. "Maybe the beach?"

"Eh."

I rolled my eyes. "Alright Mister, you got a better idea?"

"How about a tower with a winding staircase?"

"What's inside the tower? A damsel in distress?"

"No. A man cave. Complete with an air hockey table, an industrial-sized refrigerator stacked with frozen pizzas, and a personal home theatre."

"I should have guessed."

We rounded the corner to find a grand piano displayed majestically against the gorgeous backdrop of the Heron's backyard. I gasped at the way the moonlight danced over the keys.

"It's gorgeous!" I ran my fingers over the black and white. The keys had just enough weight to them as I pressed down.

"Joe got it for his mother's eightieth birthday after her old one quit. When she passed away he got it back. My mom forced me to take piano lessons when she married Joe. I'm the only one that plays it around here."

"You?"

"Don't get ahead of yourself. I only know a couple of songs."

"Show me, please." I patted the bench. He groaned but joined me anyway.

"Here goes nothing."

He played the introduction to a love song I'd never heard before. I was surprised when he began to sing along to it, his tenor voice rich, the tough drug-dealing persona slowly drifting away to reveal yet another layer of the complicated Julian Rossi.

He stopped abruptly.

"Oh, please don't stop."

"I have to."

D.S. Fisichella

"Why?"

"Because that's as far as I got."

"You mean... you wrote that?"

Julian smiled. "Don't sound so surprised. I told you music was therapeutic to me, didn't I?"

I crossed my arms. "It's quite a long jump from beatboxing to playing ballads, don't you think?"

He shrugged. "I'm not much of a lyricist; I just come up with the track. Come on, I'll show you."

I followed Julian down a hallway. He opened a door to reveal a sparsely decorated room, with a loveseat against one wall and top-of-the-line recording equipment with several computer screens against the opposite one. A large window was placed above the recording equipment, but I couldn't see through the glass. The only other thing in the room was a door that presumably led to a closet.

"Wow. Is all this yours?"

"Yeah, thanks to my old job."

"Oh."

He shrugged. "The pay was good."

He stepped inside and opened the closet door, revealing a recording booth. The walls were covered with acoustic soundproof panels against dark purple walls. In the center stood a stool and a professional recording microphone. A headset hung from a hook on the wall.

I'd written so many songs over the years but never had the connections to record any of them. The musician in me itched to step into the booth. Julian must have sensed my excitement.

"What do you think?" he asked, looking pleased.

"I think I need to get in there."

"What are you waiting for?"

That's all I needed to hear. I stepped inside and closed the door. When I took a seat on the stool, I realized I was facing a dark curtain. I moved it aside, for the first time catching a glimpse of the frame that hung on the wall behind Julian's head. Cased inside the frame was a single word, one I knew well.

BEATZ.

Dreamer

My mind traveled back to the train tracks when Beatz's music almost moved me to tears, and later on, when Julian stopped talking to me for a while, that's when Beatz came into my life. And then…

The Bandshell.

I thought Beatz had stood me up, but it'd been Julian all along.

Julian gave me a half-smile from the other side of the glass. He put on a headset and motioned for me to do the same. When I did, his voice came through.

"You figured it out." His voice was so crisp that it felt like he was standing right next to me. I spoke into the mic.

"How long have you known?"

"When I got those recordings of your voice with my tracks, I couldn't get it out of my head. Then one day I walk into a classroom to fulfill my first day of community service, and there you are, singing just like the mysterious girl whose voice I'd fallen in love with." He cast his eyes downward, and let out a short laugh, his cheeks turning a slight shade of red. "Wow, I can't believe I said that."

I laughed too, thinking of how cute he looked when he was embarrassed.

"So, um, now that the mystery is over… do you still want to work with me?" he asked.

I didn't hesitate.

"Absolutely."

I recognized the introduction, but after the first few bars, it was accompanied by a sad melody an octave higher. Then the beat dropped. I couldn't believe this was the work of someone my age, as I could picture this being something that might play on mainstream radio. My favorite part by far was Julian's singing voice.

I was a shadow of myself
I never thought
I could be anyone else
I was ready to die
Ready to die

After an instrumental, he came in with a chorus.

Then you found me

And you loved me
Called my name
Took me in your arms

When his voice fell silent, I heard a click in the headphones.

"Think you can help me out, Song Girl?"

I smiled at Julian through the window.

"Yes, Beatz. Let's go."

He started from the beginning and when it was my turn to take over, my head and my heart let out all I wanted to say. When I was done, Julian's voice came through my headphones again.

"That was incredible. Come out here and listen back to it with me."

I stepped out of the booth, excited to hear my recording, but Melissa put her head through the door and got Julian's attention.

"Honey, Dylan's here."

Julian nodded and turned to me. "Wait here. There's something I have to take care of."

"Okay," I said. When he left, I snuggled up on his swivel chair, breathing in his cologne all around me. I smiled, still unable to believe I'd been befriending Beatz all along. I drummed my fingers on the table for a few minutes before deciding I'd better find the nearest bathroom. I heard the sound of running water coming from the kitchen and poked my head through. Melissa stood at the sink, her back to me.

"Hey, Melissa. Where's your nearest bathroom?"

She called over her shoulder. "The one downstairs is just a mess, you're better off going upstairs. First door on the right."

"Thank you!" I ascended the stairs, my fingers tracing the stylish railing. Everything about the Herons' place screamed wealth, and although I knew that Julian and Melissa merely inherited everything I was looking at, it was hard not to feel a little bit jealous of the kind of comfort they enjoyed. Once again, I wondered why Julian would rather make his money illegally. When I reached the top, I heard voices coming from what was presumably Julian's bedroom, but hurried past it to my destination.

On my way back toward the staircase, the muffled conversation caught my attention once again.

"Did you know Bianca broke up with Paxon? Now's your chance to win her back. Am I right?" The nasal voice carried clearly through the

Dreamer

closed bedroom door by the stairs. My foot hovered over the steps, my hand clutching the railing.

Julian responded. "What makes you think I'd want her back?"

"Because she's the hottest girl at school."

"It can't be all about looks, Dyl."

"But you guys were together since, what, kindergarten?"

"Fourth grade."

"So, did you find a rebound or what?"

"Shut the hell up, Dylan."

"What's her name?"

"It's *none of your business*. Drop it."

"Come on, Rossi."

Julian must have sensed Dylan wasn't going to let it go. "Her name is Elleni and she's *not* a rebound, you idiot."

After a brief pause, a husky voice spoke up. "I've hooked up with an Elleni."

If Julian heard the second speaker's remark, his tone didn't betray the fact. Instead, he spoke neutrally. "I uploaded all of Tekky Mel's stuff onto your cloud, even the underground stuff. It'll take you a year to sort through everything."

A cell phone rang, and Dylan spoke up. "Thanks for giving my man the hookup. I have to take this call. Cal, I'll meet you in the car."

The name pierced through me like an icicle to the heart. I ducked back into the bathroom as the scrawny Dylan emerged. He walked with his shoulders hunched over, a large cell phone to his ear, and a flashy watch floating loosely around his wrist. He left the bedroom door ajar, allowing the voices from inside the room to carry. A moment later, the front door closed with a heavy sound.

"Does she ever mention me?"

"Who?" Julian sounded distracted.

"Elleni."

"Look, man. I don't know who you hooked up with, and I don't care, but I guarantee it's not the Elleni I know."

"When's the last time you heard of someone with her name? I'm just saying, you should ask her about me. If it turns out to be the same girl, let me be the first to offer you my congratulations."

Julian was quiet for a long few seconds before replying.

"You've got my number. Message me if you need anything else. I have to get back to work."

Cal only chuckled in reply. A moment later, there was the sound of a bedroom door slamming shut followed by footsteps down the stairs.

As I heard the front door opening and closing again, I collapsed, lifting a trembling hand to my face, a trickle of tears against my hot skin.

*

Four Years Earlier

In—two, three. Out—two, three. In—two, three. Out—two, three. In—
"Leni?"
—two, three. Out—two, three.
"Someone's here to see you."
In—two, three. Out—two, three.

"He says he wants to pay his respects," Daniel said, moving aside to let him pass. "I'll leave you to it. Let me know if you need anything."

"Hey, beautiful."

I stopped counting my breaths long enough to look at the speaker, but I said nothing.

"Where are your parents?" he asked.

"Reception," I mumbled.

"I saw you at the church. Sorry about your friend." He closed the distance between us, reaching up to touch my hair.

"Thank you," I whispered.

"Are you okay?" he asked, twirling my hair sweetly around his finger. It was the way he asked, not like everyone else who'd uttered that same question in the last week. When I looked into his face, his expression didn't seem rehearsed. It wasn't painted with an attempt at remorse that no one could convey except me. When Cal asked if I was okay, I knew he was asking for real because he didn't try to hide his true self. Someone else might find his easy grin off-putting, but I found it authentic, and comforting.

"Not really," I admitted.

With those two words, I got a taste of my own realness. However brutal it was, at least it was *real,* and that had to count. All I wanted was to feel something other than pain, other than guilt or the reality that my childhood was gone, and with it, my innocence.

Dreamer

It was for this reason that when he brought his lips to mine, I didn't protest. This was my first real kiss, and while I didn't know exactly how to do it, I followed his lead, mimicked his motions, and through it all, I began to forget. Forget the day. Forget the pain. Forget *her*. When his kiss deepened, I didn't complain. But then his hand found my zipper, and without a hint of hesitation, he pulled it down.

"What are you doing?"

"Shh." He brushed his hands over my bare skin.

"Stop," I whimpered against his hot breath. When he looked at me, the playfulness in his gray eyes was gone, replaced by steel. I swallowed. "I—I don't feel so good." He didn't move. "I think you should—" I didn't finish the sentence because just as those words were leaving my mouth, he shoved me onto the bed.

"This will only take a minute," he grumbled.

"No."

He clamped a hand over my mouth Panicked, I bit down as hard as I could. He jerked his hand away and examined the bite mark.

"B*tch."

He backhanded me across the cheek, before sending a second blow to my gut. I gasped, the wind knocked out of me. I lay, looking up at the ceiling, unable to utter a sound as he climbed on top of me, hiking up my skirt in the same movement.

Daniel called from the living room, "You guys want something to drink?"

I inhaled sharply, my nostrils filled with the smell of weed and body spray. With a tight jaw and venom in his eyes, Cal got off me, pulled my skirt back down to my knees, and straightened out his tie.

"Waste of my time," he hissed.

"Hello?" Daniel's voice was just outside the door now Cal put one finger to his lips, making sure I got the message before he opened the door.

"Hey, we're good on drinks, but thanks for asking," he said, a smile in his tone.

"Oh, okay. You're welcome."

"I'm headed out now," Cal said, running a hand through his hair. "I have some errands to run."

That's when Daniel caught a glimpse of me on the bed. "Leni?"

"She said she wanted to be left alone to take a nap," Cal said coolly.

"Oh. Well, thanks for stopping by."

"Not at all. Thank *you*."

*

Suddenly, sure I was going to scream, I looked around for something to stuff into my mouth. My eyes landed on a neatly-folded hand towel on a silver rack. I bit down on the cloth and let out a muffled wail. I wanted to shriek at the top of my lungs, throw things, claw out of my skin, disappear, but this was not the place to lose it. If I could get back down to the recording studio or even the piano, I might be able to use the music to pull myself together before I had to face Julian again.

When I'd regained enough of my composure to stand without my knees giving away, I gathered up the courage to check that Julian's bedroom door was still closed before bolting down the stairway. I reached the first floor just as the front door reopened and Cal came through.

Standing at about six feet, his dirty-blonde hair was styled differently than I remembered, and he'd grown a five o'clock shadow. A whimper escaped my lips as he looked up from his cell phone, recognition registering on his face.

"So it *is* you," he hissed, sliding the phone into his pocket. His expression was a mix of glee and surprise. His gray eyes snaked along the curves of my frame, lingering on my bust for two seconds too long. "You look grown-up." His tone was smooth, like that of a car salesman, oozing with flattery, a hint of rottenness just under the surface. I gripped the railing as he prowled in my direction. "Do you remember me?"

How could I forget?

"No?" He cocked his head to one side, showing his teeth. He was just inches from me, raising one hand to my neck. With two fingers, he lingered on my pulsing vein before moving his hand backward, toward my hair. He took hold of a lock and followed it down to its end, near my chest. The movement, as harmless as it was, made me feel utterly and completely violated. I inhaled sharply, involuntarily breathing in the familiar scent of weed, sweat and body spray. How did I ever forget that smell? If I had a name for it, it would be *Hell*.

"Elleni?" Julian's voice brought me back. I wanted to turn to him, ask for help, but Cal's soulless eyes had shackled me in place, the steel piercing through my heart, rendering me completely helpless.

"What are you still doing in my house, Calvin?"

Cal smirked. "I left my wallet," he sassed, not looking up.

Julian flung it toward his head, but Cal caught it without taking his eyes off me.

"*Get out,*" Julian growled.

"Alright." Cal yanked me forward by my hair. "But Elleni is coming with *me,* aren't you baby?"

What followed happened fast; Cal was thrown down the stairs, a clump of my hair still around his finger. The sick *thud* of his head against the tile. The strike of Julian's fist into Cal's nose with a *crunch*, and the sight of blood spouting down his face and jaw.

"You're going to regret that," Cal snarled.

I tore my feet from the stairs and darted blindly through the house, trying to put as much distance between me and the brawl as possible.

"Julian, get off him!" Melissa's stilettos clicked furiously behind me, her voice calling for her husband. "Joe!"

"Joe, let me go!" Julian shouted.

"Kid, I can't hold him much longer. Get out of here!"

Cal cursed, "All of this over that—"

"Finish that sentence and I'll kill you."

"*Keep her*. Everyone else has had their turn."

"JULIAN, STAY DOWN!" Joe's bellow echoed through the house, followed by the slamming of the front door and the screech of a car speeding out of the driveway.

"You heard what he said! Why would you let him go!?"

"Because you need to make sure she's alright!"

Julian found me sobbing on the floor beside the piano, my hands pressed against my ears. He knelt at my side.

"Are you okay?" His hair was disheveled, a button or two missing from his shirt, but otherwise, he looked fine. He tipped my chin toward him and lowered my hands from my ears. I flinched at his touch. Hurt flashed across his face, but it was replaced by empathy. "You're safe now," he breathed, pulling me into his chest. "It's over."

I wanted to believe it. With every molecule in my body, I wanted to allow his warmth to wash over me with promise.

But it wasn't over.

Not for me.

Chapter 11

"So flee youthful passions and pursue righteousness, faith, love, and peace, along with those who call on the Lord from a pure heart."
2 Timothy 2:22

Miss Josie once explained to me why I had these 'episodes' as she called them. In times of extreme stress, my mind disconnected from the rational part of my brain and tapped into my fight-or-flight instinct. In plain English, my mind would control me and not the other way around. The worst part for me was when I came to my senses because I didn't want to remember any of it, but I did.

I remembered breaking out of Julian's secure embrace and running to the bathroom where I cried for a solid half hour. Melissa checked on me a couple of times, asking if she should call my parents. I begged her not to every time.

I was spiraling, and I knew it. The tunnel was as dark as I remembered, and in it, I couldn't recall ever being happy. It didn't matter. Nothing mattered. If I was gone, I wouldn't be remembered, and if my family missed me, they would get over it, because if I wasn't around, that would mean fewer problems for them.

"When peace like a river attendeth my way, When sorrows like sea billows roll… Whatever my lot, thou hast taught me to say, 'It is well, it is well with my soul.'"

Dreamer

My ears perked up at the sound of the familiar hymn, goosebumps coming over my arms. It was a familiar tune, one I'd heard a million times, but this rendition was new and different because it was sung by Julian. I felt my heart rate start to slow, and I breathed deeply as his voice brought me back to reality one verse at a time. When he finished the old hymn, I unlocked the bathroom door to find him sitting on the floor across from me, relief washing over his face.

We'd been driving for a few minutes when I posed the question, "What made you sing that song?"

"My grandmother used to sing it to me when I was a little boy. I hadn't thought of it forever, but something told me that it was what you needed to hear. Are you sure you're okay?"

"I feel better."

Julian pulled into a gas station.

"I'll be right back," he said.

As he disappeared into the store, I leaned my head back on the seat and took out my cell phone to text Mami.

"I know it's close to curfew, but we are on our way. Julian had to stop for gas. Be there in 10. I love you."

"Ok, mi amor. I will leave the door unlocked. Nos vemos pronto."

Before long, Julian was getting back in the driver's seat and handing a bag to me.

"What's this?"

"Open it."

When I opened the bag, I found aspirin, a bottled coffee drink and a large chocolate bar.

"Is this for me?"

"Of course."

"Who taught you about the healing power of chocolate?" I asked, thinking it may have been his ex.

"My mom."

I snuck a glance at him, but he just kept his eyes forward as he pulled back onto the road. "When I was a little kid, I used to think chocolate was magical. My mom told me it was."

I smiled.

"After dad lost his job, he was angry and drinking all the time. Mom had to get a job. She used to dress nicely for work, so my dad got jealous. He thought she was trying to look good for someone. If she got home even a minute after she was supposed to, he'd beat her up."

My stomach twisted into a knot. Why would anybody hurt *her*?

"My mom knew when a beating was coming, and if she couldn't get me to my grandmother's house, she would lock me in my room until it was over. But I could still hear the blows. On my sixth birthday, my mom bought me an old MP3 player. I was able to drown out the noise with the music in my headphones. The beating didn't take long, but sometimes my mom was knocked unconscious and wouldn't come to get me for hours."

He drove with one hand on the steering wheel, while the other lay on the center console. I slipped my fingers through his. He turned his face in my direction and nodded, squeezing my hand.

"As I got a little older, I started wanting to fight back, you know? I wanted to protect her."

"So brave," I said, "but that's a big burden to carry on little shoulders."

"I know," he replied, "and so did my mother."

"What did she do?"

"She told me I could only help her afterward." He nodded at the bag on my lap. I let go of his hand and rummaged through it again. "She sent me down the street with ten dollars and instructions to come back with chocolate, coffee and an individual packet of aspirin."

Peering into my lap, I was touched to see he'd given me the same thing.

"When I got back home and realized she was in the bathroom, I slid the pills and candy bar under the door. The next I knew, she was coming out of the bathroom with the half-eaten candy bar, and the bruises on her face were gone. Poof! Magic."

"So, make-up?"

Julian gave his half-smile. "Naturally. It became a routine that afterward, she would take me back to my room and help me with my homework, all the while sipping on her coffee and smiling as if nothing had happened. She had no idea I could hear her crying herself to sleep late into the night. The only thing that helped was the music."

"I can't imagine what that must have been like." I opened the plastic wrap around the rim of the bottled coffee drink. "You didn't have to do this, you know."

Dreamer

"Sure I did. I can't have you showing up at your house a wreck."

"True. You wouldn't happen to have tissues, would you?"

"Center console."

Impressive. I reached for a tissue and let the visor down. The mirror on the inside had small lights on either side. I rummaged through my purse for my make-up and got to work.

"So, you turned down a Mustang," I said. "There had to be a good reason."

Julian turned up the stereo, a soulful song coming through. "My dad is a piece of work. You know, he's the reason I started selling drugs. He used to do it for extra cash, but when he was too drunk, he would have me make the drop-offs for him down the neighborhood. I couldn't have been older than seven." He cleared his throat. "He would stick something in my Spider-Man backpack and tell me, go to Craig's or to Kevin's, always one of the neighbors, and I would go. They would grab the drugs from my little hand and hand me a stack of bills in return which I would take home to Pop."

I put my makeup away and watched him silently as he drove, eyes ahead. Light and shadow washed over his features.

"I got a letter in the mail a few weeks before my sixteenth birthday. Dad found Jesus and wants to reconnect. Hasn't forgotten my birthday. Has a fixer-upper that we can work on together and he plans on giving it to me. I should've known it was too good to be true. Anyway, I give him a call and he gives me the address of where he is working. I show up there on my birthday only to find out he's been fired for coming to work drunk out of his mind." Julian chuckled. "I was such an idiot for believing him. I came home that day to a surprise party and here comes Joe with a Mustang. I swear it was like the whole school had shown up and everyone was clapping and cheering about my new car. I just couldn't take it anymore. So I locked myself in my room until everyone left." His voice broke.

I reached for his hand again and we rode wordlessly until turning onto my street. "We're here," he said as we pulled up to the driveway. He turned off the engine. We sat in silence for a beat. "Since I didn't get to give you the tour, you have to come back. I want to show you what I'm going to do with the song."

I'd forgotten about the song. And the fight.

"Okay. Thank you for everything, Julian. I feel much better."

"Yeah. Nothing like hearing someone else's crappy life story to cheer you up." He winked.

"I'm serious. What you did for me, coming to my rescue like that..."

"Nobody deserves to be talked to like that," he said, meeting my eyes. "*Especially* not you."

I don't know what came over me, but I unbuckled my seatbelt and placed a kiss on his cheek. When I pulled back, I realized I'd caught Julian off-guard. There was no hiding his surprise. I surprised myself, too. Smiling, I said, "See you later."

Before my feet hit the ground outside of the vehicle, he caught me by the hand and forced me to look at him. My mind traveled back to the first time we met, how his eyes caused a quietness to come over me. This time his face was partially covered in shadow, but there was no mistaking the look in his eyes. I knew what would follow, but as much as I wanted my lips to meet his halfway, this was one time I did not have the luxury to throw caution to the wind.

I slid my hand out of his grasp and dashed through the front door. He called after me, but I shut the door, and with my back pressed against it, I suspired.

Even after the emotional calamity of the last hour, I knew one thing to be true: the only thing more frightening than facing my past, would be to repeat it.

SUNDAY SCHOOL

"Okay, crew! It's time to go over our duties for VBS. Teachers, raise your hand if you received your lesson plan packets back in March." Todd looked around the room, nodding at each person with their hand in the air.

"Elleni, since Leah is needed for snacks, I'm assigning you a new helper." He scanned his clipboard. "Mr. Rossi, I hope you don't mind volunteering to be Ms. Salgado's classroom manager on Friday."

Whether he minded or not, I couldn't tell, mainly because I'd been too afraid to make eye contact with him from the moment I arrived. I was rummaging through my bag when his sneakers appeared beside my own, his cologne causing my mind to swim. I bit my lip and pulled a lesson plan and lanyard out of my bag, pretending to be totally unaffected.

"Hey," he said before sitting down on the chair across from me.

Dreamer

I handed the materials over to him. "Make sure you write your name in permanent marker. I'm teaching Friday, so I need you to read over the materials in each age group."

He leaned forward in his seat. "So, are you going to look at me at all, or…?"

I cracked a small smile and allowed my eyes to find his. "Can I leave you in charge of markers?"

Julian put on a thinking face. "Oh, I don't know. Is it worth the risk of getting interrogated by the Dollar Mart security guard?" I let out a giggle. Julian winked before leaning back in his chair. "Can we, uh, talk about what happened?"

"I'd rather not." I fished for a change of subject.

"Alright, fine. But you can't avoid me, you know that right?"

"Oh?" I replied teasingly. "You're sure about that?"

"I am. For one, my mom invited your family over for our Fourth of July Barbeque."

"What?"

Todd called over his shoulder on the way out the door, "Mr. Rossi, I'm glad you decided to come to camp with us." When he was gone, Julian turned to look at me with a smirk. "Right. And there's *that*."

"What?" I repeated. "How did *that* happen?"

Julian shrugged. "Joshua showed me the website. They have some cool stuff." He looked like he had more to say, but the bell rang to mark the end of Sunday School hour.

Chapter 12

"Do not be unequally yoked with unbelievers. For what partnership has righteousness with lawlessness? Or what fellowship has light with darkness?"
2 Corinthians 6:14

The Sanctuary of Agápē Baptist Church was decked out in festive jungle decor. Paper mache trees covered the high walls, each with dozens of green leaves. Large stuffed animals gathered around the altar which was decorated like a watering hole. Once again, the ladies of the church had outdone themselves.

We'd all received our schedules at the sign-up table. Jake and I were in charge of the music, Mark and Dakota were manning the outdoor activities, Selah was on crafts, and Amanda on snacks. Then there were the floaters: Julian, Leah, Joshua, Daniel, and my cousin, Macho.

The teachers each had to take a turn teaching the Bible classes one day in the week. On the day of their lesson, they would be assigned a helper from the group of floaters, and a second floater would take their place in their usual station.

Today was Mark's day to teach the Bible lesson. Joshua would take his place at Dakota's side for the outdoor activities, and Leah would be his classroom helper. While Jake and I were teaching music class, our helper would be Julian.

Dreamer

In my mind, no one from the Youth Group was as qualified to teach the Bible lesson as the PKs: Selah, Leah, Mark and Dakota. But it was Todd's idea to make sure all of the older teens with the most church experience would have an equal opportunity to do so.

PK stood for preacher's kids. There were different levels to PKhood. There were the PKs: *P*reacher's *K*ids (highly knowledgeable about Churchianity, musically inclined), the MPKs: *M*issionary *P*reacher's *K*ids (cultured, multi-talented, and often adventurous), and the PSKs: *P*astor's *K*ids (smart, sheltered, and most likely to rebel or surrender to the Ministry themselves — at times both).

Although I was not a PK, my parents always stressed the importance of church attendance, and they led by example. Not one day went by when I didn't come out to find my dad reading scripture at the coffee table. My mom read at work on her break; I knew this because she discussed her daily reading over the dinner table. I was comforted by the fact that I had four days to get *in the zone* before it was my turn to teach the Bible lesson.

When it came to the music class, I'd read and re-read the plans Jake and I had communicated back and forth to each other through email. Somewhere along the way, I discovered that Jake did his best work away from the limelight. Over the last few months, we'd found the best songs to teach each age group. Everyone had to learn two: the VBS theme song and a second song, picked out for them by us, the children's choir directors.

Jake was already on stage with his guitar strapped on when I made my way over to Brother Steve, the music director. He smiled brightly behind his large glasses. "How's my favorite musical prodigy?"

I shrugged. "I don't know, but *I'm* doing fine."

"Don't be coy. Are you ready to lead the children's choir?"

"I hope so."

"Elleni…"

"Kidding!"

"Good. It's time to start."

Shortly after Julian showed up, we kicked off the assembly time with our VBS theme song. The children in the front were quick to wiggle and clap along with me and Brother Steve, but the older children opted to point and giggle instead.

I looked over to my left where Jake mirrored the concern I felt. As I studied the difference between the tots and the pre-teens, I was reminded of a verse of scripture: *"Whoever humbles himself like [a] little child is the greatest in the kingdom of heaven." Matthew 18:4*

From his place behind the drums, Daniel played a jungle drumbeat, the music picking up speed. This was day one of VBS, our only chance to set the mood for the rest of the week. It was now or never.

With a running start, I slid across the stage, using my microphone stand as an air guitar. A big *whoop* followed from the crowd as I hopped back up just in time to sing and boogie to the chorus. I boogied like it was my day job.

That's when I caught sight of Julian off to the corner, beaming at me with his snow-white teeth.

In the first ten minutes after assembly time came to a close, I decided I was going to enjoy my job as the children's choir director. The little ones were too cute for words, but as the children got older, our songs became more difficult to teach. Halfway through directing the third and fourth graders, we found ourselves at a standstill thanks to Miles, the cockiest boy in the class. As I tried to teach the hand motions for one of the songs, he rolled his eyes and shouted, "I'm not doing that. I'll look stupid!"

The other children joined in with protests of their own. I felt my face get hot as I looked over to Jake who only shrugged. Sister Suzy and Brother Steve told the children to settle down, but it seemed to be in vain. Just as I started to rethink my life choices, Julian raised his hand. "Excuse me, Ms. Salgado?"

"Yes, Mr. Rossi?"

"I was just wondering, how do you do that dance again? Is it like this?" He joined me at the front and started to move his arms robotically, causing some of the children to burst into laughter.

"No, Mr. Rossi, I'm afraid that's not it."

"Huh. How about this?" He put a hand to the back of his head, and jerked his other arm from right to left, causing the rest of the children to join in the giggles. I had a hard time keeping my composure.

"No, Mr. Rossi. That dance move is called, The Sprinkler."

"Oh. Can you show me the dance move I'm *supposed* to be doing?"

I did. He nodded. "Oh… yeah. That's *way* cooler than what I've been doing. Who else wants to try it?" Hands popped up all over. I smiled at Julian, who winked and shrugged as if to say, 'It was nothing.' A bell sounded throughout the building, signaling snack time. The children made a line behind Sister Suzy, who led them to the fellowship hall.

"Well done, Julian. I'm impressed." Brother Steve gave Julian a high five before disappearing into the music room.

I bumped his shoulder playfully. "I'm sure it helps that the girls have a crush on the TA."

"The what?"

"Teacher's assistant."

Julian grimaced. "No way."

Jake snorted as he walked past us. "Way."

Tuesday was Joshua's turn to help us with the lesson. Although Joshua was obviously older than our students, he still didn't have the same effect on the older kids that Julian did, but luckily for Jake and me, by the time our lesson was done, the kids had already gotten into the groove and had actually started to enjoy themselves.

With each day of VBS, the numbers grew until every class had almost reached capacity. Wednesday had been Daniel's day to help out with the class, but between his goofiness and two left feet, he'd been more of a distraction to the children than an asset to the teachers.

With that in mind, I arrived Thursday evening with a sense of uneasiness. Jake was teaching the Bible lesson tonight, which meant that I'd be left to teach music without him. Luckily, I'd have a helper.

I checked the schedule on my clipboard, finding the day with my index finger.

Thursday, July 4th. Leah.

That's when I remembered. We were supposed to be spending the evening with the Rossis! I gulped, feeling even more jittery than before — whether from nervousness or excitement, I didn't know.

"La-la-Lenicious!"

"La-la-Leah!" I called back, trying to match her tone. "How's it going?"

"It's only the *best day ever.*"

"Doubt that."

She wiggled a sparkly nail in my face. "Don't be so negative, Leni. We get to spend the whole day together! This is going to go down in the books as historically the best day of our lives."

D.S. Fisichella

"You're putting a lot of pressure on me."

Leah only beamed. "Don't feel pressured, silly. Every day with Lenicious is my new best day ever."

"Thank you, Leah. You're every inch as sparkly as the clothes you wear."

"Oh, Leni. That's the nicest thing anyone has ever said to me." She threw her arms around my neck. I was surprised at how light she was. When she let go, she looked teary-eyed. My heart turned to mush.

The sound of children finding their seats for Assembly time filled the sanctuary. Leah squared her shoulders and lifted her chin up, a picture of determination, from the big bow in her hair to her bokeh fanny pack. "It's showtime."

I'd been dreading spending time with Leah, but the more I got to know her, the more I realized she was so much more than a tiny person with a huge personality. I'd always considered her to be very child-like, but while I may have expected her to be as distracting as my brother, I was surprised by her mother-like approach to the little ones. The girls loved her clothes, and the boys seemed surprisingly taken by her as well. In the end, she turned out to be my best helper, and for the first time since she made the announcement about our slumber party, I found myself looking forward to it.

LATER

Joe and Melissa Heron had spared no expense for the small get-together. When we arrived, I watched as my parents *oohed* and *aahed* over the enormity of the house like I had done my first time there. After a quick walk-through of the first floor, Melissa led us to the backyard.

Although it was only our family and theirs, they had an abundance of food as well as red, white and blue decorations around the yard. A red vase held sparklers and a lighter. We had our burgers and hot dogs around the minibar by the pool. I looked around, my eyes wide, still not quite believing the enormity of the place.

"Mister Joe, are you rich?" my father asked.

Joe chuckled, raising his beer. "It's a nice place, right?"

"Very nice." My father nodded, taking a sip of his Sprite.

Melissa said, "I hope you all brought bathing suits!"

Already in his swim trunks, Daniel didn't miss a beat, stuffing his face with the rest of his cheeseburger and running to the pool. "*Cawowbaa!*"

Dreamer

He leaped into the air, his knees hugged to his chest, sending up a mini tsunami in our direction.

"*Daniel!*" my parents shouted in unison.

"Melissa?" I called. "Where did Julian go?"

"He's grabbing some drinks from inside. Do you need to change into your bathing suit? There's a bathroom through that door." She pointed. "Feel free to use one of my robes."

I went through the door and changed out of my clothes and into my bathing suit before slipping my arms through the soft cotton of a pink robe. The bathroom had two doors, one leading into the inside of the house and one leading out to the backyard. I walked back outside to find my parents in the hot tub with Joe and Melissa, staring up at the fireworks show. Daniel floated on the surface of the pool, presumably doing the same.

"I believe I still owe you a tour of my house."

The sight of Julian leaning against the side of his house shirtless, water dripping from his hair, caused my heart to leap. I was glad it was now dark and he couldn't see my blush.

"Lead the way," I said.

He grinned and stepped past me, reaching around me to close the door shut. We stood in the dark for a second, and just as my pulse had elevated to the point that I thought Julian might hear it, he opened the door that led into the house, the light flooding into the small space.

"Come on," he said from inside the house, now wearing a dark robe which he must have grabbed while we were in the dark.

I let out a sigh of relief and followed him into the brightly lit home. He led me through the first floor, stopping even at the kitchen and dining area. Joe's office had high walls covered in books. I felt a tinge of jealousy mixed with enthusiasm, thinking I'd only seen offices like this in movies. Next, we headed upstairs, opening the door to every bedroom except for his parent's master bedroom.

"Trust me. I've barged in there before and… well, I'm never going in there again!"

I laughed.

After going through the upstairs hallway, we headed to Julian's bedroom. I looked around at the elegant black-and-white scheme throughout: three white walls offset by one black accent wall, one large bed with black and white stripes, and so on.

"Come in."

I hesitated, remembering my parents' advice never to go into a boy's bedroom by myself. Thinking that it was just Julian, I ignored the warning in my head and stepped inside.

His large window had a seat with a soft cushion. Other than a desk with a chair, a bookshelf on one wall, and a framed autographed picture of a soccer player, there was not much else in his room that caught my attention except for the little teddy bear perched on his nightstand. Julian followed my gaze, moving to where the little bear sat. He placed it in my hands.

"I can't believe you kept him!"

"Of course I did. I know I was a real jerk to you at the hospital, but I honestly didn't think about how I hurt your feelings until you threw this little guy to the side and ran out of the room." I looked down at the little bear again before handing him back to Julian.

"I get it. You didn't even know me."

He put it back on the nightstand, turning back to me. "That's no excuse."

I hugged Melissa's robe to my body. "It was a while back, lots has changed."

He visually relaxed and proceeded to open his large bedroom window.

"Sit," he said, motioning toward the window seat. I did as I was told.

The view over the front yard was spectacular. Below us, the cars on the driveway encircled the beautiful little fountain. Across the street, a glistening waterfront with narrow docks was embellished by private boats floating peacefully in the moonlight.

"I might have to borrow this place for inspiration to write my songs."

"You're welcome to use it anytime," he said from his desk, as he hit some buttons on his laptop. Taking off his robe, he draped it over the chair to dry. My eyes traveled over his chiseled features as a familiar melody began to play. He took the seat next to me. "This is my thinking spot."

"What do you think about?" I asked, tearing my eyes away from him. He noticed me looking at him. I wondered if he knew the effect he had on me.

"Oh, I don't know. My plans after high school. My music. But lately, I've been thinking a lot about you." The beat dropped on the song, followed by a soulful tenor voice.

Dreamer

"Wait, is this—?" But I didn't have to finish my question. I already knew. This was our song. Julian's voice carried through the room.

I was a shadow of myself
I never thought
I could be anyone else
I was ready to die
Ready to die

My response was sweet. I may not have realized it at the time I was recording the song, but my lips sang the longing of my heart.

You came in, saw all my brokenness
I was a mess but you saw me and
Helped me,
You helped me to cry
Helped me to cry, oh

The sad piano rose to a crescendo, while the sound of violins coming in added to the dramatic effect as Julian and I harmonized the chorus together.

Then you found me
And you loved me
Called my name
Took me in your arms

The violins ceased, the sound of the bass increasing as Julian came in with a rap.

Standing at a crossroads between life and death
One day you showed up and gave me back my breath
I knew I messed up on the day that you left
You took my heart with you, babe, I call that theft
I cried to a God I did not believe in
But since I met you, I feel like I've seen Him
I'm afraid this heart will not change easily
But for Song, I promise, I'd do anything.

The laptop fell silent, replaced by the calling of seagulls through the night. A few fireworks blasted through the sky.

I felt a familiar sensation on my hand and looked down to find his long fingers wrapping gently around mine.

"Elleni."

I lifted my eyes to find his gaze on me. I couldn't believe I was here with him, the most gorgeous yet haunted boy I'd ever met. "I don't know what I believe," he whispered, "but when I'm with you, I know there *has* to be something more out there. In a short amount of time, I went from hating my life and wanting to end it, to wanting to live my life as long as you were in it."

I loved the tone of his voice, the sincerity in his eyes, his easy smile, and the way he carried himself with masculine confidence. I loved that he confided in me as if we had known each other all of our lives. I loved that I felt like I could tell him anything. His eyes wandered over me, his expression like that of an artist examining a breathtaking masterpiece.

The breeze picked up a little, causing a lock of my hair to fly in front of my face. I broke eye contact, ready to pull it back in place, but before I could, Julian reached up and tucked it behind my ear, bringing my attention back to him.

Bursts of color from the pyrotechnics illuminated his face with warm light, his perfect eyes glistening with their fire. His hand lingered on the side of my face, his thumb tracing a soft line over my lips before stopping on the small black freckle right above them. I breathed in his scent.

His hands slid down my neck and shoulders, to my waist, before coming to rest at my hips. I ran my fingers through his hair, willing him to lean his face closer until we were nose to nose. A protest began in my core, but I ignored it, as I turned my face slightly, positioning myself for what I hoped would follow. It was all the encouragement he needed before bringing his lips to mine.

My breath caught as the ardor of his kiss rippled through me like lightning. He was tender, disarming me, and giving me back my air simultaneously. He tasted like spearmint and desire. I couldn't get enough of him. He must have done this many times before, but I didn't feel threatened. I felt… free.

Elleni.

I ignored the tug at my heart as Julian's kiss grew deeper, stronger and maddeningly more passionate. Time seemed to stop as my senses heightened. I could feel everything. The slight pressure of his hands on my

Dreamer

sides. The water droplets still in his hair. The warm summer breeze touching the few parts of our bodies that didn't meet.

"Elleni, Julian, where are you?" my brother's voice echoed through the enormous house.

Startled, I let go of Julian's hair and put my hands up against his bare chest, tearing myself from his lips. We looked at each other, both breathing hard, an expression of glee mixed with guilt coming over our faces.

"He's going to kill me if he finds me shirtless," Julian whispered. I nodded in agreement, struggling to regain my composure as Julian dug through his dresser for a clean shirt.

"Bathroom?" I whispered.

Julian pointed to a door I almost mistook for a closet. "Through there, babe."

Babe!

I smiled, disappearing inside.

"There you are!" I heard my brother's voice coming from the other side of the door. "What are you doing?"

"I promised your sister a tour of the house," Julian responded coolly.

"Uh-huh. So, where is she?"

"In here, Dani!" I called. "Had to go to the bathroom before we headed back."

"Are you guys going to swim?"

"Yes. I'll go with you, man," Julian said. "We'll meet you outside, Elleni!"

"Okay!" I called back.

I looked at the mirror over the sink and examined my face, my cheeks pink and my brown eyes glistening. I couldn't stop smiling. I removed the bathrobe I wore, for one last look at my bathing suit. It was a vintage-style one-piece with a sweetheart neckline. The material hugged my body in all the right places. I ran a hand through my hair once more before heading out.

My brother was doing a backstroke when I came outside. Julian sat at the edge of the pool, feet in the water. He looked ready to say something when he saw me in the shadows, but the moment I stepped into the light of the lanterns, he seemed temporarily at a loss for words.

I tiptoed to the pool, which gleamed merrily with the underwater light system. Moving past Julian, I could still feel his eyes on me as I braced for the cold. I stepped onto the top step, but was surprised to find that the water was warm! Upon further inspection, I watched how a layer of steam danced above the surface.

"It's heated!?"

It was all the encouragement I needed to dip the rest of my body in. Once in the water, I watched how the light changed colors from white, through all the colors of the rainbow. I felt a rush as Julian jumped into the pool near me. Swimming to the surface, I blinked the water out of my eyes.

"Hey."

I turned to the sound of his voice.

"I'll race you to the other side."

"Are you sure you want to do that?" I replied. "My parents had me in swimming lessons when I was two!"

"I'm not scared of you, you're like a walking butterfly."

I laughed. "Alright then, on the count of three. One..."

"Three!" He dove in, moving his arms and legs as fast as he could.

"Hey!" I submerged, gaining on him quickly. Once I made it to the other side, I kicked off the wall, passing him on the way back to the starting line. Victorious, I sat on the steps with my legs crossed, arms resting casually on the edge of the pool.

Julian sputtered, breaking through the surface, out of breath. "How did you do that?"

I shrugged. "I warned you."

After a while, my parents and the Herons made their way out of the hot tub. Joe called, "Julian, a little help distributing towels?"

When Julian went inside to get the towels, I leaned back into the water, my eyes closed. I felt Daniel's eyes on me.

"What?" I asked, not opening my eyes.

There was a ripple as Daniel swam closer. "Something going on between you two that I should know about?"

"What do you mean?"

"I've never seen you act so *girly*."

I snorted. "Gee, *thanks*." A light came on from a nearby lawn chair, accompanied by a vibrating sound. "Julian, someone's calling your phone!"

His voice came back muffled. "Can you get it? I'll be right out."

Daniel went back to his backstroke as I climbed out of the pool and headed for the blinking cell phone. The caller ID read 'Unknown.'

"Hello?" Silence. "Are you calling for Julian?"

"And who might *you* be?" a sultry female voice inquired, causing my throat to tighten.

"Elleni. And you are?"

"Bianca. Could you ask JuJu if he's still planning on spending the night this weekend?" I grimaced at the odious nickname, unsure what to do about her request.

"Here." I swiveled around to find Julian holding out a white towel to me and Daniel drying himself off just past him. I handed Julian his cell phone without saying a word.

"Hello?" His face darkened. "Hey."

"We'll meet you inside," Melissa called as she ushered my smiling parents into the house, each holding a towel. My brother followed after them.

Julian stole a glance in my direction. "Look, Bee, I can't talk right now. I'll call you later. Yeah, fine. Bye." He hung up the phone and put it back on the lawn chair.

I thought back to our kiss, to how easily I felt myself losing control. To how badly I'd wanted it never to end. Those feelings scared me. It wasn't just me and Julian. I knew all too well that actions had consequences, but with Julian, like with Cal, I'd lost my head, not thinking any further than my own selfish desires. I couldn't give in, not again.

"It's not what you—"

"This was a mistake."

We both stopped speaking at the same time.

"Wow," he said, scoffing to himself. "A mistake? Really."

I looked at the floor, a sinking feeling in the pit of my stomach. "Yes."

"You told me that day on the bridge that you believed God wanted you to be there for me. Do you really believe that? Or was *that* a mistake too?"

"Of course I believe that," I said, meeting his eyes again.

"Look, I know I'm not a good person, but I can be better."

Tears flooded my eyes, my voice quivering. "I know you've been trying really hard to change your life around…"

"But you don't want to be with me?"

"That's not true!" I exclaimed. "But I told God I wanted to wait for the person He chose for me and lately, I haven't been doing that."

D.S. Fisichella

"What can I do to be that person?" He sounded hurt, willing to do whatever it took. Isn't this what I wanted? No! A false conversion was *not* the answer.

"It doesn't work that way. I'm sorry." I began walking past him.

"Did you feel *anything* when we kissed?" he asked without moving.

"Of course I did."

He didn't respond.

I went inside and closed the door.

Chapter 13

"Consider him who endured from sinners such hostility against himself, so that you may not grow weary or fainthearted."
Hebrews 12:3

Miss Josie's Office

Miss Josie must have sensed something was up because she took one look at me as I walked through the front of the building and turned to Sister Bev sitting next to her.

"I'll be back, Bev. Remember, all we need is their name and the time they signed in."

Sister Bev beamed, waving a plump hand in my direction, her neon fingernails matching her bedazzled baseball hat and VBS T-shirt. Miss Josie put a hand on my back and muttered in my ear, "Thank goodness you're here. My retinas need a break. An astronaut could spot that getup from space." I said nothing. Instead, I walked through her office door and sunk into one of her armchairs. It took me a couple of tries to get the words out, but Miss Josie listened intently the whole time.

"Oh, honey-bee, I'm sorry! Heartbreak is the pits. I'm fixin' to make me a coffee — you want one?"

I sniffled, dabbing my eyes with a tissue. "Mmhmm."

"Alrighty then, be right back."

I looked around at the familiar little office, unable to stop thinking about the last time I'd been here, smiling down at my cell phone like a lovestruck doofus. Why hadn't I listened to Miss Josie? It was only an hour before the last night of VBS and the musical presentation that would follow. But instead of being excited about teaching my first Bible lesson and directing the children's choir, my stomach was in knots because of my last conversation with Julian.

"I'm back! So, where did we leave off? Oh, right. You gave him a smooch."

"Miss Josie!"

"What? Ain't that what the kids call it anymore?" She placed a mug on the desk in front of me. "Coffee with your cream and sugar. Can't help noticing you like your coffee like you like your man."

"*Miss Josie.*"

"Strong, tan, and sweet as candy."

"Miss Josie."

"But after you have a cup, you're left with a bitterness in your belly and full of…"

"Miss Josie!"

We looked at each other for a moment before bursting into laughter. Miss. Josie always knew how to make me laugh.

"I'm terrified of what I'm going to do when I see him tonight. No. What am I saying? I'm going to be stuck in a van with him for eight hours next Saturday! And then we're going to be at camp together, for a full week!"

"Yes, yes, it's a sticky situation. Love makes everything more complicated."

"Love?"

"Oh, sure. Society will tell you to follow your heart, but don't listen to them. God says our heart is wicked. Deceitful, even. But love… love is a whole other thing. You wait around for God's timing and he'll get it right for you. He's the Author of Romance, little chicken, not to mention, your loving Father. You think he's gonna leave you pinin' for Mr. Right all your life?"

"I hope not."

"No. He won't. It's your heart's desire. It takes a very special person to have the gift of singleness."

"Like you?"

"Yeah, I'm special, alright. 'Specially not fond of the menfolk!"

"You don't like any man? Not even your dad?"

"Oh, I like men just fine, but I'm through with datin'. I'm married to Jesus!"

*

The plan later that evening was that every age group would attend my Bible class once that evening, and I would present them all with the same lesson, tweaked only to accommodate the age group I was teaching. Julian would be the classroom manager, in charge of attendance, enforcing the rules and pointing the older students to the restroom. His first duty, however, was to buy markers, which is why when Daniel walked in with the markers, I became immediately alarmed. He was already on his way out the door, heading to the snack area of the church when I posed my question.

"Daniel, have you talked to Julian in the past three hours? We were supposed to meet here half an hour ago, but he's not answering my texts." For the first time that day, I noticed something was off about my brother. His shoulders were rigid, fists clenched. This was out of character, even for him. "Dani? What's the matter?"

"I meant to talk to you about him," he said through his teeth, turning to look at me. "We went to the store to get the stuff you wanted, but while we were there, we ran into some of his old friends, and… things got weird."

"What do you mean? Weird how?"

I got up from my chair, pulling another one out for him to sit on. Daniel stepped forward, accepting my invitation. It was a small chair made for little ones, but he didn't seem bothered. Instead, he sat and let out a frustrated sigh.

"Well, the first thing that happened is that a girl recognized and snuck up on him. You should have seen him; he looked pale as a ghost at first. But then they got talking, and I noticed she was all over him. I couldn't even look at her; she was dressed so inappropriately. She was really rude too. Didn't even say hi to me. He said her name… I think it started with a B."

"Bianca?"

"That was it!" Daniel said, nodding his head.

"Then these two bone-headed guys walked up and started teasing him about his Bible School shirt. At first, I started to say something to defend him, but he asked me if I'd go looking for the materials you wanted while he caught up with them. I was like, 'yeah, sure,' but as soon as I was out of sight, one of the guys called me a loser, then asked Julian why he was hanging out with me. I thought Julian would punch him in the face like any decent friend would have done, but instead, he *laughed*!"

"*What?*"

"Yeah. I couldn't believe it either, so I peeked around the corner to see if I heard right. Sure enough, he was *laughing* with them! You know I don't take that crap from *anyone*, but I felt like I'd been punched in the gut. So I just grabbed the markers and headed for the cash register. When I finished paying, I took one last look at him before I walked out the door. I called dad to pick me up."

I froze.

"*Oh.*"

Daniel must have seen the distress in my face because he immediately grew from disgusted to playful. "Don't worry, Leni. I'm sure he had more than enough time to think about what a jerk move that was. I saw his face before I left. He looked like he regretted not standing up for me. I'm sure he will be here soon."

I knew I needed to trust that whatever had happened between us, and between him and my brother, wouldn't get between him and his work, but my brother had gotten his feelings hurt. If everything he said was true, then did I even *want* Julian to be here with me? Even if he *did* show up, he would have to explain himself and apologize to my brother. Nobody treated my twin like that. Not if I had anything to say about it.

After Daniel left, I eyed the clock, watching how the minutes ticked by, closer and closer to class time. I listened for even the smallest creak of the floor out in the hallway, watching the door handle in hopes that any moment, Julian might walk through the door with an apology. My hope evaporated the moment the first group of children walked through the door.

My first class was with the kindergarteners. I watched how they skipped into the room, each holding hands with a partner. They sat on the carpet, wiggling, chattering and unable to keep still. I looked into their bright eyes and couldn't help but smile. Thanks to the music class, I already knew their names. Each little boy and girl had their own personality, but the more

Dreamer

timid children always seemed to shy away from the spotlight. I decided those were the children I would call on to help me with the lesson.

In half an hour, I watched how those who mostly kept to themselves transformed in front of their classmates, blooming when showered with praise for a job well done.

During my snack break, I ran into Todd. He asked me about Julian's whereabouts.

"You should talk to my brother."

Todd groaned when Daniel joined us and relayed to him the same story he had told me.

"You know what this means."

I nodded. Julian was no longer eligible for the camp scholarship. My brother took me off to the side to ask me how I was feeling. "It's taking everything for me not to cry right now. I can't believe he would bail on me. I thought he was my friend."

"Maybe he has a good excuse."

Daniel came upstairs with me, staying as my helper the remainder of the evening.

I let the events of the afternoon slip to the back of my mind as I gave the children the best news they would ever hear: the message of the gospel of Jesus Christ. I knew that most of the children who received the message joyfully were probably too young to understand the penalty of sin versus the sacrifice He made, but as I taught the lesson, and later directed the children's choir in front of the congregation and their families, I was overwhelmed with a feeling of purpose.

As the children performed with bright smiles and all the right dance moves, remembering their songs by memory, I realized I wanted to stay in this moment of joy forever. But good things never last forever.

THE SLUMBER PARTY

Never had a two-bedroom townhouse looked more ominous. It wasn't the light gleaming from each window or the sound of an automatic sprinkling system coming on. It certainly wasn't the night sky adorned with a myriad of stars, but somehow I couldn't help a panicky feeling from rearing its ugly head. I pushed my large black-rimmed nerdy glasses up my nose before clutching my duffel bag like a life preserver.

"This is awkward," Macho said.

I turned to him. "I can't do this. Take me home."

"Why? The place looks nice enough."

"It's not about the place."

"Is it the people?"

"No."

"Is it the geekazoid glasses?"

"Hey! That's not nice. My eyes need a break from contacts once in a while."

Macho chuckled. "I was kidding. They look cute on you. But, come on, Cuzzo… why won't you go in?"

"It's me. The last time I went to a slumber party…" I trailed off.

"Is this about Blondie?"

I looked over at him, surprised. "I haven't heard that nickname in forever."

Macho smiled. "You and Blondie, 'The Two-Headed Teeny-Bopper.' You didn't really think I'd forgotten that, did you?"

By that point, we hardly treated sleepovers like special occasions anymore. The sight of Monica eating cereal at my breakfast table, or the sight of me emerging from her bathroom with a towel on my head, had become as common as Saturday morning cartoons.

One day, my uncle came by with cousin Macho, back when we called him *Machito*. He'd gotten his tough-guy nickname because he always seemed to be picking fights. Monica had emerged from the bathroom in a pair of pajama pants and an oversized custom T-shirt with the name 'Elleni' printed across the front. He'd raised his eyebrows at her and completely ignored me as I came out of my bedroom.

"Elleni? When did you dye your hair?"

Monica raised an eyebrow. "Uh…"

"Did uncle Marcos trade you for a blondie? You look much better now."

I chose that moment to interrupt his one-sided conversation. "You think I'm ugly?"

I must have cried for ten minutes before my uncle took me aside and whispered, "Ay *Chiquita*. That's just your weird cousin's way of telling your friend she's pretty."

Dreamer

When it entered my head that my cousin had a crush on Monica, I used the knowledge to my advantage, embarrassing him at every possible opportunity by chanting, *"You like Monica, you like Monica,"* until he refused to get near her while I was around.

Those were the days.

"So are you ready to go inside now?"

I'd forgotten I was still in Macho's beat-up Lancer and not in my ten-year-old body anymore.

"Yeah, I'm ready."

Macho turned off the engine and got out of the car just as I was opening my door. He met me at the passenger side and engulfed me in a bear hug. "Love you, *prima*. Tell Jake I'm waiting."

"I love you too. I will."

"If you need us to stage a good kidnapping, we've got your back. Don't get me wrong, I like your church friends, but that little cheerleader gives me a headache."

"She's not a cheerleader."

"She should be. She has enough pep for a whole squad."

I couldn't deny how true that was.

The front door of the townhouse was slightly ajar, music coming from the other side. I cracked it open a bit more, identifying the source of the music. Jake and Selah sat cross-legged on the floor, their backs to the living-room couch, singing a duet.

Jake's long fingers moved effortlessly over the neck of a Spanish guitar, his deep voice reverberating through the room. Selah's charming alto voice complemented his perfectly, sending shivers up my arms. The only thing more breathtaking than their harmony was the way they looked at each other as if life itself hung on the existence of the other's song.

"LENICIOUS IS HERE!"

Jake and Selah stopped singing abruptly and looked up to find me halfway through the door. Leah twirled through the room decked out in pink pajamas, her hair held up by fluffy pink scrunchies into matching ponytails on either side of her head — instantly bringing me back to Macho's cheerleading comment. Selah got up from her place on the floor and smiled brightly.

"Welcome! Come sit down." She motioned toward the couch, but before I could take a step forward, Leah was at my side, pulling me forward. I was surprised at her strength as she pushed down on my shoulders so I would sit. She presented her face inches from mine; I smelled strawberry bubblegum.

"Love the specs. Very vintage-chic."

"Thanks."

"Just wait until you see the room. It's adorable! I've been working on it for hours, since before VBS and a little bit after. You can't go in yet, 'kay?"

"I'll just sit here."

"Goody! I'll be back in a few." She disappeared back up the stairs.

Selah looked at me apologetically. "I tried to restrain her, but you know, it's Leah."

"Leah."

"Leah," Jake and I said at the same time as Selah.

"Right," she said. "I'm on snack duty, so I'd better get back to it. Jake, stay one minute. I'll be right back with pizza slices for the road." Jake nodded and sat down on the opposite side of the couch from me.

"So, a guys' night at my house, huh?" I asked. He nodded and smiled. "That should be fun. What are you going to do?"

"Play manhunt and maybe some video games."

"Cool. I didn't get to tell you, great job this week. We make a good team."

"All I did was play music. You're the one that got the kids to sing. You're a natural."

"Thanks, Jake." I looked down at my hands, folding and refolding them in my lap, "Can I ask you something?"

"Sure."

"How did you and Selah first become close?" Jake shrugged, and for a moment, I thought that was all I was going to get from him, but he surprised me.

"We have similar interests. We both like music and I guess that's where it started."

"Makes sense."

The room was quiet again, but just as I decided to keep it that way, Jake spoke up again.

"I heard about Julian not showing up today. It was nice of your parents to open up their home for our party last minute, but I'm sorry he wasn't there for you."

Dreamer

I looked at my bracelet. "It's fine. Maybe he had a good excuse." Although I knew it was unlikely, somehow I preferred that response to admitting I'd been stood up because of his ex-girlfriend.

"For what it's worth, I may not know him as well as you do, but it doesn't seem like him at all."

"Yeah," I mumbled. "I would have said the same thing yesterday."

"Pizza, anyone?" I hadn't seen Selah standing there with tupperware in her hands. I wondered how much she'd heard. She handed the plastic container to Jake who kissed her softly on the forehead before turning to me. I thought he might add something else but instead, he just nodded at me and left through the front door. A moment later, I heard Macho's car start up again and drive away.

"How did you turn my boyfriend into a chatterbox?"

I laughed. "Yeah, right. Where are your parents?"

"Under room arrest per Leah's orders."

At precisely that moment, we turned to the sound of a door creaking open and watched as Pastor Tim poked his head out. He looked toward the staircase and then to us, a finger to his lips. I wasn't used to seeing him in anything but his Sunday best, so the sight of him in plaid pajamas tiptoeing toward the smell of pizza made it almost impossible to bite back a laugh. Sister Kimberly appeared a moment later, rollers in her hair, "Psst! Timmy, don't forget my ice cream!" She then caught sight of me. "Oh, hi Elleni! Great job tonight. New glasses?"

"Hi, Sister Kim. Not really," I said.

"Mom, you know the rules."

Sister Kim looked at her eldest pointedly. "I brought you into this world. You don't get to separate me from the one thing that got me through my first pregnancy!"

"I thought dad was the one who got you through the pregnancy."

"Of course. He's the one I sent for ice cream runs at all hours of the night."

We giggled.

"What's so funny?" Leah stood at the top of the stairs just as her dad was exiting the kitchen area, a pizza box in one hand piled high with a bag of chips, a jar of dip and a tub of ice cream. He used his other hand to hold a pizza slice halfway in his mouth.

"Dad!"

Pastor Tim made a break for his room as his wife held the door open, frantically waving him in. The door slammed shut a second before Leah made it to the bottom step.

"Grownups." She swept her ponytails behind her shoulders before announcing, "The room is ready!" I made it up the steps with her as Selah went back into the kitchen for our goodies. When we entered the bedroom, I wondered if I'd gone blind, except instead of everything going black, everything went PINK! Pink curtains, pink bedding on two beds, pink streamers, pink balloons — you get the idea.

"Leah, I like pink as much as the next girl, but it looks like a unicorn barfed in here."

"Don't be a sourpuss, Leni."

My eyes traveled to a white desk on the far end of the room, its legs clearly visible under the pink scarf Leah had flung on it. Over the desk was a bulletin board with a slightly faded picture that immediately caught my attention.

I made it across the room, my eyes locked on the photograph. I carefully removed the thumbtack from over it, sticking the small needle back into the board before bringing the photograph closer to my face.

Staring back at me were the faces of eleven-year-old me in a yellow dress, Selah in a skirt and blouse combo, braces on her teeth, and Leah in a fluffy dress and white shoes with socks. Holding her hand and peering sweetly down at her was none other than…

"Monica Josephs." Selah's shadow loomed over the photograph. "She was one of the nicest girls I'd ever met."

"I remember her!" Leah piped in. "She braided my hair every time I asked her, and she was really good at it. She must have known every braid known to womankind."

I'd forgotten about her doing Leah's hair.

"When was this picture taken?" I asked.

Selah took the picture from me. "It was after our first Sunday Morning Service at Agápē. My dad had just recently accepted the Pastor's office after we moved from Clearwater."

"That's right. You and Leah were new."

"Yup." Selah sighed. "Leah never had trouble making friends, but it was difficult for me, seeing as I was a total introvert."

"*Was?*" Leah mumbled.

Dreamer

Selah stuck her tongue out at her sister before turning back to me. "Monica was the first person from Junior Church to come up and introduce herself. She made me feel totally at ease."

I jiggled my charm bracelet. "She had a way of doing that, didn't she?" I looked up again, only to catch a reflection of the same sadness I felt mirrored back at me.

Leah tiptoed to me, burying her face on my shoulder, her arms around my waist. A moment later, Selah joined us in a group hug.

When somebody dies, the only thing you can try to wrap your head around is how they're not there anymore. If you can make it past that stage, other things about them will come back into your mind. Sometimes you will be happier for it, but sometimes you'll simply realize the size of the void they left behind.

Selah interrupted our board game with, "Ooh, I have to go get—that thing."

"What is it?" I asked. She looked nervously from me to her younger sister, who scowled some inaudible message to her.

"N—nothing. Never mind. I'll be right back."

Once she was out of the room, I looked at Leah. "She's a horrible liar."

Leah rolled her eyes. "I know, it's pathetic."

A moment later, Selah returned with a small bowl of ice cream in her hands, topped with whipped cream, sprinkles and a glowing candle. The sisters broke into a sweet birthday chorus, leaving me temporarily speechless. "So *that's* why Leah wanted the sleepover today. Sneaky, sneaky."

Leah wiggled her eyebrows. "It's also why it just so happens that Jake and Macho wanted to have a guys' night! I knew both your guards would be down since it's technically not your birthday yet. Besides, you're the only person on the planet that doesn't like birthday parties."

Unsure of what to say to that, I blew out the candle.

"What did you wish for?"

Selah elbowed her in the ribs.

"Nothing. I just thanked God for opening my eyes and helping me to realize what wonderful friends I have."

"*Awwwwwwwww!*"

"Presents." Selah rummaged under her pillow as Leah stuffed herself into the closet, wrestling with something as big as she was.

Selah handed me a little gift. "Here's mine."

I admired the golden wrapping paper, adorned with a perfect white bow. I carefully undid the wrapping, laying it aside as I turned the small jewelry box over in my hand before opening it to find a necklace with a single charm hanging from it.

"A Backwards Treble Clef?"

Selah smiled. "It makes an S for Salgado." I reached over to give her a hug.

"Here's mine!" Leah huffed, plopping down a large lightweight object on my lap.

"A— Piano—" she held up one finger as she regained her breath, "Body Pillow."

"You know, Leah, if you would declutter your closet like I've been telling you to, you wouldn't need to hold your breath just to find something in there."

The rest of the evening was divided between more snacking, another board game and several romantic comedies. At some point during the falling action of *A Cinderella Story*, I stopped fighting sleep.

I dreamt I was Cinderella, wearing a puffy white gown in a forest. I'd walked until my glass slippers started to hurt my feet; that's when I reached a fork in the road. On one side stood my family and friends, each dressed for the ball. I called them, but they didn't recognize me. I brought a hand to my face and realized I was wearing a mask over my eyes. No matter how hard I tugged, I couldn't get it off. That's when I heard someone call my name from the other side. I ran toward the voice.

The road got darker, branches and thorns littering my path. That's when I saw him, Prince Charming. He stepped out of the shadows, and I realized he wasn't a prince — he was Julian. Julian stepped toward me and brought his lips to mine, a perfect kiss, except I tasted alcohol. When I opened my eyes, I realized I was not kissing Julian anymore. I was kissing Cal. He took a step back and grinned at me maliciously, his eyes glimmering red. He faded into the shadows and was replaced by a mirror. When I walked closer to get a better look, I realized my gown had been replaced by a tattered dress. My mask was gone, but my face was smeared with something dark. I wiped it with my hands and looked down to find them dripping with blood.

I gasped, opening my eyes, temporarily confused by the sight of a pink balloon floating over my head and the sensation of something on my face. I touched it to find that I'd slept with my glasses on. The small TV on the

Dreamer

dresser was stuck on the Main Menu screen of the movie we fell asleep to, a happy pop song playing over and over.

I breathed to the music until my own heart had slowed its tempo. After about a minute or so, I looked around the room, the chaos coming into focus for the first time since last night. The floor was littered with *Solo* cups, open cookie packets, empty candy wrappers and an open pizza box with a single slice of pepperoni still inside.

"Breakfast is almost ready, girls. Get dressed and come down!"

Leah held up her palm, her face buried in her pillow, her voice muffled. "Five more minutes, mommy." Seconds later she was snoring again.

I unzipped the sleeping bag Leah had loaned me the night before, the face of a Barbie smiling broadly at me.

"You're up!" Selah came through her bedroom door, a towel wrapped around her head. She smelled of cocoa butter.

"Barely."

"Bathroom's unoccupied if you want to take a shower."

I looked around for my duffel bag, stepping over a couple of pink paper plates and a large bowl that still held some popcorn kernels. I gathered my belongings and made it to the bathroom, still steamy from Selah's shower. I undressed and stepped into the tub, shivering under the hot water running over my aching neck and shoulders, unable to shake the dream.

Between a huge pancake breakfast and scrambling to get my belongings together, I'd thrown my cell phone in my duffel bag and forgotten about it. Around ten-thirty I was waving goodbye to Leah and Selah from the back of their father's minivan. Pastor Tim hummed along to the Christian radio station from the driver's seat, tapping his fingers on the steering wheel along with the music.

"Did you get any sleep, Elleni?" I looked up to find his gentle eyes watching me from his rearview mirror.

"Um, I guess so. Still kind of tired though."

"Oh sure, by my calculations, there wasn't silence coming from that room until at least three o'clock in the morning."

I grimaced. "I didn't realize you could hear us."

"I was up, but not because of the noise. I was working on my sermon."

"Oh, okay."

"You know, Sister Elleni, I've never heard you laugh quite as much as you did with my daughters last night. It made me very happy to hear you all having a good time together. You were unusually quiet over breakfast though. That's why I had to ask about your sleep."

I turned up the corners of my lips and shrugged, hoping he wouldn't press the issue.

"It's funny how well I know the voice of my daughters. I was thinking about that before bed and about the Good Shepherd and His sheep. The sheep hear His voice, and He knows them each by name, and they follow Him. Isn't it comforting to know that our Shepherd holds us in the palm of His hand?"

"His grip is too tight."

Did I just say that out loud? If Pastor Tim was bothered by my comment, he didn't let it be known.

"*For the moment all discipline seems painful rather than pleasant, but later it yields the peaceful fruit of righteousness to those who have been trained by it.*' That's Hebrews chapter twelve."

"So…"

"So, you may not see the upside of a storm while you're in the middle of it. But God is sure to use it all for your growth, your ultimate good, and most importantly, His glory."

Chapter 14

"The Lord has made everything for its purpose, even the wicked for the day of trouble."
Proverbs 16:4

I noticed Tio's truck parked in front of the house long before we pulled up to the driveway; what I didn't expect was to hear his voice before I reached the door. I waved goodbye to Pastor Tim and let myself in.

"What were you thinking Mauricio!?"

This was bad. My uncle never used cousin Macho's real name. I walked slowly into the living room but stopped abruptly at the sight of Macho and Daniel sitting on the couch with their heads down and ice packs on their faces. When Daniel re-adjusted his ice pack, I noticed his lip was swollen to twice its normal size. Macho had a black eye. Tio and Papi took turns laying in on their sons.

"*Daniel, teniamos un trato.* Our deal was that you could study Wing Chun as long as you never used it to pick a fight." Papi was clearly exasperated with my brother, pacing back and forth in front of him.

"Your mother is going to kill you when you get home!" Tio exclaimed, wagging a finger in Macho's direction.

"And you're not going to camp. Even if by some *milagro* Todd let you go, we sure are not," Papi said to Daniel.

"If there was even the slightest chance this fight could have been avoidable, your behavior is inexcusable," said Tio.

"¡Y no más video juegos!" Papi and Tio yelled at the same time.

Both Daniel and Macho cringed but knew better than to say a word in their defense. It was only after Tio grabbed Macho by the ear that he turned around and saw me standing by the door.

"Why couldn't my son be behaved like you, my niece?" He reached past me and opened the door, all the while still holding on to Macho's ear. I cringed at the pained expression on Macho's face.

"Ouch. Bye cuz."

Tio slammed the door behind them. I turned to see Papi storming into Daniel's room long enough for me to exchange a glance with my twin. He mouthed, "Help!" Papi reemerged with my brother's headset, power cord and controllers.

"One year!" he shouted in English.

My brother's eyes widened as our dad went to the back of the house and slammed the door of his bedroom shut. Daniel buried his face in his hands.

"It's over. No more Wing Chun. No video games. No TV. No camp. My life is over."

I sat down next to him on the couch, a hand on his back. Papi hardly ever had to lay down the law, but when he did, he brought it down with a hammer.

"What in the world did you and Macho do last night?" When Daniel didn't answer, I pressed. "Come on, tell me."

He sighed. "Have you checked social media?"

"No. You know I never log on."

"Well, it's on there." He started to get up. "Oh, and by the way, she called again."

I cleared my throat. "Oh. Did you talk to her?"

"Yes, I did. She wanted to wish us a happy birthday."

"Yeah. Thanks. I'm going to check my socials now."

He looked like he wanted to say more but instead, he got up and retreated to his room.

I rummaged through my duffel bag for my cell phone and charger. As soon as the home screen came on, I went on Daniel's Instagram page. A recent upload by someone from Pinellas Park High School had tagged him, Macho and a few others. The ten-second video clip had been shared one hundred and twenty times. The thumbnail displayed someone lying on the pavement, straddled by my cousin. In the background, my brother could be clearly seen under a streetlight, mid-kick.

I pressed 'Play.'

Daniel's body came alive, sending his opponent flying with the strike of his foot. The voice of a few spectators rose with excitement in the background, including a few female voices. At the bottom of the screen, I made out Macho, punching the face of his challenger, only to be blindsided by a fifth person ramming into his side and throwing him off his rhythm. The video ended with Daniel tackling Macho's foe and putting him in an arm lock. Even *I* had to admit, this did not look good for my brother or my cousin.

My phone vibrated as the messages I'd missed while it was off started to come in, one after the other, repeating the same name over and over: Julian.

*

"*Elleni, please. Pick up.*"
"*Elleni?*"
"*I'm really sorry. Let me explain. Please.*"
"*I can't believe I flaked on you. I'm such an idiot! Please, let me apologize.*"
"*Your voicemail is full. Please call me back.*"
"*...Elleni. I'm sorry. I understand if you don't want to talk. I'll leave you alone, but I would really like it if you gave me a callback.*"

*

I spent all Saturday morning turning down phone calls, ignoring texts and listening to music. After hours of my phone interrupting my thoughts, I finally put it on 'Silent' and let it all go to voicemail.

That night, I dreamed a series of nightmares, waking up every hour. I watched how one day turned to the next on the face of my alarm clock. Midnight, July seventh. It was my seventeenth birthday. How in the world was I going to be able to drag myself to church that morning? I knew Julian would most likely be there. I decided to skip the morning service before finally surrendering myself over to sleep for the last time.

*

"What do you want for your thirteenth birthday?" Monica asked from her bedroom floor as she went through her books. I laid on her bed, flipping through a magazine, my hair cascading over the edge. I stopped when I reached the centerfold of Nick Francis, my celebrity crush.

"For my thirteenth birthday, I want to have my first kiss," I said.

Monica laughed before responding, "I meant something that I could get you."

I made a face and rolled onto my stomach. "Ew. You could have been more specific."

We both giggled.

"What about you?" I asked, offering her the magazine. "What do you want?"

She laid it neatly on top of her desk. "I don't know what you should get me, but I think I know what my parents got me," she said, beaming.

"Oh my gosh, is it the guitar?"

"Yes!" she squealed, throwing herself on the bed next to me. "Mom asked me to grab her keys out of her purse yesterday, and a receipt fell out. It was from the music store in Tampa that I always want to go to. They bought me guitar strings and a strap!"

"Yay!" I said. "It's about time. You've been wanting to play guitar forever."

"Maybe not forever," she said. "I don't know of a lot of things that really last that long."

I rested my head against her arm. She smelled of *Roxy* perfume. "Do you remember how my brother always complained that he wasn't invited to our slumber parties?" I said with a chuckle.

Monica let out a laugh. "Yes, I do. Remember when your cousin wanted to join too?"

"Duh! He likes you."

Monica blushed. "No, he doesn't."

"Oh yes, he does. But I think the real tragedy is that you like him too but you're both too shy to admit it."

"He's kind of cute. I love his dark curls."

"Ew!" I scrunched up my nose.

Monica threw her head back and laughed. "Okay, okay, change of subject. We have to start planning our slumber party, you know. Let me look at my calendar."

Dreamer

"I'll grab it," I said, getting up and walking over to the wall by the door. The calendar had cutesy pictures of dressed-up puppies. I took it down and handed it over to Monica. She sat up and turned to July. The picture was of a fluffy pup in a spangled tux and star-shaped red sunglasses. She gasped. Curiously, I peered down at the page. Next to a picture of a birthday cake was a frowny face with a tear.

"What does that mean?" I asked.

"It means we can't have our slumber party on our birthday."

"Why not?" I asked.

Monica didn't meet my eyes. "I didn't know how to tell you. I thought we had more time."

"More time for what?" My chest began to tighten.

"We're moving."

The words came out as a whisper but hit me like a ton of bricks.

"What?"

"Our moving day is July 8th." I closed my mouth and felt a tickle in my nose as my eyes brimmed with tears.

"Oh Leni, please don't cry!" Monica said, sitting down next to me and taking my hand. "I'm really sad too, but my parents feel called to start a new ministry in Atlanta. They said you can come to visit!"

"But how am I supposed to start seventh grade without you?" I rubbed my nose on the back of my hand.

"Oh, it's going to be okay. Honest. You'll make new friends."

"You're my only friend at school."

"That's not true. Lots of people are nice to you at school."

"That's not the same, and you know it. Please, Monica. You can't!" I cried.

Monica put her arms around me. I didn't have to say it. She knew I didn't like goodbyes.

"Leni, I promise it's going to be okay. We can still write letters back and forth and visit each other. We're best friends," she said as she wrapped her pinky around mine, "forever."

*

I let out a ragged breath, my vision was blurry. It took me a moment to realize that I'd been crying in my sleep. The sound of heels on the hardwood floor approached my bedroom door. "Wake up, *Mi Amor*," Mami said as she walked into my room. She was dressed in a navy blue polka-dot dress and black heels, a chocolate cupcake balancing on the palm of her hand. I groaned and pulled the covers over my head.

"*Que te pasa?*" Mami asked while gently drawing the covers off my face. Her hair was pulled back on the sides, revealing tiny white stray hairs over her ears. Her red lipstick matched her nails. She sat on the edge of the bed and brought her face close to mine, smelling of perfume, her laugh lines disappearing as she ran the back of her hand over my wet cheek. "You're not supposed to cry on your birthday." She offered me the pastry. I examined the tiny heart-shaped sprinkles, probably leftover from Valentine's Day, before blowing out the candle.

"I don't want to celebrate this year."

She put the cupcake on my desk. "Because of Julian?"

"How did *you* know about that?"

"*Soy tu Madre.* It's my *job* to know."

"Julian is only part of the reason," I mumbled.

"And the other part?"

I twirled my bracelet around my wrist. 'Forever,' it lied. "She would have been eighteen," I whispered. Mami nudged me toward the wall as she slipped off her heels and put her feet up on the bed, laying her head down on the pillow. I rested my ear against her chest, her heart beating reassuringly. We stayed that way, her hand caressing my messy hair, and me, breathing in the smell of freshly baked cupcakes until I felt myself drifting back to sleep.

There was a knock on the door. "Come in," Mami called sleepily.

Papi walked in decked out in a short-sleeve blue button-down and black slacks, his thick hair brushed to one side. "*Feliz Cumpleanos, hija.* Would you like to go to your favorite restaurant tonight?"

"What does Daniel want to do?"

"*Tu Hermano* is not going anywhere."

"Not even on his birthday?"

"He can go to church," he said in Spanish. "He's going to need more of the Lord if he's going to get through the next year without video games."

Mami rolled her eyes. "Marcos, *no seas malo.*"

Papi smiled the tiniest smile under his mustache before turning back to me. "It's getting late, *Chiquita*. Shouldn't you be getting ready for service?"

Dreamer

"Do I have to?" Any other day, I wouldn't have dared to ask, but today was not just any other day.

Papi started to object, but Mami spoke up. "*Podemos hablar afuera?*" Papi agreed to speak to my mother privately. When they stepped out of the room, I got out of bed and pressed my ear against the door.

"What are we teaching her when we let her stay home from church on a difficult day?" Papi asked in Spanish.

"I know what you mean, Marcos. I just think it's more important to be empathetic right now."

"Empathetic?" he asked. "It's been four years, Marta. She should be over this by now, but you insist on coddling her when she has these moments. When we were kids, hard things happened all the time. Did we lay down to die because of it? No. We were taught to get up and move on with our lives. We are making our daughter weak."

"I will not risk losing her again," Mami said sternly, a quiver in her voice.

Papi exhaled heavily. "I know, I know. But this is the last time she misses church because of this. Got it?"

"*Si.*" I heard the front door open. My mom called out, "Elleni, we will be back in a couple of hours! I love you."

"I love you too," I called back, slipping back under the covers. There was a knock at the door, followed by Daniel's voice. "Are you decent?"

"Yes."

"Happy birthday, sis," he said, draping his arm over my shoulders in a sideways hug. His mouth was dotted with chocolate crumbs.

"Happy birthday to you too. Clean your face." He wiped the back of his hand over his mouth. "Anything planned?" I asked, already knowing the answer. He put on a thinking face.

"I'm deciding between reading mom's collection of *Home Remodeling Magazine* or watching paint dry."

"Yikes."

"Yeah. Dad's not even letting me read for fun. At this rate, I'll be lucky if he lets *Sister Bev* sing "Happy Birthday" to me. Anyway, I'll see you later, Leni."

He was almost through the door when I called him back. "Dani, wait. What are you going to do if you see Julian?"

"I honestly don't know," he said before closing the door behind him.

D.S. Fisichella

As I heard my parents' vehicle pull out of the driveway, I looked at the little cupcake on my desk with a new sense of appreciation and bit in. I devoured the pastry before throwing myself back down on the bed. When I woke up an hour later, I went to the bathroom and undressed, stretching out my aching limbs. I studied my shoulder in the mirror where the hand-shaped bruises had been but were now no longer visible.

I stood motionless under the showerhead, allowing the hot water to travel down my back, noticing for the first time that my hair now reached my waist. When I was done with my shower, I toweled myself dry and went back into my room to get dressed. I slipped on a sleek black dress and emerged shortly after in a bun and full makeup. After stepping into some flats, I headed out the front door.

*

We could have been around nine and ten years old when our parents finally trusted us enough to let us wander outside of our own street.

"I have to show you this little place I found when I was riding my bike!" Monica said over the phone one evening.

"Does it have a name?" I asked.

"I don't think so."

"How do I find it?"

"It's by Kailey's grandma's house. I'll bring my chalk and draw an X on the sidewalk right in front of it. X marks the spot!"

The X faded with the first rain shower that followed, but the name did not. In the beginning, we were content to get to the Spot and sit down on the grass, watching how the little critters made their living, but we soon discovered that feeding the ducks was more entertaining than just watching them.

As time went by, the families of ducks grew in number and stature. Each time a new member joined the family, Monica named them. I could never keep the names straight, but she always did. She saw so much beauty in our little corner of the world.

It was our last time visiting the Spot together before the scheduled big move. I didn't want to think about it. I wasn't ready for her to go.

The air was full of moisture, and I could already feel my shirt sticking to my back under the hot July sun. "I'm going to miss it here," Monica said, her golden hair pulled up into a braid crown. She wore a pretty flower-pattern sundress, her feet dangling bare over the murky water of the canal.

"It's just a ditch," I said.

"It's not just a ditch, Leni. We grew up here. Don't you remember swinging from the old tire swing that used to hang from the train tracks?" She stood up, balancing on the edge, her hands out as if to embrace all the memories.

"Yeah, until it snapped under my weight. Remember *that*?" I countered, determined to stay grumpy. Monica laughed, as carefree as ever.

"Okay, how about the time I got to hold one of the ducklings?" she asked.

"You mean before its mom ran us off the property?"

"Oh, I forgot about that too."

"Face it, Monica. Whatever your parents plan on doing in Georgia, it has got to be better than living in this dump."

Monica grew quiet, making her way over to where I sat on the grass. She sat also, putting one hand on top of mine. "Leni, it's not goodbye. I will really miss you, but it will only be a 'see you later.' One day, you will come to visit me, and it will be just like it's always been."

Like it's always been.

*

My feet were now firmly planted where Monica once stood with her arms out. I spread mine out in the same manner, hoping to get back some of what I lost this day four years ago. The Spot was unchanged in appearance, but in contrast to that last sunshiny day here together, today was overcast, the ducks nowhere to be seen. As I stood with my arms out, I got a rare chill as the wind picked up speed, rustling the leaves of the oak trees overhead and the blades of grass around my ankles. Monica was gone and I was completely alone.

"Elleni?"

Or not.

Dropping my arms to my sides, I turned to face Julian who was standing only a few feet away. He wore a plain tee and jeans, his hair was without product and slight circles were beginning to form under his eyes.

"I hope you don't mind," he said. "Daniel told me where I might find you if you weren't at home." When I didn't answer, he closed the distance between us, his head down. He didn't look up until he was close enough for me to touch. I hated how much I wanted to reach out, to be engulfed in his arms, that place I'd come to know so well.

"About Friday," he began. "There are no words. No excuses. I wasn't there for you, and worse, your brother and your cousin were put into danger because of me."

I said nothing, instead, looking over the Spot. I waited for him to continue.

"Daniel came to a party to confront me about not being there for you when you needed me. Instead, he found me getting beat to a pulp by Cal and his lackeys. If your boys hadn't shown up, who knows what would have happened," he said, trailing off.

My heart warmed at the thought of my brother rushing to defend Julian, even after he'd done Daniel so wrong earlier in the day.

"Elleni?"

I turned to look at him again. He looked so apologetic, the lines on his face deeper than usual. He ran his fingers through his hair.

"Not being able to talk to you the past couple of days has been torture." He walked forward until there was no longer any distance between us. He moved his fingers from his own hair, trailing the tips against my temple, before cupping my face in his hand. "Even now, seeing you here, looking so good, and knowing you want nothing to do with me is unbearable." He tipped my chin upward. "I'm sorry."

The earnestness in his face made any lingering resentment slip away with the breeze. His touch against my skin ignited a small kind of hope within me.

"I missed my chance to make you my girlfriend, but if I lose you as a friend, I'll be completely lost."

I slipped my arms around his waist. He reciprocated by pulling me closer, crushing me just slightly. I breathed in his scent, my ear against his chest, his heartbeat centering me with its pulse. The wind whistled softly in my ears, reminding me that no matter how lost I also sometimes felt, I was still *alive*.

"Can I ask you something?" Julian murmured into my hair.

I took a step back. "Sure."

Dreamer

"Why would Daniel protect me after what I did to him?"

"Because he's done worse to God," I said, remembering my conversation with Miss Josie all those weeks ago after Julian had rejected me at the hospital. "And just like Christ showed us grace, we are to do the same."

Julian nodded slowly.

"There's something I have to tell you," I said. "When we were at the Bandshell, you asked me about my bracelet. I told you it was from my friend."

"The friend who moved away, right?"

"That one. Except she didn't move away. It was her parents that moved." Julian gave me a confused look. "They moved one day after her funeral."

The confusion on his face turned to dismay as my words registered. "Oh, Elleni." A silence fell over us as the wind stopped howling. The only sound now was the trickle of the water below.

"Her name was Monica Josephs. She died on her fourteenth birthday, four years ago today." Julian slipped his long fingers through mine, the warmth of his hand filling me with something that gave me the courage to push forward. "I tried to commit suicide a couple of months after her death," I said, remembering. "There was a presence there that day, a dark ominous thing. It watched and waited, accusingly, reminding me of all the reasons everyone would be better off without me. It drained my energy; I hadn't slept in days. And there it was, filling me with dread and fear that I would never wake up from this nightmare. The hopelessness felt like too much, and when I felt it was heavy enough to break me, I just gave up."

I could feel Julian looking at me, but I didn't stop for fear that I'd never be able to talk about this again.

"Mami walked into my room to find me falling asleep on my bed, an empty pill bottle in my hand and blood trickling down my arms. All I remember was her screaming for my brother to call 9-1-1 before I lost consciousness."

"I spent some time in a mental health facility before I was released. Brother Todd came by with his wife Amanda, and together, they opened scripture to 2 Corinthians 5:17:

"Therefore, if anyone is in Christ, he is a new creation. The old has passed away; behold, the new has come."

I turned to look at Julian, who'd fixed his eyes on the bridge. "That's the day I realized that I needed God's forgiveness. And His help."

"Do you think that Jesus would wait… for me?"

*

Text Conversation

Julian: *"Did you have a good dinner with your family?"*
Elleni: *"Yes, I was surprised that my brother was allowed to come. I suspect you had something to do with that? But what was so important that you didn't want to join us?"*
Julian: *"I owe you. But there was something I had to talk to Joe about. It really couldn't wait."*
Elleni: *"Oh. Is everything ok?"*
Julian: *"Yes. I'll tell you in person when I see you on Tuesday."*
Elleni: *"Tuesday?"*
Julian: *"Your brother is off on Tuesdays, right?"*
Elleni: *"…yeah"*
Julian: *"I'm taking you and Daniel out to Jubilation Station as my belated birthday gift."*
Elleni: *"Are you serious? Does Dani know?"*

As if on cue, Daniel burst through my doorway, completely out of breath. The largest, goofiest grin I had ever seen was painted across his face.

Elleni: *"Never mind."*

Chapter 15

"Also henceforth I am he; there is none who can deliver from my hand; I work, and who can turn it back?"
Isaiah 43:13

Jubilation Station

"Pizza, laser tag, unlimited coins for games AND go-karts? This is the best. Day. Ever!" My brother may have just turned seventeen, but his tastes hadn't changed much from the time he was twelve.

I watched from our booth with amusement as he strutted to the prize counter with a long scarf of tickets around his neck, a paper birthday crown on his head and oversized neon sunglasses on his face. He leaned coolly over the counter, flirting with the cute employee behind the register. She smiled politely at his compliment, taking out the prizes my brother wanted, but she turned down his request for the ultimate prize: her number.

"He'll find someone soon," said Julian as he followed my gaze, "I know people say that good guys finish last, but it's just a matter of time before some nice girl finds out how great he is."

I smiled in agreement. "Hey, didn't you say you had something to tell me today?" I asked between bites of pizza.

"Ah, yes! But let's wait till Daniel sits back down."

A moment later, my twin materialized with a medium-sized goody bag in one hand, from which stuck out an oversized pencil decorated with skulls. In his other hand, he held an inflatable blue electric guitar. Gone was his ticket scarf.

"Please tell me that's not all you got for a thousand tickets."

"For your information, *Elleni*, I got *lots* of cool stuff. I could have gone for a larger prize, but I decided to go for a bunch of small stuff instead. I even got you guys something."

Julian said, "Aw, Dan, you didn't have to get us anything. We have our own tickets!"

"I wanted to say thank you for bringing us here. So I got *you*…" He rummaged through his bag. "This!" He proudly held up a red whoopee cushion with the Jubilation Station logo on it for Julian to see. Julian laughed, slapping Daniel a high five. I rolled my eyes. *Boys.*

"And for you, my dear sister, I got this." From his bag, he extracted a sparkly pink harmonica, a pen with musical notes in its design and a plush purple teddy bear with the words '*Happy Birthday*' across its tummy. I gaped at my little treasures, looking up to see my brother smiling sweetly at me.

"Aw! I love them!"

He leaned back in his seat, throwing his hands behind his head, clearly pleased with himself. "*Nailed it,*" he said smugly.

Julian cleared his throat. "I want to give you some good news."

Daniel and I exchanged quizzical brows.

"As you know, due to my royal knuckle-headedness, I've lost my camp scholarship."

Daniel placed his neon sunglasses on the table, folding his hands together. "I'm failing to see the upside."

"I talked to Todd after church on Sunday. He said that if I'm able to pay my own way, I can still go."

Daniel looked at me eagerly, but I wasn't ready to celebrate just yet.

"How are you going to come up with the money by this Saturday if you haven't been working except for your community service hours?"

"On Sunday, while you guys were dining out with your parents, I was sitting across from Joe in his office, asking for a loan so I could cover my camp expenses."

"So he loaned you the money?"

"No. Instead, he asked me to allow him the '*pleasure*' of sending his only son to summer camp for the first time ever. His words, not mine. I

Dreamer

couldn't say no to that." So that settled it. Julian was coming to camp with us on Saturday. I couldn't wait.

We spent the rest of the afternoon in great spirits — finishing our pizza, running from laser tag to mini-golf, back inside for some more arcade games — before finishing out the night with go-karts. Strapped into my pink vehicle, I stomped down on the gas pedal when my turn came to zoom onto the racetrack. I wondered if driving a real car was anything like this.

I loved the thrill I felt with the wind coursing through my hair, as I swerved from side to side in an attempt to drive past my companions. We were all surprised to find that my girly cart was faster than their 'hot rods' as I managed to take the lead. I laughed, hearing their protests coming from behind me. With this new sense of freedom, I pushed forward, racing toward the finish line.

Wednesday Night Youth Group

Jake met Daniel at the door of the Youth Room and motioned for him to get closer. They hunched over with their backs to me. When Daniel turned back in my direction, he was visibly shaken.

"Have you seen this?" he asked. He handed me the green pamphlet Jake must have slipped him during their exchange. The words 'Grace Place Camp' stretched across the top of the cover page. Underneath, I saw the happy faces of about twenty campers in matching shirts with some counselors in between. But wait, was that—?

I gasped.

Julian emerged from the Youth Room, took one look at me, and asked, "What's going on?" When I didn't respond, he looked at Daniel and tried again. "What is it?"

Daniel held up his palm at Julian and nodded before turning to me. "Leni," he said slowly, "we knew where they were going, right? And that they were buying a big property?" He turned the pamphlet over in my hands, two familiar faces smiling brightly under the title: 'Meet Our Founders, Bill and Tracy Josephs.'

Julian took another step, bowing his head to peer at the pamphlet I was holding before snapping his attention back on my face, waiting for me to confirm what he was already putting together. "Josephs? As in—?"

"Monica," I said, and then everything went black.

Chapter 16

*"Remember not the former things, nor consider the things of old.
Behold, I am doing a new thing; now it springs forth, do you not perceive it?
I will make a way in the wilderness and rivers in the desert."*
Isaiah 43:18-19

The sensation of fingers softly raking through my hair was followed by the smell of musky cologne. I inhaled deeply and smiled, content in the familiar warmth.

"Hey beautiful," whispered Julian. I opened my eyes to the sight of his honey-green eyes gazing lovingly at me, his arms cradling me securely. I exhaled happily.

"What's with the goofy grin?"

I turned to look at the speaker. Macho's tone was taunting. On either side of him, Selah and Leah hid giggles behind their hands.

Amanda hunched over me, moving a small light from left to right. "How are you feeling?" she asked.

I squinted. "What happened?"

"You passed out," she said. "Your parents are on the way."

"Do you need to borrow some of my lip gloss?" Leah asked, kneeling at my side. She wore a tutu over mermaid leggings and sparkly flats, her hair up in a perfect bun.

"Your lip gloss? Really, Leah?" asked Selah.

Dreamer

"What? It always makes *me* feel better," Leah shot back innocently.

Macho snorted. "Figures." He then turned his brown eyes on me, one of them still slightly bruised, his black curly hair spilling onto his forehead under a red beanie. "You okay, cuz?"

"Yeah, yeah. Fine," I said, sitting up. "Where's everybody else?"

"Daniel and Todd are waiting for your parents downstairs," Julian said as Amanda retrieved a hot pink stethoscope from her bag. "Mickey D.'s throwing a ball around in class."

Amanda listened to my breathing and my heart, each time wrinkling her forehead in concentration, before putting the stethoscope away. "Sounds good! Let's get you some ice."

Macho and Selah grabbed hold of my hands and hoisted me to my feet. Selah studied me with concern, her freckles dark against porcelain skin. "Are you sure you're alright?" she asked.

"You heard Amanda," Julian said, coming up beside me.

"Yeah, I know. It's just that Jake showed me the flyer." My heart sank. She must have seen it on my face because she put one freckled hand over her mouth. "I'm sorry. I didn't mean to make you think about it again."

"It's okay, Selah," I reassured her.

"We should go in," said Julian, his hand on the small of my back.

I nodded.

Once in the Youth Room, I sank into a chair, a blue ice pack to my head. Julian had gone off to wait for my parents with Daniel. In the meantime, Todd had returned and was now kneeling in front of me, his bald head reflecting the fluorescent lighting above us.

"What happened back there?" he asked.

"Nothing," I said, then, "On an unrelated note, I'm not going to camp."

Todd raised his eyebrows but kept his mouth serious. "I see. Is there anything I can do to change your mind?"

"I don't think so."

He nodded and got back on his feet, calling his wife to the side. Macho sat down next to me, his beanie now in his hands. He cleared his throat. "Your boyfriend is something else," he said.

"My what?"

"*Por favor!*" He rolled his eyes. "You can pretend with everyone else, but not with me."

"Are you off house arrest?" I dodged.

"That's what I'm tryna' tell you, Cuz."

I put the icepack on my knee, my hand red from the cold.

"He called my old man and told him it had all been his fault."

"He did? Is Tio letting you off the hook?"

"Yes and no. He says one punch would have been justified, but the other five were just *'overkill.'*" He made air quotes with his fingers. I bit my lip. Tio had a point.

"Who'd you punch, anyway?" I asked.

"The meathead that knocked Julian unconscious. Your brother seemed to know him."

"Why do you say *that*?" I asked, a pit forming in my stomach.

"Because Daniel was the one who knocked him to the ground. He yelled, *'I've got this one!'* like he had some personal beef with him or something. I never got around to asking him why because one of the other stooges tried to knock him down; that's when Daniel kicked the living daylights out of him. I wish the video had shown all that," he said. "It might've landed me a girl."

Amanda made her way to the podium while Todd slipped out the door. "Alright everybody, let's get started with prayer requests." Macho turned his eyes up front, and Dakota's hand shot up.

"Yes, can we pray for Elleni? If she faints at camp, it'd be kind of a *drag.*" Macho laughed next to me. Another voice spoke up.

"Hey 'Kota, didn't they tell you that to make jokes, you have to be *funny?*" I turned toward the voice to see Julian winking at me. Dakota slumped back against his seat, his arms crossed. Mark, his identical twin, slapped his arm, jeering.

Daniel, Mami and Papi appeared in the doorway behind Julian. He stepped to the side to let them through. Mami got to me first, her hands on either side of my face.

"What happened, *Mi Amor*?"

"Apparently, I passed out. Help me up?" Papi steadied me as I emerged from my chair. I handed Mami my ice pack before I gathered my belongings. We were getting ready to leave when Todd approached us.

"Marta, Marcos, can we step into my office?" he asked. My parents looked at each other before following him to the open door of his office, near the Youth Room. As I passed Julian, he caught me by the hand.

"Hey, you okay?" he asked.

Dreamer

"Fine. Just a little shaken up."

He gave me a heartbreaker's smile, his dimple making an appearance. "Don't worry. I'll be with you at camp no matter what happens."

I opened my mouth to say something, maybe to tell him I wasn't going, but was interrupted by Brother Todd who was still waiting by the open door to his office.

"Elleni? You coming?" Like I had a choice. I smiled at Julian and squeezed his hand before following Todd inside.

A blonde head turned in my direction. "Hey lil' chicken."

"Miss Josie!" I exclaimed, taking the seat next to her. The office was snug, Miss Josie and I sitting on two foldable chairs against the wall and my parents on comfy armchairs facing Todd's desk. The way my parents sat motionless in their chairs made me nervous. Something was up and I didn't like it. I squirmed. Miss Josie leaned down close to my ear. "Bless your heart, honey pot. You're fidgeting worse than a sinner in church."

"Last time I checked, I *am* a sinner. And we *are* in church," I whispered back.

She smiled and shook her head, tapping her feet to some praise and worship song only she could hear.

Todd closed the door and sat behind his desk. "Thank you all for joining me," he said, folding his hands together.

I'd never been sent to the principal's office, even when I attended primary school, but as I sat in my chair watching how Todd's words hit my parents, who seemed just as tense as I felt, I wondered if this is what it felt like to be in trouble with the highest authority.

He rested his steady eyes on me. "Elleni, I want to commend you for all your work with the music," he said, "not just with the youth, but with VBS as well."

I felt myself relax.

"Everyone looks forward to learning your songs, young lady. What you're doing is nothing short of genuine service for the Lord. Well done."

"That's my girl," Miss Josie whispered from beside me. Todd was turning to my parents now.

"Marcos, Marta, it should come as no surprise that Elleni is at the top of the list for a full camp scholarship." Mami and Papi raised their eyebrows in that, *wow, will you look at that,* kind of way. I bit my lip, knowing their excitement would dissipate soon enough.

"There are only two problems." *Here it comes.* "The first problem is that Elleni missed church this past Sunday." My mouth fell open. How did I forget about that?

Mami spoke up, "Sunday was Elleni's birthday, Brother Todd. If anything, Marcos and I told her she could stay home."

"I still would have granted her the scholarship, Mrs. Salgado, but I'm afraid this brings us to point number two: she doesn't want to go." Miss Josie's happy foot-tapping stopped abruptly. The room was suddenly quiet, except for the low hum of the air-conditioning and the muffled worship music coming from the room next door.

Todd gave my parents a hard stare. "Marcos, Marta, I think it's time you told Elleni what's been going on." I was only half-listening, wondering if it was Selah's voice who was now singing lead and wishing I was there to see it when Todd said this last part. As his words registered, I brought my focus back to the here and now. I looked from Todd to my parents, but nobody met my eyes. "What does he mean?" I asked. "Papi, what's he talking about?" After a few more seconds of the air conditioning humming its happy seventy degrees and a few grunts and failed starts by Papi, my mother spoke up.

"It's about Grace Place."
"What about it?" I asked. My mom grew quiet, suddenly a shade paler than usual.

Miss Josie groaned and sat upright in her chair. *"Oh for Pete's sake."* She turned to look me square in the face. "They set it up, Elle Belle."

"They set *what* up?"
Mami put up one hand to stop Miss Josie before addressing me again. "We knew the camp was managed by the Josephs." My heart drummed deafeningly in my ears, the dizzy feeling from before returning. "We were the ones who asked Todd to take the group to their campground this year." I blinked, once. Twice. But nothing seemed real anymore.

I scanned the knick-knacks on Todd's desk: the worn baseball glove, the oversized paperclip, the bulldog bobblehead. It all seemed foreign, misplaced. I thought of Betta Bob's plastic world, only this time, I was the one in the bowl, exposed, my fate already decided. I looked down at my feet. Small, insignificant fish. That's what I'd become. My world, a mere illusion of safety.

I balled my hands into fists. The only evidence that I was still there was the pain of my nails digging into my palms, and even more so, the pain of

Dreamer

my most trusted people in the world going behind my back like I shouldn't have a say in my own life. Like I didn't exist. Like I wasn't alive to make my own decisions. And maybe I wasn't, maybe I hadn't been for a long time. Thank God I could at least feel the pain.

"They have been so worried about you. It's been years, Elleni, and you're still not well. You won't even pick up Tracy's phone calls," Mami was saying now, faintly. After a few more breaths, I realized Mami had stopped talking. Nobody was talking, and yet, the silence… the silence was screaming.

"Are you kidding me?" said a shaky voice. It took me a second to realize the voice had come from my lips.

Papi placed a hand on Mami's arm, speaking to me in Spanish. "We wanted you to move past this. We want to see our happy girl again." *Nuestra niña Feliz.* My mind flickered with images of myself as an eight-year-old crying myself to sleep nightly, homesick for Costa Rica. At ten, examining myself in the mirror convinced no boy would ever like a chubby girl like me. At twelve, struggling to fit in at school. The only times I could remember being happy, *truly* happy, was when I was with *her.*

"Elleni," Miss Josie uttered softly, "they were just doing what they thought best."

There was a burst of heat coming from my chest, the grinding of my teeth so intense that my jaw throbbed under the pressure.

"What's *best?*" I spat. I could feel myself losing control, the heat in my chest bubbling up, threatening to spill over like lava, oozing with the ugliest thoughts from the depths of my wicked heart. My hands closed around the arms of my chair, tightening harder and harder, adrenaline coursing through my veins like fiery poison. I wasn't just feeling sad or disappointed. Oh, no. For once in my life, I was *livid.* "Did any of you think that the best thing would be to stay *out* of it?"

"We were trying to help," Miss Josie said evenly, her chin unwavering, her soft blue eyes resolute. I narrowed my eyes on her.

"Well, that's not what you did. Is it? You didn't help. You lied."

I turned my attention to my audience, Brother Todd behind his desk, a look of grave concern over his features, Mami, looking small in her chair. She had twisted her torso around to face me, her big brown eyes moist, her nose red, and her lips, usually curved into a smile, now pursed into a frown. Papi sat sideways in his chair, his head bowed, avoiding eye contact.

"You *all* lied. You tell me you're proud of me, you try to convince me that it's all good. But I see the way you look at me when you think I'm not looking. Mami, always so scared that I'll spiral again. Papi, wondering when he'll have to do damage control. It's because you *know* that I'm not okay. But you're good at pretending that we can just move on… and *you*," I turned my eyes on Miss Josie, "you hide in your office, dealing with everybody's problems but your own. I should have known better than to trust a *hypocrite*."

She flinched. My hands flew to my mouth, but it was too late. The words had already reached their target. A heartbreaking detachment fell over Miss Josie's face, and instead of responding, she gathered up her belongings and walked out the door, leaving me to drown in an ocean of regret.

People deal with distress in different ways. Take my parents for example. Mami, who always saw the glass half full and glistening in the morning light, was now polishing off a travel-sized pack of *Kleenex* which, by my count, she'd only just opened back at Todd's office. Papi on the other hand, drove stiffly, his eyes burning holes through the windshield. All the while, I, the culprit responsible for their despondency, sat sandwiched between Macho and Daniel, sporting a blotchy face and a wedgie deep enough to make the Grand Canyon look like a crack on the sidewalk.

Speaking of cracks...

"Stop squirming like a worm," Daniel murmured, elbowing me in the ribs.

We arrived to find Tio's car already in the driveway, the motor running and windows down. Papi had barely hit the brakes when Macho threw his door open and flashed across the lawn and into his father's vehicle. "Step on it, *Viejo*!" we heard him say.

Tio turned in his seat. "Who are you calling old?"

"Trust me, Pops, you want none of what's about to come out of that car. Just go!"

Tio looked in our direction, where my dad was still sulking in the driver's seat, his knuckles white on the steering wheel, my mom dabbing her face dry beside him and me, stumbling out of the open car door, both hands on my behind. By the time I fixed my little problem, Tio and Macho had peeled out of the driveway and were already halfway to the stop sign at the end of the street.

Dreamer

"Lucky," Daniel muttered next to me, looking after them. I hurried past him, shoved my key in the door, turned it, and let myself inside, leaving it wide open as I made a beeline for my bedroom. I slammed my door shut and stepped over an empty suitcase on my way to the bed.

My white headphones were laying on my pillow, inviting me to drown the rest of my evening in music, but as my fingers curled around the cord, there was a knock on my door. I froze. Another knock. The door handle turned, and the door opened to reveal slacks and a button-up. My eyes widened. Papi was the last person I'd expected to come in after me. Mutely, he walked over to my desk chair and sat down. He leaned back in it, his arms crossed over his chest, his eyes downcast.

I waited.

A minute passed on the face of my digital clock, then another. I looked out my window. A homeless man with a curly gray beard and tattered clothes pushed around a shopping cart filled with tin cans, stopping at each blue recycling bin he came across to peer inside and move around its contents. The sky above his head was getting darker.

When I looked back at my dad, I found him watching me, his mustache looking whiter than I remembered, his eyes tired.

"*Hija,*" he started, then stopped, uncrossing his arms and leaning forward in the chair. "At the time, not consulting you about our plans with the Josephs seemed like the right thing to do, but we should have trusted you to make the right decision to confront them on your own."

"No, you shouldn't have," I blurted out.

He raised an eyebrow. "Why?" he asked in Spanish.

"Because I never would have done it on my own. I'm too stubborn, and I don't like change or conflict," I said, looking at the floor. Papi let out a chuckle. I raised my head in surprise. "What's so funny?"

"There's more of me in you than I realized," he said, his teeth making a rare appearance under his mustache. I smiled back, cocking my head to the side as he peered over at the only framed photograph on my desk: one of me as an infant, snuggled up against a younger version of himself, both of us inside my crib. I could picture it perfectly in my mind, even as he took it off the desk to examine it closely.

In the photo, my father had thick jet-black hair and a much fuller mustache than he now sported. There were no bags under his eyes, and he wore a vibrant shirt. He cracked another smile and I saw a glimpse of the same youthful radiance. I crossed the room and knelt at his feet, taking a peek as he balanced the frame on his lap, trying to see it through his eyes.

"I was not blessed with your mother's personality, but I always believed you were," he said.

I wrinkled my nose. "Me? I'm way moodier than Mami."

"I think that if your circumstances were different, that would not be the case," he countered. I shrugged and looked back at the picture.

"Today, I saw something else of myself in you," he said, returning the frame to its place before turning back to me. "We both can be intentional about our words. God can use that to bless people, but as you saw today, those words, sharpened in bitterness, can also be misused to wound."

I sat back on my heels and picked at my shoelaces in an attempt to hide the crimson in my cheeks. "I know, Papi. I'll apologize to Miss Josie."

He nodded. "Good." A part of me knew what his tone meant; he was finished talking, had said his bit, and was ready to wrap it up, but I couldn't remember the last time Papi and I had conversed for so long, and I wasn't ready to let him go, not while there was still so much unsaid.

"It's just that—I really miss Monica, and I wish she were here. I feel like—" I swallowed. "Like it shouldn't have been her. She should have been the one to live." I looked up to find him shaking his head, his chin quivering. "It's true!" I cried. "You know it is. The Josephs shouldn't have lost her."

"And *we* should have lost *you?*"

I opened my mouth, but no words came out. I knew that was essentially what I'd said because no matter what, I'd never wished death upon anyone but myself. Without thinking, I slid a finger under my sleeve and ran it over my scars.

"*SUFICIENTE!*" Papi roared, yanking my wrist forward with one quick move. My hand looked small and delicate in his square palm as he slid my sleeve up to my elbow, my scars in full view. I wanted to roll it back down, to hide my past. My shame.

"I was working," he said, his eyes hard. "I got the call when you were already on your way to the hospital. I drove to meet your mother and brother there, and it was the longest drive of my life." His voice broke. "I cried and begged God to preserve your life." He stopped, struggling to find his next words. I was shocked to see my father, always strong, never wavering, on the verge of tears. He cleared his throat, the next words coming out in broken

English. "You don't know how helpless I felt, *hija,* to wonder if my little girl would ever open her eyes again. And how I, *tu padre*, could let this happen." Tears streamed down his cheeks. "You are my world, Elleni. Don't take away the *gift* that God has given *me*."

He rested his face on my scars, and for a moment I imagined him crying over my casket. How could I be so selfish? I bowed my head and touched it to his.

"I'm sorry, daddy," I whispered. "It wasn't your fault."

He produced a handkerchief from his back pocket and ran it over my cheeks before bringing it to his own face, but before the cloth touched his skin, I took it gently from his hand and did my best to dry his tears once and for all.

Chapter 17

"And I am sure of this, that he who began a good work in you will bring it to completion at the day of Jesus Christ."
Philippians 1:6

The first thing I noticed was the eerie feeling of someone watching me, the second was the smell, that pungent-sweet smell. When my eyes adjusted to the darkness, I realized I stood on a deserted street, gravel underneath my feet. The only light was one facing me from the large front window of a two-story house. There was no movement coming from the house, only a single couch, visible through the glass.

All was quiet, no wind, not even the sound of crickets. The only thing that set this reality apart from a still-shot photograph was my breathing and the wild thumping in my chest as the feeling of being watched only grew stronger. Thick static energy threatened to suffocate me, the hairs on the back of my neck stood on end.

I took one step, and my foot hit a low barrier. In contrast to the street, it felt soft against my bare feet. I didn't look down. I didn't have to. I knew it was a body. It was *her* body.

My throat tightened, but I didn't scream. Instead, I squeezed my eyes shut and tried to will myself awake by uttering the only name powerful enough to bring me back.

Dreamer

"Jesus," I said, my voice weak to my own ears. "Jesus," I repeated again, this time a little louder. If I had ruby slippers, I would have tried that too, but I wasn't in Oz. Oz wasn't real.

"Jesus?"

"Yes?" the reply came, calm, authoritative, and yet gentle. I turned my head in an attempt to make out the Speaker.

"Where are You?" I called, my voice echoing.

"I am still here, Elleni." He sounded close, not in a particular direction, but instead as if He inhabited the very atoms that made me up, was the very glue that held me together. I breathed, His voice speaking into the depths of my heart and soul.

"Help me, Lord. I can't do this. I'm not strong." My voice was raw, the pain palpable in my own ears. I waited for a moment, but there was no sound. No voice. Nothing. "Lord?" my voice sounded weak, faint. "Please, God. Don't leave me here. Not like this. I need you," I pleaded with him, my pulse growing quicker and my eyes spilling over with moisture. "God!" I called, my hands cupped around my mouth, my voice fading into the night. When there was no reply, I let my arms fall back to my sides.

"Don't leave me here. Not again," I whispered. "I'm scared and empty. I've been trying to do right by you, by my parents, by Miss Josie, by Julian… and I'm done. I can't anymore. Those small glimpses of you that I get here and there, that little bit of peace is not enough." I looked down at the ground. "I'm sorry, but it's not going to cut it anymore, because what I want is You." With these last words, I realized the truth behind my confession. This whole time, I'd been wrapped up in my grief, shackled by my fear, and distracted by a yearning for a romantic relationship with Julian, but what I actually needed was the Lord. Instead of turning to music or people to find worth and contentment, I needed to start turning to Him wholeheartedly. "I want to hear You," I called out. "I want to recognize You from a distance. Take me deeper, Lord."

Without thinking, I moved my feet forward toward the house as I talked, but that's when I realized that the body that had blocked my way before, had vanished. I looked around, straining to see if I'd somehow side-stepped it without thinking, but no. It was truly gone. In the silence, having said everything I needed to say, I sat down on the ground and waited.

"I began a good work in you," He said, his voice crisp and clear. "I will be faithful to complete it." A part of me revived as I drank this in.

D.S. Fisichella

"What do you want me to do?" I asked.

The answer came without hesitation: "Tell them."

*

It wasn't my intention to be a hermit for the days following Wednesday night church, but between praying and packing, I had remained in my room for the most part and had neglected to take my phone off 'Silent.' I was a wreck, but at least I could pretend otherwise as long as I busied my mind with what to bring on the road, that is, as long as I could stop myself from unpacking.

Every day, my brother would pop his head through the doorway to tell me Julian was asking how I was. Every day, I told him the same thing. "Tell Julian I'm fine, I'm busy, I'm sorry, and I'll see him Saturday." I had expected brutal nightmares in those last nights, but there was a surprising silence that overtook me and carried me until morning. Perhaps this was because God knew that I was one more doubt away from running in the opposite direction.

And then it came: Saturday.

I woke up with a sickening feeling in the pit of my stomach and ran to the bathroom. An hour later, I was back there again, getting sick, unable to keep down my cereal. My brother knocked impatiently, insisting I was hogging the bathroom. I let the water run after brushing my teeth, putting my hands under it to splash my face. This was not a good start to my day. A few minutes later, there was a different knock at the door. Papi.

"*Elleni, estas bien?*"

I reached for the knob. Papi's face turned from curiosity to concern in an instant.

"You don't look too good," he said in Spanish.

"I don't feel too good," I replied in English.

He asked if I was well enough to go camping. I shrugged.

"I'll be okay, Papi. I just need to take some nausea medication."

He came back with a bottle before heading for the dining table where a book and a cup of coffee waited for him. I took two small tablets before heading back to my bedroom, barely dodging my brother as he jumped off the couch towards the bathroom door, flying through the air like a ninja. Once inside the bathroom, he kicked the door behind him with a loud,

Dreamer

"Hiya!" I gaped. From the dining table, Papi didn't bother looking up from his book.

"He told you he had to go."

Agápē Baptist Church

Upon arriving at the church parking lot, I looked around to see the church van, all doors open, being hooked up to a small *U-Haul* which I assumed would carry everyone's luggage. Todd barked last-minute instructions as the teens crowded around the van. Jake, Selah, and Joshua helped, while Mark and Dakota goofed off to the side, playing with a frisbee. I spotted Julian leaning up against his mother's Volvo, carrying on a conversation with her while looking very camp-ready with his aviator sunglasses, white V-neck and grey swimming trunks. Catching a glimpse of my dad's car, he fell into an easy run towards us, opening my passenger door.

"Hi, Mr. Salgado!" he called across from me, leaning down to see my dad.

"*Hola* Julian, *cómo te va?*"

"*Muy bien, señor. ¡Gracias!*" Then looking over at me, in a softer voice: "*Hola Elleni. ¿Cómo te sientes?*" (Hi Elleni, how do you feel?)

I sighed.

"That bad, huh?"

"I'm fine. I guess I'm just not looking forward to the long ride," I said, hoping I sounded convincing. He offered me his hand. I let him help me out of the car. He then made his way over to Daniel, who was holding out a suitcase for him to load into the trailer. I stretched, reaching back into the car for my pillow and backpack.

"Elleni!" I turned to see Melissa pulling up next to us, waving out the window. I walked over to her as she stepped out for a hug. She sported a striped yellow-and-white V-neck over crisp white shorts and leather sandals that showed off her French pedicure. Her hair was pulled back into a high bun over large brown sunglasses. She smiled widely at me.

"Hi Melissa," I said, taking a step back after our hug, "you look awesome."

"Oh, that's right! You're not used to seeing me in my play clothes," she said lightly. "I'm meeting Joe for brunch after I drop off Julian. But you know I couldn't leave without saying goodbye to you, Leni girl!"

Leni girl.

I felt a hollowness in the pit of my stomach. Where had I heard that phrase before? I snapped out of it, saying my goodbyes to Melissa before helping the boys carry the rest of the luggage into the trailer. Having kissed Papi *adios,* I made my way to the van, mentally preparing myself to hit the road. Amanda strolled over to me, looking flushed but excited in Bermuda shorts and an airy white top. Her hair flowed loosely around her shoulders.

I waved.

"Hey you, how are you feeling?" she asked.

"Better," I admitted. "Still surprised I came."

"I'm not," she said with a smile. "I knew you had it in you. We have about ten minutes before we leave, why don't you take a bathroom break before finding your seat?"

"Good idea," I said.

I put my pillow inside the van, next to a striped black-and-white pillow I recognized, before making my way toward the church building. Julian jogged up to me. "Hey," he said, a bead of sweat already falling down his temple.

"Hi," I said. "You need to use the bathroom too?"

"Water." He held up a tumbler.

"Ah. Smart." We stepped into the building in time to meet Sister Bev on her way out, a pinched expression on her face. As usual, her nails matched her bedazzled hat and outfit. Today's color of choice: hot pink.

"You okay Sister Bev?" I asked.

She sniffled. "No. Some women in this church don't know how to talk to people," she said, turning her nose in the air before waddling away. Julian and I looked after her in surprise.

"What was *that* about?" asked Julian.

I shrugged. "No idea."

I looked down the hall that led to the bathrooms, noticing a light under Miss Josie's door. Julian walked over to the water fountain mounted on the wall.

"Hey, do you mind getting me when they're ready to go?" I asked him. "I'll be in the counseling office."

"Sure."

"Thanks."

I went down the hall and into the bathroom, exiting a minute later with hands that smelled of lavender soap, attempting to dry them on my jeans since the cleaning crew wasn't scheduled to come in to replenish the paper towels until that afternoon. I stopped short at the sound of something heavy hitting the floor.

"Dagnabbit to bits!" Miss Josie's muffled drawl carried through the door.

I knocked before slowly opening the door to find her on her hands and knees, scooping colorful paperclips back into a mason jar.

"Steve, if this is about me tellin' Bev to pipe down that thing she calls a singin' voice, I promise you, I'm doin' the Lord's work. That woman puts a whole nother meaning to 'joyful *noise.*' Not even her dead and gone mama would blame me — bless her cremated heart..."

"Miss Josie?"

She stopped cold, finally taking a moment to examine my scuffed-up pink sneakers, her eyes traveling up until they landed on my puzzled face.

"Oh. Sorry, girl. Thought you were Steve."

"Yeah, I gathered that," I said, getting on my knees to retrieve the last of the paperclips as she got back on her feet. I slid them into the jar and placed it back on its usual place on her desk, only to realize the rest of her mason jars were gone. I looked around for them but was instead met with a sparse room. Besides the desk, the jar, a box of tissues, the rug under my feet, and the chair, the only other things around the room were a cluster of boxes lined up against one corner. The top box had a roll of lights poking out. Miss Josie watched me quietly as I walked the perimeter of the room, dodging boxes and trash bags filled to the rim.

"Are you going somewhere?" I asked, afraid to hear the answer.

"Yes."

"But—you're not—*leaving,* leaving, are you? I mean, it's temporary, right?"

Miss Josie turned her sad cobalt eyes on me. "Oh, Elleni. I'm no good with goodbyes. I was hopin' to be out of everyone's hair before you got back from your little trip."

I felt the air go out of me. Had I chased my mentor away? "If this is about what I said on Wednesday, I am so sorry, Miss Josie! It was stupid and I didn't mean it, I swear." As I said this, Miss Josie crossed the room and pulled me into her arms. I buried my face in her shoulder, returning her embrace.

"I know, baby doll. All is forgiven. This is not your fault. God called me to my next mission is all. You can understand that, can't you?"

"Well, yes, I guess. But, where are you going?" I asked.

"Kentucky. I've been offered a job as an in-house counselor for a ministry that helps young women with troubled lives. You know, runaways, young mothers, recovering addicts and such. I've been praying about it for a while, asking the Lord to show me if it was His will, and He has."

"Really? How?"

"Well... with *you*."

"Me?" I asked, surprised.

Miss Josie smiled warmly. "Yes, you. I asked God to show me that you were going to get along fine without me, and He has. You're not my only client, but you're my favorite. Everyone knows it."

"This doesn't make any sense."

"Sure it does! You've grown so much in the time I've known you, and the fact that you're willing to face the Josephs once and for all only confirms that you will be just *fine*. That scared little girl with sad eyes has turned into a brave, gentle, and caring soul, one who would look past the tough exterior of a young thug and be a light to him in his darkness. More importantly though, you're learning how to overcome your own darkness as well. My work here is done."

"But—I'm *still* working on it," I insisted. "I'm not ready for you to go! I have so much more to learn."

"We all do, sugar. Jesus teaches me new things every day! The difference now is that you are *willing*. That's all God wants of you. He'll take it from here. And don't worry, other people will come along to help you on your journey. You just wait on the Lord. Until then, I'm just a phone call away."

"But—" I scrambled for an excuse, a reason, anything — but my mind was blank. I knew she was right: if this is what the Lord was leading her to do, who was I to keep her from doing it? I knew better than anyone else that Miss Josie was the perfect person for the job. I felt my throat tighten up and a tickle in my nose, the tell-tale signs of soon-to-be waterworks. Miss Josie knew it too.

Dreamer

"Oh, no you don't," she said, wiggling a perfectly polished finger at me. "If you cry, I cry, and we'll need Noah to come to the rescue. No, no, little chicken, I'll be around come Christmas time, ya hear? And I promise to fly you up to see me from time to time. How's that sound?"

I sniffled but nodded my head.

Miss Josie cleared her throat. "Good."

There was a knock on the door.

"Who is it?" she called.

"It's Julian. Is Elleni there?" Miss Josie's eyes brightened at his name, and she swung the door open.

"Well hello there, handsome," she cooed. "Aren't you a sight for old eyes?" She stuck out her hand. "I'm Josie."

"*You* are the famous Miss Josie?" Julian asked with his full dimple in view. "I've heard so many great things about you!"

"Likewise, young buck." Miss Josie turned to me with a twinkle in her eye. "Girl, I see the dilemma you got yourself into. If they sculpted guys like this back when I was a hormonal teenager, I woulda got myself into a whole mess o' trouble!"

"Miss Josie!" I exclaimed. Julian smiled down at the floor. Miss Josie cackled, tears of joy in her eyes. "Look at y'all! Red as a couple of strawberries in the middle of February." She pinched our cheeks.

"I'll, uh… go wait for you outside," Julian said to me, his eyebrows raised. "Nice to meet you, Miss Josie."

"Nice to meet you too, cutie pie. She'll be right out for ya." Julian nodded and waved, walking away with a chuckle. Miss Josie turned back to me, fanning herself. "Oo-wee, girly. Good for you."

I laughed. "What happened to 'unequally yoked'?"

"Well," she said, "just cause you can't marry the man, don't mean you can't appreciate God's handiwork. Besides," she continued in a low whisper, "we'll keep praying he gets saved. If he does, he'll fit right in with all the hunks in Heaven. David, Samson, Boaz…" She'd started to count on her fingers.

"Miss Josie," I interrupted. "You're stalling. Also, the Bible doesn't say Boaz was handsome."

She winked at me. "Who needs beauty when you're Godly *and* loaded?" I smacked a hand to my forehead, only to hear Miss Josie erupt into another fit of laughter. "I'm just kidding, honey. Come here and give me some love."

D.S. Fisichella

I gave her a big hug, hoping it would communicate all those things I didn't have time to say: how she filled my life with joy, warmth and laughter for so long.

"Can't breathe!" she gasped. I let go.

"Miss Josie, there's so much I wish I could say."

"I know."

"I love you," I said.

"I love you too," she replied, lightly pinching my nose. "Hold on one second, I have something for you." She went behind her desk and reached underneath, retrieving a medium-sized gift bag. She came back around and handed it to me.

"Here you go, my Sunshine Gal. Open it in the van." She kissed my forehead, her eyes moist as she took a step back. "Go on." She shooed me with her hands. I started to walk away but stood in the doorway one more second, memorizing her just like she was. Her short blonde hair, barely past her shoulders, brown roots starting to show. Her eyes were tearful and full of love.

"I said go on now."

"Okay. Bye, Miss Josie."

"Until next time, honey pot."

I started to close the door behind me but opened it back up in time to see her reaching for a tissue. "Oh, and Miss Josie… thank you."

Chapter 18

"I have said these things to you, that in me you may have peace. In the world, you will have tribulation. But take heart; I have overcome the world."
John 16:33

When I stepped out of the church building and into the morning sun, I was met by happy chatter and the sound of Todd attempting to get us all into a circle for prayer. After he finished praying, I mounted the van and situated myself in the second row back, next to the window. Julian followed after me, then Daniel.

"I like Miss Josie," said Julian with a grin. "She doesn't have a filter, does she?"

"Not even a little bit."

"What's in the bag?" he asked.

"I don't know yet," I said. "I'll open it later."

When everyone was situated, I counted twelve people in the van. First was Todd, the driver and the bossman. Amanda was the DJ and road-trip activity expert. We were all extremely impressed with her arsenal of card games, adult coloring books and cheesy road trip sing-along songs. Jake was the only one besides me that had brought his musical instrument. While he had packed his guitar in the trailer with mine, he had brought into the van his ukulele, playing along to every song that was sung on the ride. Selah sat next to him, singing along sweetly and looking lovely as ever, her soft brunette tresses pulled back, a few locks framing her sweet face and doe eyes. Leah was road-trip ready with a stack of magazines poking out of her *Hello Kitty* backpack. She wore a purple headset, bopping along to some poppy song.

Just behind Leah, Joshua stole glances at her from behind his tablet. Joshua was only fourteen, his father the pastor of the Philippine Church down the street. They were fine with Joshua attending our Youth Group since they thought his technical skills would be put to better use with us. At first, it was difficult for Todd to convince him to come to Georgia with us, but when he found out Leah would be coming along, he signed up with no further hesitation. He pushed his glasses up the bridge of his nose, before going back to his screen.

Mark and Dakota took up the rear of the van. They had been attending for about as long as I had. Their mom and dad were our in-house missionaries, so they had seen the world. They were also the only other pair of twins in the Youth Group; however, these two were identical, with blonde hair, deep blue eyes, athletic frames and picture-perfect smiles.

Years ago, when Monica first brought me to church with her, we'd been in awe of these two perfect-looking boys walking into our Sunday school class, having just moved to Pinellas Park from somewhere in Europe. Their 'dreaminess' quickly turned to 'annoyance' as we were constantly taunted by the two class clowns. While over time they had grown and matured, it was always hard for me to look past the gum they put in my hair one Sunday morning in the fourth grade. It took my mother several tries and almost a full jar of peanut butter to scrape it out. I'd hated peanut butter ever since.

The only girl I didn't know very well was Annie; she sat in the front row. We'd been introduced only that morning before getting into the van. Apparently, Annie was Amanda's niece and a bit of an anomaly. She was petite with straight brown-and-purple hair; she wore bangs over the thick black glasses that framed her sweet face. She had a slender nose and big brown eyes. She wore a grey baggy T-shirt over denim shorts and dark purple *Converse* shoes. Her nails were a silver sparkle.

"*Call of Duty?*" I asked, leaning over the seat in front of me to take a closer look at Annie's shirt. In my peripheral vision, I noticed my brother's head shoot up. She shrugged coolly, taking out a headphone. "I stole it from

Dreamer

my brother's closet before he left for college last year. He was my gaming buddy."

"That's right!" called Amanda from the passenger seat. "I stopped being able to buy her dolls when she was four. She insisted on playing with her brother's *Ninja Turtles*." My eyebrows shot up.

A female Daniel.

When I looked back, Daniel was sitting at the edge of his seat pretending to read a comic book, his cheeks flamingo pink. Julian followed my gaze. As I turned back to Annie, I heard him whisper to my brother, asking if he was feeling okay. Daniel nodded, before remembering that he was supposed to be reading (and breathing). He quickly let out a jagged breath, turning the page.

Annie and I carried on an easy conversation. She was sixteen, had an older brother and a pit bull she had adopted that she named Lola. She liked playing video games, but she also enjoyed playing her grandpa's old violin. Annie was a church-goer, but only because it was expected of her.

"Well, I hope you have a good time with us," I said. Annie only shrugged her shoulders and put her headphones back in.

I grabbed my pillow and fluffed it up before gathering my feet up into the seat, curling up under a soft pink blanket. I was lulled to sleep by the motion of the van and the sound of lazy chatter floating up from the back of the vehicle.

*

"Well, aren't you just cute as a button? Call me Josie, little chicken."
"Okay. Hi, Miss Josie."
"Hi, sweetpea. Looks like life's got you down. Oh no, why are you crying? Tell me what ails you, Sugar Cookie."
"M—my best friend died."
"Oh, Jesus, heal this little heart. Sit here, baby doll. You want some coffee?"

I woke up to the sound of the van doors slamming shut and sat up in my seat, only to find that the van was empty. Through the window, I could make out Todd, his back to me, standing in front of a highway rest area. I rummaged through the items at my feet until I found what I was looking for, a polka-dot gift bag. I pulled out the first item, a card. The front of it was a simple design, mason jars and lights, just like her office.

Elle Belle,

Pinellas Park was never meant to be a destination. It was just a stop along the way in my journey... but you are the one that made staying worthwhile. I never told you this, but I gave birth to a daughter while I was married to my husband. She only lived an hour after birth, at which time she died in my arms.

Sometimes things happen, terrible things, but it isn't until later on that God shows us exactly how He uses all that hurt to make us better people. Her name was Belle and had she lived, I imagine her being just like you. Guess I'll find out when I meet her in Heaven. Until then, I'll always love you as my own.

—Josie

The second item in the bag was a framed photograph of Miss Josie in a hospital gown, surrounded by pillows and holding a bundle in her arms. I traced her features, her naturally brown hair in disarray, her smile radiant, and her eyes, gazing at her child in a most familiar way.

MOTEL

"Alright gang, we made it to Atlanta. Boys are rooming together with me, girls with Amanda. Let's go!"

We stumbled out of the van one by one. Leah was the first to speak up. "Um, where are we?"

"The Motel where we'll be spending the night," Amanda replied.

Daniel took one look at the building and frowned. "A bed bug metropolis. Charming."

Selah swiveled around to look at Amanda, fear in her eyes. "Bed bugs? Amanda, has anybody considered bed bugs?"

"Calm down, I'm sure it's fine," said Todd.

"Oh no. Have you watched that recent investigation into motels on the news? Some cleaning ladies don't even change the sheets and pillows!"

Amanda grimaced, turning to her husband. "Todd, do you suppose we could get the front office to change our sheets and pillows before we go down for the night?"

"But we haven't even walked into the rooms!"

"Please!" Selah begged. "You don't understand. Bed bugs are the devil."

"Really? The devil?"

"Yes! They get into everything!"

"Alright, fine. I'll go talk to the front." Todd jogged over to the office.

I stretched again, turning in a circle to take in our surroundings. It was nighttime, and the only thing I could really see was the bright sign of the motel and one for a nearby gas station. Across the street, I could make out a twenty-four-hour diner. My stomach grumbled. Todd reappeared a few minutes later with room keys. "They assured us they would change the sheets right away. Is anybody hungry?"

Julian threw up his hand. "Yes!"

Daniel, who up to this point had been rummaging through Amanda's snack bag, looked up, and with a mouthful of chips, muffled, "I'm starving!"

Mark yelled out, "A man shall not live on *Cheetos* alone."

I spoke up. "There's a diner across the street."

Todd said, "Good, let's walk. We need to get our blood flowing."

I crossed the street feeling a little unstable, like my legs were made of jello. At one point, I felt my knees giving way, but before I hit the ground, an arm looped through mine and steadied me.

"Come on," said Julian. "Let's get off the street." We moved hastily to the sidewalk.

"Thanks."

"Don't mention it." He started to walk away, but I reached out and caught his hand.

"Julian, wait, can we talk?"

He said yes but kept walking, squeezing my hand gently as he tugged me along. We walked inside to find the rest of our group pushing tables together.

"Want to get a booth?" he asked. I nodded.

We sat at a booth by the window, rummaging through sticky menus for a few minutes before a server came by to take our drink orders. As she walked back toward the kitchen, Julian turned to me.

"So, are you okay? You seemed a little out of it after you talked to Miss Josie."

"She's moving away," I said, my lip quivering. I stopped talking, all of a sudden sure I was going to lose it. Julian looked as shocked as I felt at the news.

"But that doesn't make any sense," he said. "She didn't tell you until today?"

I shook my head just as the waitress came back, setting our drinks down on the table. "Are you ready to o—oh..." She had caught a glimpse of my expression. "I'm sorry, should I come back?" she asked.

"Don't bother," I said before heading for the door.

"Elleni, wait!" Julian called after me before turning back to the waitress. "I'm sorry, we'll be back soon." I didn't stop until I was outside. Julian ran out after me.

"Elleni."

I turned on my heel to look at Julian. "I'm fine," I said.

"You're fine," he repeated.

"Yep, totally fine."

"Really..."

"Sure, I just have one request," I said, pacing back and forth. "Could you maybe tell me, like... oh, I don't know, a week ahead of time before you walk out of my life?"

Julian crossed his arms but said nothing.

"Because for once, I'd like to know ahead of time, you know?" I continued to pace, twirling my bracelet around my wrist. "A month ahead would be better. Or you know, like, right now." I stopped moving and directed my attention to him. "Tell me now, Julian. Are you going to leave me too?"

Somewhere in Georgia

My neck felt tight, my shoulder blades were rigid from hours upon hours of being crammed in a van full of sweaty teenagers, and my butt was stuck to the floor of the dingy rest stop bathroom.

"Are you okay?"

No.

"Elleni, don't make me crawl under this stall!"

"We only have an hour to go!"

"Everyone is worried about you!"

It didn't matter that Leah, Selah and Amanda were hollering. It didn't matter that I had locked myself in the bathroom for over twenty minutes.

Dreamer

Every conversation I had with God, every pep talk I'd directed at my mirror, and every time I resisted unpacking my things no longer mattered because today was by far the *worst* day to face my past. Miss Josie left me, my parents tricked me and Julian… don't even get me started on Julian. I could hear the disappointed trombone in my head:

Wah—wah—WAHHHH!

I thought I was strong enough to face Bill and Tracy again, but now I was equally convinced that to do so would mean my demise. The trauma was four years in the making. Was it really any surprise that in a few days, I still hadn't gotten over the fact that I would have to face the two people in the world that I'd been trying to avoid at all costs?

If I get through this, I deserve a gallon of ice cream and a spoon.

I heard the girls shuffle away, the door closing behind them. A couple of minutes later, I heard it open again. I cleared my throat. "Look, I can't do it, okay?" I called shakily. I looked over at the shoes that stood on the other side of the stall, surprised to see worn black *Converse* with blue laces. *Daniel.*

"Leni, I know this is difficult for you. You've avoided these people for years, but they're like parents to you. The only thing they're going to feel when they see you is love."

"Monica is *gone*. Them seeing me is not going to bring her back!"

He was quiet for a moment.

"I know you snuck out of the house the night Monica died."

What? My heart began pounding violently in my chest. *Did he know all this time?*

"It was late at night, and I was going to say goodnight, but when I realized your door was locked, I picked the lock, thinking it would be funny to barge in while you slept and scare you. Stupid, I know. But when I opened the door, I realized your room was empty. I saw the window was unlocked, and I figured you probably snuck off with Mo." I didn't know what to say. After all this time, I thought the whole ordeal was just *my* secret.

"Did you ever wonder why I started going to the WCA?" he asked. The question surprised me.

"I figured you just liked the idea of kicking butt," I said.

"Well, yeah. One butt in particular. I got my chance a couple of weeks ago, and I took it."

"*Calvin?*" I asked, shocked.

His voice broke as he said, "Ever since mom found you nearly dead in your room, I realized there was a whole lot more going on than any of us realized, only I didn't know what. I started asking around school, gathering bits and pieces from people who were at the party, until I got a name... the name of the person I let into your room. I should've known better than to leave you alone with him, Leni. Did he...?"

"No," I said. "No, he didn't."

"But did he hurt you?" His voice was so soft, so afraid of my response that my heart broke with the realization of the huge burden my brother had been carrying for so many years, and suddenly, it made sense. Why he was so overprotective, why he had learned how to fight, and why he couldn't seem to mind his own business. And for once, I was grateful. With one final sigh, I found my footing, walking over to unlatch the stall door. I opened it.

"Not too much," I replied.

"Well, I hurt *him*," he said with fire in his eyes. "A lot, and it felt good."

"Dani..."

"It killed me that I didn't do anything to protect you when we were younger, so as I swung at him, hit him time and time again with everything I had, I did it wanting him to feel it too, wanting him to feel what you felt after he got done stomping on your heart. I wanted him to *want* to die."

In my life, I'd heard my brother deliver all sorts of empty threats, but this time, his words chilled me to the bone.

"Do you realize what you could have *done?*" I demanded. "What if you'd succeeded, huh? Then you would have gone to prison, and I would have lost *another* loved one. Is that what you want?"

"Of course not! But I wasn't thinking, that's the point. The only reason I stopped hitting him was that God showed me the truth."

"And what's that?"

"That the only person you blame for everything is yourself." Daniel watched me, not angrily, not with disappointment. He just watched me as his words traveled from my ears, through my veins and to my heart. I didn't speak. I didn't move. I didn't deny it.

"Whatever happened that night, with him, with Monica... you were just a kid, Elleni. And I think God wants you to put it behind you once and for all."

I tapped my foot impatiently. "Why?"

"Why what?"

"Why do you say that? Why do you think it's true? Why do I have to be here, Daniel? Why? Why is He doing this to me?"

"I don't know, but it *can't* be a coincidence that you're walking right into the Josephs' campground after all these years."

"You're right, it's not. Mom and Dad made sure I would."

"You know as well as I do that God has the final say."

I sighed in defeat. I knew it, alright. It was the only reason I'd come. Daniel had won this match. He beamed and opened his arms to his sides. I walked into them and breathed in the smell of home.

"I love you, my barely-little sister," he murmured into my hair.

"I love you too, my barely-big brother."

On our way out, we were met by an elderly woman who nearly toppled over at the sight of a teenage boy and girl walking out of the same public restroom arm in arm. Daniel and I looked at each other, mortified.

"It's not what you think!" I said.

"Yeah, she's my sister!"

The lady pushed past us into the restroom, muttering something about teenage hormones under her breath. Dani and I stood there, speechless, not realizing we had an audience until we looked over at the van, where the entire youth group erupted into hysterical laughter at the scene they'd just witnessed.

Chapter 19

"For I know the plans I have for you, declares the Lord, plans for welfare and not for evil, to give you a future and a hope."
Jeremiah 29:11

Welcome to Grace Place!

The sign loomed just up ahead as the van rumbled over the dirt road, shooting up clouds of reddish-brown dust. I couldn't tell if I was shaking because of the motion of the van or if I was just terrified of what lay ahead. In contrast to the previous combined ten hours in the van, everyone seemed to be wide awake now, craning their necks to take in the camp for the first time.

In the distance, we could make out acres of woods towering over cabins and a pen echoing with the sound of farm animals. The smell in the air was of freshly cut lumber. We drove past a little hill topped off with a fire pit, aligned with large makeshift benches made of old tree trunks. A sign by the road dubbed it "Campfire Hill." The skies were blue up ahead. Although quite hot, the day could not have been any prettier.

We slowed down at the sight of church buses parked outside of cabins across the campground. It hadn't occurred to me how many people could actually fit in a campground this large. Workers in matching purple shirts with the 'Grace Place' logo ran from vehicle to vehicle with clipboards in hand, assigning cabins to each group. Youth groups that had already been assigned their places to sleep were unloading their vehicles, lugging their things inside.

A tall college-aged counselor sauntered over to our vehicle, introducing himself as Alex. He was very tan with dark brown hair and light honey-colored eyes. He spoke to Todd for a moment before being drawn by the intensity of my stare. He nodded at me before turning back to Todd.

All of a sudden, I was painfully aware of the fact that I hadn't run a brush through my hair in several hours and was probably looking like a hot mess. In a hurry, I started to pile my hair up into a ponytail, while admiring Alex's chiseled features. Julian cleared his throat from the seat behind me.

"You like what you see?" he growled.

I blushed, hiding my smile.

Alex took a step back from the open window, pointing us toward two cabins at the far left of the property. I resisted the urge to look at him again as we drove past. Todd turned to Amanda. "I don't remember him on the counselor list, do you?"

His wife shrugged. "I know one thing for sure," she said, "there weren't any pictures of him in the brochure. I would've remembered *that* face."

Once parked in front of our cabins, a collective sigh of relief was heard around the van as Leah reached over to unlock the double doors.

"I swear on my *Hello Kitty* backpack that if I don't get a shower in the next twenty minutes, I'm going to kill something!"

Todd looked over his shoulder with a raised eyebrow. "Leah, that's not very Christian of you."

"Well excuse me, Brother Todd, but I think Christ would agree, especially if he was just stuck in this smelly van for the past thousand years!"

"Ten hours hardly constitutes a thousand years. And there were no vans back then."

"Exactly!" she said as she hopped out. Todd began to say something else, but Amanda put her hand on his shoulder to stop him, mouthing the words, *'Don't bother!'*

Cramped between pillows, blankets, and my carry-on backpack, I dug my way out with difficulty, my sweaty shirt stuck to my back. I stretched my arms, experimenting with movements I'd been unable to perform since that morning. The boys were instructed to unload the trailer, the girls to stand in line to receive their luggage. I stood with Annie.

"Have you met my brother?" I asked.

"Your bathroom buddy?" she said, picking at her nails. "Haven't had the pleasure."

"He's somewhat of a gamer himself. I think you guys would have a lot to talk about," I said nonchalantly. Annie looked over at Daniel, examining him as he unloaded an oversized suitcase.

"Who brought the bag of bricks!?!" he huffed. Amanda yelled back, "It's my first aid stuff!"

"Yeah? Well, I hope you packed an extra pair of lungs in here! And maybe a new spine." He blew his hair out of his face. "I'm gonna need it!"

Annie laughed. When Daniel realized who the laughter was coming from, he lost his grip, the suitcase falling on his foot with a muted *thump*. We froze, bracing ourselves for what would come next. His face turned white, then red, then about three shades of blue before settling on bright indigo. He opened his mouth, sucking in his breath.

"YEEEE—OOWWW!"

There was an odd moment of silence surrounding Daniel, as his scream seemed to echo through the cabins, the woods, the state of Georgia and beyond. Then, just like that, we snapped out of it and rushed to his side. I was the second one there; Annie was the first.

"I am so so sorry, this is all my fault!" she fussed, trying to get the suitcase off his foot and clearly underestimating its weight, as she accidentally let it slip through her fingers. Annie and I gasped collectively as it fell back down. Daniel's face went white again, his eyes rolling backward in his head.

Annie brought her hands to her mouth. "Did I just…"

"Yep," I replied.

Amanda slung Daniel's arm around her shoulders in an attempt to steady him while Todd carefully hoisted the suitcase off his foot and let it drop a considerable distance away.

"Julian, assist Amanda with him. I'm going for help."

Julian ran to Daniel's other side as I lifted his pant leg under the knee so he could get the weight off his injured foot. Once I was sure Daniel could keep his foot elevated, I stepped to the side to allow the trio past me down the ramp. Annie wasn't far behind, groveling her apologies.

"Elleni," Amanda was calling over her shoulder, "find some ice, stat." I hurried down the ramp and trudged uphill to the main office in hopes of finding someone with a purple shirt. As if on cue, Alex appeared, crossing the distance between the cafeteria building and the office.

"Alex?" My voice came out too timidly; he didn't hear me. I tried again. "Alex!" He turned to look at me. I gave a little wave and jogged in his direction.

"I'm Elleni. Sorry to bother you, but we could use some help. My brother got hurt, and we need ice."

"I'll be right back." He ran inside, re-emerging a few seconds later with a small blue cooler. I reached for it, half expecting to bring it back on my own, but Alex didn't seem to notice as he walked past me, his eyes fierce. I struggled to keep up.

"What happened?" he asked, his voice gruff.

"He dropped a heavy suitcase on his foot."

Alex grimaced. "It wouldn't be the first day of camp without an incident."

"Really?"

"Most times, it's a misunderstanding or a dispute, but sometimes it's physical, at least outwardly."

"What do you mean by that?"

"A lot of things go on around here," he said, his eyes still aimed forward, "most are not as they seem." At his words, a scripture verse entered my mind.

"For we do not wrestle against flesh and blood, but against the rulers, against the authorities, against the cosmic powers over this present darkness, against the spiritual forces of evil in the heavenly places."

"But we're at a Christian camp," I protested. "Wouldn't the devil try to stay away from here?"

"This is just a place, Elleni."

"I hope this doesn't keep my brother from participating in physical activities throughout the week," I said.

"It wouldn't be the first time," he replied.

My heart sank for Daniel, he would be crushed if he didn't get to do all the fun things he'd been rambling on about since he read the pamphlet.

We made our way back to the cabin, but about halfway there, I tripped over a brick-sized stone. Instinctively, Alex reached over, closing his hand around my arm to steady me and pulling me toward him. "I'm used to this uneven ground, so stay close." As we neared the cabins, I made out a couple more purple shirts. Julian looked in our direction, his gaze zeroing in on Alex's hand still on my arm, his expression indecipherable.

Alex spoke up, "Oh good, Mama T is here. Looks like she's already got a handle on the situation."

I didn't respond because just as he said this, *Mama T* looked up from her place beside Daniel. She turned in our direction, and my heart stopped cold.

"Leni girl, is that you?"

Mama T was none other than Tracy Josephs.

*

Four Years Earlier

The sequence of light and darkness through my bedroom window resembled a bad game of peek-a-boo, with each day showing its ugly face like a jump-scare surprise. *Peek-a-boo!* You've been without a best friend for one day. *Peek-a-boo!* Two days. *Peek-a-boo!* Six days.

On the seventh day, I found myself sitting between my parents, surrounded by a cloud of black dresses, slacks, and shoes that resembled the chaotic storm inside my mind. And then, like a single jelly bean in a jar of black licorice, a lavender casket disrupted the darkness. As if its color alone could liven up this horrible situation. I had to give the Josephs credit for trying.

I spent the whole service twirling my new bracelet around my wrist and avoiding eye contact, with a *Kodak*-moment smile framed for all to see. The longer I thought about my friend's image plastered on shiny paper and encased in glass, the angrier I became. It was a single moment, framed in forty dollars worth of metal and paint, and somehow that was supposed to make up for a lifetime of *her*? I balled my hands into fists.

When it was our turn to offer our condolences to the Josephs standing up front, I tried to hide behind my mother like a bashful child. But that's when a glimmer caught my eye, and I forced myself to look inside the casket. Around the wrist of the embalmed version of someone I loved, was a bracelet that resembled mine. 'Best Friends,' it accused. I sprinted down the center aisle and out the double doors to empty myself of childhood memories and last night's lasagna.

*

My neck had grown tense, and there were strange aches all over my body that I couldn't explain, but even that wasn't enough to motivate me to move from the corner of my bed. The doorbell rang.

"*Dios Mio*. Tracy?" I whipped my head towards the sound of the front door opening and Tracy saying a tearful hello to my mother. "Tracy! How are you feeling?"

"Oh, you know, as well as can be expected. I've come to drop off Leni's sleeping bag and to say goodbye."

"So soon?" asked Mami.

"Afraid so. The movers arrived in Georgia last week and unloaded everything at our new place already. We were supposed to have been there to greet them, but a friend did us the favor. We can't stay here anymore. We don't even have a bed to sleep on. How are the kids holding up?"

Mami dropped her voice as if to let Tracy in on a secret. Too bad our walls were paper thin.

"Daniel has immersed himself into his video games, but I'm most worried about Leni. She hardly touches her food, and when she does, it just comes back up. She doesn't leave her bedroom. I don't hear a peep coming from there all day. Every time I go to check on her, she's right where I left her last, curled up on her bed, and staring blankly at the wall."

"That's terrible. May I see her?"

"Of course. But first, can I get you something to drink? I have some water bottles in the fridge."

"Water for the road would be lovely, thank you."

As Mami's footsteps grew fainter on their way to the kitchen, I sprang into action, struggling quietly to stretch out my aching limbs in preparation for my escape. I lifted my bedroom window as quickly and quietly as I could manage. By the time my mother returned, I'd slipped out, hugging my knees to my chest on the ground beneath the open window.

"That's odd," Mami said, her voice carrying out the window loud and clear. "I thought she was here."

"Did I miss her?" Tracy asked, the disappointment unmistakable in her voice.

"Can you stick around? I'll try her cell phone. I'm sure she'll be here soon."

The sound of a car horn sounded from our driveway.

"I wish I could, Marta. But Bill is adamant we make it over the bridge before rush hour."

"I understand. What a pity. It may have done her good to see you."

"Would you do me a favor?"

"Of course, anything."

"Would you give her this?"

"Absolutely. Are you certain you don't want to keep it?"

"Yes, I am. There's no use in us taking it to Georgia. It would only collect dust. Monica would have wanted her to have it."

A minute later, after Tracy had said her goodbyes, the front door closed. I peered around the side of the house as Bill's Nissan backed out of the driveway. From where I was crouched, he was almost unrecognizable without his trademark good-humored smile. Tracy sat next to him, crying softly into her hands. And then, they were gone. I waited a few minutes before hoisting myself up and through the window, only to be met by what Tracy had left behind for me.

Monica would have wanted her to have it.

As I faced the last of Monica's dreams, neatly zipped up in a bohemian-patterned gig bag, I was forced to face the fact that nothing could save me from my new reality.

I didn't blame the Josephs for leaving. Maybe in their new setting, they would have a chance to start fresh, to move forward. They deserved that. Even Mo's six-stringed instrument was moving on to me, the next person in line. And didn't I want to move on, too? So why did that feel so wrong?

And why in the world did it suddenly hurt so much to breathe?

Chapter 20

"Blessed is the man who remains steadfast under trial, for when he has stood the test he will receive the crown of life, which God has promised to those who love him."
James 1:12

Camp (continued)

Alex let go of my arm and ran over to Daniel's side, past Julian who was still watching me. I couldn't move.

"Leni?" Although I was looking right at her, when I saw my name come out of her lips, I jumped. "It's me, Tracy."

I nodded slowly, trying to let her know I understood. Without warning, she reached her arms toward me and pulled me close. I stiffened at the gesture. "You have no idea how long I've been waiting to hug you, sweet Leni girl." At the nickname, I relaxed slightly, the warmth in her voice flooding me with emotion. I breathed in cherry blossoms.

The familiar scent triggered a trail of sun-bathed flashbacks I thought I'd forgotten: Sunday lunches after church, Tracy serving her fresh-squeezed lemonade as Monica and I lounged by the pool in one-piece bathing suits and plastic sunglasses, Bill flipping burgers at the grill and cracking dad jokes for our groans and amusement, summer outings, Daniel tagging along to the beach or the water park, sand on the inside of Bill's Nissan Altima as we sat on old towels to keep the seats dry.

Tracy took a step back and looked me up and down. "Look at you! From a girl to a woman in just a few short years. I feel old."

I knew that this would be the time to jump in with some objection to her 'old' statement, but it was taking concentrated effort for me not to fall apart. I held my breath, fearing that one more whiff of cherry blossoms would send my molecules into derision, and I would be no more.

Tracy seemed to pick up on this because her smile faltered as she examined me.

"Are you alright, hon?"

"Is that little Leni!?" Bill appeared from behind Tracy, sporting a new scruffy beard along with his familiar smiling eyes. At the sight of the two of them standing together, I was suddenly sure I would flip. Whatever that meant. My eyes traveled over Bill's shoulder where Julian was now approaching, pushing a wheelchair.

"Bill!" Daniel exclaimed, breaking my awkward silence.

"Dani Boy! C'mere!" Bill's bear hug was enough to lift Daniel off his seat. Tracy tittered at the sight, a hand over her heart. "How the heck are ya?" Bill asked, crossing his arms over his chest.

"Well, you know. Rolling along."

Bill guffawed at Daniel's pun. I'd forgotten how easy it was to make him laugh. Julian grinned at Bill's reaction and extended his hand.

"Hello sir, I'm Julian Rossi."

Bill raised his eyebrows. "Well hello, Sir Julian." He clapped one hand on his shoulder while shaking his other hand. "You are a proper fellow, aren't you?"

"Not sure."

"Only well-mannered young men introduce themselves in that way. *That* or they're trying to impress their sweetheart's father."

Julian shoved his hands in his pockets and met my eyes, but looked away so quickly I wondered if I'd imagined it. Bill seemed to pick up on Julian's sudden change of attitude toward me, a knowing smile making its way across his face.

"A new friend plus a long-lost son and daughter that have come back into my life. Father God is gracious, and my heart is full," he beamed. From beside him, Tracy fixed her misty green eyes on me, as I pretended to be fixated on the red dust now sprinkled on my shoes.

*

Bill Josephs stood in front of the dinner line in the dining cabin, his arms extended like he wanted to embrace the whole camp. "I want to welcome all of our new friends who have come from far and wide! The Lord has amazing plans for your stay here." His voice projected through the cabin like a megaphone. "If you have any questions or need any help, please approach one of our counselors in purple. Nightly devotionals and testimony time start at ten thirty, so be back at your dormitories by then. Lights out at eleven. Tomorrow, we meet at Campfire Hill for morning devotions at eight o'clock."

"IN THE MORNING!?!"

"Yes, Mr. Salgado, in the morning." Bill chuckled. My brother huffed, leaning back in his seat. Annie patted his shoulder sympathetically. They would make a cute couple, but it concerned me that Annie didn't have a relationship with Jesus. It was at this thought that a twinge of guilt caused me to look down the table at Julian, only, he wasn't there.

*

We weren't supposed to have electronics at camp, and even if we did, our cell phones wouldn't pick up a signal for miles. Luckily for me, I'd found my mother's *iPod nano* buried in the back of her nightstand drawer. It had been a well-intentioned gift by Papi, but as far as I knew, she fidgeted with it only a couple of times before declaring the music downloading process "impossible" and giving up. I'd downloaded her favorites on there anyway, plus some of mine as well, but she'd grown bored of it, stuffed it in her nightstand, and forgotten about it.

Since I had my cell phone for music, I never saw a need to rescue the neglected electronic, but before going to bed on Friday night, I'd plugged it in to charge, and now, as I powered it up for the first time in years, I was really glad I had. Without thinking, I tried to swipe the main menu, before realizing I had to use the buttons instead. *What a dinosaur.*

With headphones hidden beneath my hair and the wire under my shirt, I made my way outside, following the sound of laughter that traveled just above my music. I'd walked for about five minutes before stepping into a clearing. Mark and Dakota threw a frisbee back and forth as Leah stood off to the side of the clearing, bouncing excitedly on the balls of her feet, *oohing* and *aahing* at their athleticism. Joshua sat at the edge of the tree line, watching them with a scowl. I jogged over and sat beside him.

"Can you believe them?" he asked, not bothering with pleasantries. I followed his eyes to the twins, now competing on who could jump over the frisbee first. "They don't go anywhere without the other, and care only about sports, but they still manage to attract the attention of the prettiest girl in our group. Meanwhile, I'm sitting here like a loser because I have no friends and no social skills." It was true that Joshua always seemed to keep to himself, but it never occurred to me that it wasn't by choice. "You don't have to sit next to me out of pity, you know," he said, throwing down a blade of grass.

"Pity?" I said. "Never."

"Then why are you sitting with me?" he asked, his brown eyes suspicious.

I examined a tiny ant as it crossed my ankle and disappeared under the grass. "Because I'm your friend."

His ears perked up at the word. "You are?"

"Well, maybe I haven't been before, but I'd like that to change that, if it's okay with you," I said. "I *do* care about you, and I think what you do for our Youth Group is important. You are very talented and someone worth getting to know a lot better." I watched as Joshua straightened his back a little and nodded. Our conversation was interrupted by a fit of giggles as Leah joined in the game of frisbee. I looked over to Joshua who was watching her too, an involuntary smile changing his appearance so drastically I hardly recognized him. My heart warmed at the sight.

"You should talk to her, you know," I said, bumping his arm.

"She wouldn't like me," he said. "I'm no good at sports."

"Who says you have to like sports?" I asked while swatting a mosquito.

"Society. It's in the manhood handbook."

I giggled.

"What's so funny?"

I clapped the bug into eternity before turning back to Joshua. "You are, Joshua. You are funny and techy and smart. You don't have to be good at sports to catch a girl's eye."

He snorted. "Right."

"I'm serious. What are your hobbies?"

"I like reading and I'm part of my school's robotics team."

"Nice. Anything else?"

Dreamer

"I guess I like watching TV with my sister, even if she *does* make me watch *Match Make Mansion*."

I grinned. "Lead with that."

"Really?" He seemed skeptical. If only he knew.

"Yes, really. Now, go get her."

"Now?"

"Right now."

Joshua still seemed a little unsure, but he stood up and straightened out his T-shirt, brushing off his shorts before taking a few steps forward.

"You've got this, Joshua," I called.

He didn't stop walking as he replied, "Call me Josh."

Chapel

It wasn't often that I sat in a service and didn't get something out of it, but when that was the case, I always felt guilty about it. Tonight was one of those nights. I kept trying to tune into the preaching, but my mind kept wandering to Julian.

In the past week, I'd been so consumed with thinking about coming to the camp and facing Bill and Tracy that I hadn't really allowed myself to think about him. Maybe part of me was trying to avoid the fact that things between Julian and I were different now. I could no longer imagine not having him around. The boy that I met on the bridge those few short weeks ago was so completely different from the boy that played the piano for me or held me as I mourned the loss of my best friend, or took me and my brother out for our birthday.

Everything I had thought about Julian changed within days of getting to know him better. He wasn't a thug. He wasn't a person who wanted to throw his life away, not really. He was intelligent, caring and real. I didn't know guys like him existed. I certainly didn't expect that he could be that kind of guy.

I thought back to our first night in Georgia and our conversation outside of the diner.

'Tell me now, Julian. Are you going to leave me, too?'

He'd stood wordlessly, with his arms crossed for what seemed like an eternity, before responding.

'Maybe.'

'Maybe?'

'Yes. Maybe. I don't know. I don't want to.'

'That's not good enough.'

'Well, I'm sorry. It's all I have.'

'No, it's not. You know there's more to it. You knew it at the hospital, you knew it when we recorded that song together and you knew it when you kissed me,' I said. 'Didn't you? Because there are only two choices. You either love me enough to stay, or you don't. Most people don't, and that's fine… but all I ask is that you let me know if that's the case.'

'I don't know what to say.'

'Then get back to me when you figure it out.'

The truth was that I wanted to do the right thing. I wanted to wait for God's timing and the person he wanted me to be with, but what had changed was that I also hoped, perhaps foolishly, that God might make Julian into that person for me.

The sun had set, and the night had grown increasingly dark as crickets chirped from the grass. I noticed little lights blinking in the trees. Fireflies! I walked past a few teens and counselors on their way to the Snack Shack before I spotted Julian standing on the side of the Chapel with his head down, his hands in his pockets. When he looked up to see me, he motioned with his head for me to follow. I did, allowing him to take the lead until we reached the top of Campfire Hill.

We sat side by side on a tree trunk, so close together that I could smell his cologne as the last remnants of twilight cast shadows on his complexion.

"There's something I haven't told you," he said. An owl let out a hoot from somewhere in the woods. The silhouette of the tree line was adorned by hundreds of little flickering fireflies. Millions of stars adorned the sky over our heads. Julian was waiting for a response, but when I didn't give him one, he continued to speak. "My community service hours were completed weeks ago."

It took me a minute to understand what this meant. "So, you didn't have to keep coming to church?" I asked. "Why did you?"

"How could I not? After all the things I put you through. First with my suicide attempts, and then with Calvin and Bianca." I gritted my teeth.

Dreamer

"And if *that* wasn't enough, I flaked on you during VBS, and your brother and cousin were hurt because of me."

It was true. I couldn't deny that. But none of that mattered now. Why couldn't he see that since he came into my life, he'd made things better? What would my summer have been like had it not been for him? I didn't realize how truly depressed I'd been until he came along and busted me out of my self-imposed house arrest. He shifted in his seat and swung one leg over to the other side of the trunk so he could fully face me.

"Remember the first time we met?" he asked, a small smile on his lips. "If I hadn't been completely on edge because of my break-up, I would have been laughing my head off at the sight of you flailing around, trying to keep from falling into dirty gutter water."

"Hey! I wasn't flailing. I fell quite gracefully."

He chuckled, and I couldn't help but smile. After a moment, he sighed. "What you don't realize is that I felt I needed to be hard around my friends, smart around my teachers, good around my family, and none of those things could overlap. But somewhere along the way, I lost sight of myself. Until I met *you*."

It was how he said it: a mix between tenderness and conviction that matched the earnestness in his body language.

"You're the only person I never had to pretend for, the only one who saw the worst parts of me from the get-go and stuck around. You were my friend when my own friends took off. When my family didn't understand me, you were the only one who really took the time to pick my brain, and not because it was your 'Christian duty,' but because you actually *cared*."

He was sitting so close to me now that I could admire the sharp edges of his jaw, the shape of his perfect nose and eyebrows, and the earnest honey of his eyes. His hair was without product and relaxed. I wanted to run my hands through it.

I bit my lip.

"I knew I shouldn't kiss you even before I did it," he said as if reading my mind. "I knew I felt too strongly for my own good, and I was right. Now anytime I close my eyes, I'm back in my bedroom with you." He must've seen something in my expression because he apologized. "I'm sorry," he said, "but I had to tell you."

I looked at the fire pit. No fire, just smoke, and dying embers.

"I was watching you and Alex this morning."

I raised an eyebrow. "What do you mean?"

"Seeing you next to him got me thinking about some things."

I thought back to the morning as well, to how annoyed Julian had been at the way I'd acted around Alex, and later, at our closeness, as we made our way to Daniel. Alex's hand had been on my arm, my face probably flushed from the heat and embarrassment of almost falling... how it must have looked.

"I don't really know him," I said. "He's a handsome guy, but I don't want to *be* with him."

"Well, I can't just sit here and wait for you to fall for someone else. I know it's selfish, but if you were ever to fall for someone, I'd want it to be me. But you need to be with someone you deserve. Someone who deserves *you*."

"Don't say that."

"Listen to me."

"*You're* the one not listening!" I said, agitated. "I want *you*, stupid. Only you I know you see me as this innocent little church girl, and maybe in some ways, I am... not innocent, but naive. About a lot of things. But don't you get it? I *have* fallen for you! Everything about you. The good, the bad, the frustrating. You're so much more than your mess-ups and your darkness and your pain. You are more than I could ever ask for, and I don't know where that leaves us, but I want to be stupid with you." I turned my eyes to heaven, "I'm sorry, God, but I can't stop the way that I feel. I need your help if I'm ever going to see Julian as just a friend."

"I don't think we should hang out anymore."

I felt my heart sink. He clutched my shoulders, shaking me slightly "I can't *just* be your friend. Don't you get it?"

"Yeah, Julian," I said, matching the tone of his voice, my hand on the nape of his neck "I get it ," I kissed him.

I was done feeling lonely. Done trying to do the right thing Done losing people I loved And I knew that here, in the cover of night, I had a decision to make When I pulled my face away, he watched me wordlessly as I grabbed hold of his shirt.

Elleni.

Dreamer

I slid to the ground, pulling him down with me, but then he grabbed me by my wrist and gritted his teeth. "Stop." My breath left me as I caught a glimpse of his face: hungry, agitated, helpless. His hair spilling over his forehead, chest rising and falling. "Please."

"I don't want to stop." I knew I sounded like a stubborn child, but I couldn't help it.

He growled and put himself out of my reach. "Once you cross this line, there's no turning back. You understand that?"

"Yes!"

"This isn't you."

"Why not?" I demanded.

"Because I love you. The *real* you." Julian sighed, his frustration giving way to defeat. "That's why I have to protect you from guys like me."

Stunned, I watched as Julian slipped his T-shirt back over his head.

"My grandmother used to say, if I gave my life to Jesus, He would fill me with light. But she never explained why I was so comfortable in my darkness. Why, when I had a death wish, I was so ready for it to consume me. Sometimes, I still wish it had."

"Why would you say that?"

"Because I could've saved myself the heartbreak of knowing you and realizing that no matter how hard I try… I can never deserve you." He rose to his feet and then, without looking back, disappeared into the night.

I had asked God for help, for self-control, for patience. I *knew* that He would have to step in if I was ever going to be able to see Julian as only a friend. But I didn't expect *this*. I never fathomed that maybe God didn't want Julian and me to be friends *at all*.

Tears began to well up in my eyes. I wanted to run after him, yell, ask him to come back… but it was no use. My tongue was paralyzed, and my feet couldn't be willed to move. In my heart, I knew that this was probably exactly what *needed* to happen and that by insisting on having my own way, I might only make things much worse.

I brought my hand to my mouth and let out a sob, feeling lonelier than I had in a really long time.

Chapter 21

> *"I form light and create darkness, I make well-being and create calamity, I am the Lord, who does all these things."*
> *Isaiah 45:7*

Tuesday

A cloud of pungent smoke hazed my view as a hand dragged me by the arm. His hot breath whispered something in my ear. I couldn't run, and I felt too clumsy to struggle. Lost in the commotion, I was relieved to get away, willing my feet forward, breaking through the crowd. I came to a halt at the sight of a body on the street: hanging from its wrist was a bracelet with two words: 'Best Friends.'

I sat up in bed with a jolt.

"Elleni?" Annie walked over to me while running a towel through her damp hair. She sat on my bed, her doe eyes scrutinizing me from behind her thick glasses. "You don't look so good."

"Thank God. It was just a dream."

"Sounds more like a nightmare. It wasn't real though." She patted me on the shoulder reassuringly.

If only that were true. I looked around, for the first time noticing that everyone else was gone.

"Where *is* everybody?" I asked.

Dreamer

"Oh, they're already at Campfire Hill. We figured you could use some extra sleep after last night. You seemed upset when you went to bed. Want to head down together?"

What I *wanted* to do was to hide under my comforter and sneak a couple of chocolate bars out of Amanda's emergency snack pack. But instead, I took a breath and braved a smile, replying with my most convincing, "Sure."

Breakfast

"Leni, come sit over here!" Selah motioned me over to her table, which she shared with Leah and Jake. I nodded at them before plopping myself down directly in front of Leah, who wore an embellished halter top with a tall neckline and glittery studs along the seams. Her strawberry blonde hair cascaded over her shoulders.

"Nice outfit, L," I said.

She flipped her hair confidently. "Thanks. I just think, why look ordinary when you can look fabulous, you know?"

Selah, sporting a V-neck and shorts, muttered, "Whatever" under her breath. Jake smiled, elbowing her on the arm. Leah shook her fork pointedly at us. "Okay, so get *this*. I've been talking to Josh, and we have so much in common. And then last night at Chapel, I caught him staring at me *four times!*"

Selah rolled her eyes. "And?"

Leah ignored her sister's tone, counting on her fingers. "First time it was nothing, you know? Except I noticed he has the prettiest eyes. Second time was during worship, which made me think, what purpose does he have for looking at me during worship?" She paused for effect.

"Right—" Selah motioned for her to get on with it.

"Third time was when Todd cracked a joke. Josh was laughing, and *I* was laughing, and it was totally synchronized. And then the *last* time it happened, I was already staring at *him*, and I guess the power of my stare made him look up 'cause he looked at me, and I smiled at him. And *get this—he blushed!*"

I looked over at Selah, who only said, *"Tsk, tsk, tsk"* and went back to her pancakes.

"*So*, I gather you like him?" I asked.

She dropped her fork back on her plate and looked at me quizzically. "Well, I was kinda sizing up the twins at first."

Jake sighed, shaking his head.

"Noooo!" Selah groaned. "Leah, that's *illegal. You're thirteen!*"

"But *anyway,*" Leah continued with food in her mouth, "I figured Josh is really cute too, and maybe he's just *shy.*"

I tried to give Leah my full attention, but my eyes traveled across the dining area and rested on Julian.

"So, what's going on between you two, anyway?"

I hadn't noticed how Leah had followed my gaze.

Selah hissed at her sister. "*Leah, that's private.*" I looked from Selah's apologetic face to Leah's expectant one. Even Jake had put down his fork to look at me.

I cleared my throat. "Nothing."

"Hey, everyone."

I turned to see Tracy smiling around the table.

Leah beamed at her. "Hi, Mrs. Josephs. Do you remember me, Leah?"

"Of course I do, young lady. You and Selah. How are your mom and dad?"

She sat next to me, as the girls filled her in on pastor and Sister Kimberly. After a few minutes and a change of subject, Tracy turned to me. "Leni girl, I hate that we haven't really gotten to talk, so I wanted to invite you to have lunch with me tomorrow. Would that be alright?"

I fidgeted nervously, fighting the urge to say no, but I'd come this far. "Sure."

"Great. What do you say I pick you up half past noon in front of this building?"

I bit my lip. "Okay."

"Wonderful, I'm looking forward to it."

She used her hands to push herself up from her seat and squeezed my shoulder before waving goodbye to the table.

A counselor in purple approached the table holding a clipboard and a red traffic cone. "Are any of you signing up to go to the creek?" She spoke with a drawl, not unlike Miss Josie's.

Dreamer

She was an angular girl with russet hair piled high into a messy bun. Her creamy skin was dotted with freckles as far as the eye could see. From her neck hung a lanyard with the name 'Juliet' printed next to a smiley face.

All three of us girls raised our hands. Jake took this as his cue to leave, pecking Selah on the cheek before picking up his tray of food and walking away. I looked around, wondering where Annie and Amanda might be. I spotted them at the table labeled 'Archery.'

Jake joined Julian and the twins at the table labeled, 'Kickball.' Juliet plopped her traffic cone down on the table. A paper was taped to it that read, 'Creek Fun!'

"Okay. Can I get your names?"

Juliet went around the table, jotting down names as we were joined by three more people. I watched her sashay her way around, with her back straight and a business-like attitude. The next person to join our table was a blonde girl in a camo hat who introduced herself as Macy, and her companions as Delaney and Nina. Delaney was heavyset with rich brown skin and hair that was braided close to her scalp. She had large dark eyes and an easy smile. Nina was slightly lighter and looked to be about thirteen or fourteen. She was thin with blue eyes. Her hair was also braided but piled up into an exquisite bun.

I was the last one on the list.

"Elleni," I said, "Salgado."

Juliet sounded out my name as she wrote it down, but, after blinking at it once, and then twice, her eyes traveled over her clipboard and focused on me, her rosy lips gaping slightly.

"Elleni?" she whispered.

"Yes?"

"Um…" she darted her eyes around the table, and when she realized the rest of the girls were busy with their side-chatter, she leaned in closer to me. "Can you come with me, please?"

She didn't wait for me to reply before turning on her heel and walking out the door. I looked around the table, but nobody else seemed to notice the sudden change in her attitude, and so, with no other choice, I followed her.

I found her pacing back and forth outside the dining hall. *Oh boy.* "Am I in trouble?"

Juliet stopped pacing.

"You were Monica's friend."

It wasn't a question. Now it was my turn to be stunned. "How did you—how could you know that?"

"She *told* me."

My stomach dropped. "But... how could that be?"

"She used to write about you all the time."

My mind was spinning, my thoughts drowned out by the sound of campers and counselors leaving the dining hall on their way to their morning activities.

"Come with me."

Once at the creek, our group was joined by another counselor that Juliet introduced to us as Yessica. Yessica was Mexican with curly light brown hair and a lighter complexion than mine. Her eyes were light brown. She encouraged us to take off our footwear and to wade in the cool water. I stepped into the creek, expecting to feel the familiar texture of sand, but was surprised to find that my feet were met with a much squishier material.

"Yessica, what am I stepping on?"

"That would be clay."

I leaned down, grabbing some with my hand. I made a fist and watched it ooze like reddish-brown *Play-Doh* through my fingers. Farther down, Leah and Nina, who seemed to have hit it off effortlessly, discovered a tree they could sit on and gossip. Selah, Macy and Delaney occupied themselves trying to catch fish with their bare hands.

Juliet came up beside me. "Can I show you something?"

I nodded.

"Follow."

She stepped deeper into the creek, motioning for me to do the same. With the water now chest high, we waded around for a little while, dodging stones at our feet and branches by our heads as we went along.

"My grandparents bought this property in the fifties," she said. "When they grew old and were ready to retire, they asked my parents to sell it to people who would use it for the glory of God."

People like the Josephs.

"Bill had an amazing vision in mind," she continued. "He and Mama T had been thinking about buying a property and starting a camp for years, and they came across this one by mistake. We never advertised it, but one

Dreamer

day, as they were heading back from a road trip vacation, they took a wrong turn, and guess where they ended up."

"Here."

"Yup. They met my grandparents then. Mama T was pregnant with Monica at the time, and Bill wasn't sure if this was God's will or his own, so they put their dreams on hold to return to Florida and give Monica a stable childhood near her own grandparents."

"Did you just say, *'pregnant?'* You mean Bill and Tracy knew about this place since before Monica was *born?*"

"Yes. Other people came along with an interest in buying the property, but none of them made an impact on my grandparents like the Josephs. So, of course, when the Josephs came knocking again after my grandparents passed away, my parents couldn't turn them down."

"I had no idea," I admitted.

"I don't think Monica did either," Juliet said. "The year the Josephs started making payments on the property is the year my parents told me that they had a daughter that was close to my age. They were the ones who encouraged me to reach out to her. We talked on the phone from time to time, but she loved to write letters." She stopped walking and turned around to look at me. "Most of them were about her friendship with you."

We'd reached a mossy tree trunk that bridged across the stream. Two canopies met over the tree, causing what appeared to indicate a dead end, but the water wasn't still. I was surprised to find Juliet taking off her glasses and sucking in her breath, then submerging under the tree trunk. There was some splashing as she emerged on the other side.

"Elleni, come on!"

I held my breath and followed her lead. It took a moment for my eyes to adjust, but when they finally did, I felt I'd been transported into a dream world.

"Where *are* we?"

Directly in front of us was a wall higher than my head, from which a tiny waterfall cascaded into the creek. As I walked forward toward the waterfall, the water became shallower. The wall circled around us in a horseshoe design. Grass covered the top, clusters of wildflowers creating a garland around the edges of the stream. Butterflies danced gracefully on the blossoms, their aesthetic wing designs as awe-inspiring as the blooms themselves.

Green vines draped over the neighboring trees, creating a beautiful canopy over our heads, which worked perfectly to shelter us from the harsh rays of the sun. I watched in awe as a family of ducks slept peacefully on the grass near me.

Juliet climbed up toward the waterfall and motioned for me to join her. I used some large boulders to climb out of the creek, to where she was. I watched as the pool beneath us became a crystal-clear vision, perfectly mirroring the canopy above our heads.

Floral scents followed me to the top of the ravine where Juliet stood. She stepped to one side, revealing a wooden sign in the shape of an X. It took me a minute to realize why the shape looked so familiar until I realized it resembled a railroad crossing symbol. As I stepped closer, I noticed some faint black markings.

"X marks the spot, right?"

I gasped.

The handwriting on the wood was as familiar as the phrase that had just left Juliet's mouth. There was no doubt in my mind that it was Monica's hand which had scripted the words on the sign, words that read:

The Spot #2

"I don't understand. That's Monica's handwriting," I said, tearing my eyes from the wood. "I thought she had never been here before."

"That's true, at least not physically. But when she told me about the place you two had in Pinellas Park, I told her there was something similar here, and I emailed her pictures of it."

"*Similar?* This is so much better!"

"Monica said you might say that. On our last conversation just days before she passed away, she told me exactly where she wanted me to put the sign. Mama T said she'd been working on it for a week. Her plan was to show it to you before she moved, but I guess she never got the chance. I believe the words she used were: 'I want this to be for Elleni what the Spot is for me.'"

I looked around at the scenery once again, my eyes stopping on the flowers closest to me. "Are those..." but I didn't have to ask. Juliet watched me as I examined them. I could tell by the color and the shape of the petals, I was looking at the Guaria Morada, the national flower of Costa Rica. "How did she do this?"

"She made a list. The Spot #2 had to have ducks, butterflies, flowers and running water. The last thing on her list was this particular flower. It wasn't easy to find, but I asked my dad to order some seeds to be imported from Costa Rica. I planted them myself after Monica passed away."

It made sense that the Spot #2 would be groomed for me by Monica's design. In all of its hues, its sounds, and its beauty, the Spot #2 *was* Monica Josephs.

I walked closer to the sign, reaching my hand out to touch it. That is when I recognized the two circle-shaped doodles, connected by the words: 'Best Friends Forever.' It was a picture of our friendship bracelets drawn to look like the infinity symbol. She must have worked so hard on the sign and the planning of everything, wanting me to be near her as much as I wanted her near me.

What in the world made me think that I could do this?

"Hey, are you okay?" Juliet asked, stepping closer to me.

"What?"

"Your nose is really red, although I can't tell if you're crying because you're still wet from the swim."

"Oh!"

Not wanting to seem weak, I turned my back to Juliet, pressing my hands against my eyes. I took a deep breath.

"Monica was an amazing girl," Juliet said from behind me. "Her loss took a toll on our family as well. I can't imagine what it must have been like for you."

I didn't respond. Too much time had gone by, too many times I'd said to myself that the worst was over. It seemed no matter how much time passed, Monica always caught up.

Chapter 22

"Have I not commanded you? Be strong and courageous. Do not be frightened, and do not be dismayed, for the Lord your God is with you wherever you go."
Joshua 1:9

Wednesday

The smell of lumber and fresh morning air wafted in from the open window of the upstairs loft. I reached blindly into my duffel bag until I closed my hand over my pack of toiletries. Swinging a towel over my shoulder, I tiptoed across the floor, stepping over sleeping bags and dodging backpacks and shoes, careful not to wake my campmates.

I was one of the first campers out of the cabin that morning, stepping out into the cool of the morning wearing a light hoodie pulled close to my body. The sun was peeking through the trees, and a light mist covered the spacious campgrounds. Florida was flat, but this camp was full of little hills and slopes that made it that much more difficult for me to fight my natural clumsiness. I didn't really mind it too much, as I made a game out of finding the most creative way to go from point A to point B. By the time I'd gotten halfway across the campground, my calves were on fire.

Tiny brown birds chirped from a nearby tree, and I prayed as a feeling of serenity came over me.

Good morning, Lord.

Hello, Elleni. You slept soundly.
It wasn't a question.
Yes, I did. Why can't I always sleep that way?
I gave you your dreams as a gift.
A gift. A gift? I thought about my dreams of late, most of them dark, all of them a constant reminder of my failures, my fears, my worst days. Memory mixed with sadness. My valleys.
In the mountain or in the valley, I will never leave you nor forsake you.
A door slammed to my left, causing me to jump.
"Hey! Sorry to startle you." Alex made his way down the steps of the Chapel toward me. "Mind if I walk with you?"
I shook my head no. We walked in silence for a moment, and then:
"Can I ask who you were talking to?"
I could feel the heat creeping up my face. "I didn't realize anyone was watching," I said, moving my hair over my shoulder. "I was talking to God."
I wondered how Alex would react to this. Would he think I was weird? I snuck a glance at him, only to find him gazing intently at the lingering colors of sunrise.
"This is a good place to do that," he said. "If you're very still, you'll realize just how *present* He is."
I breathed in deeply, knowing exactly what he meant by that. As we reached Campfire Hill, Alex excused himself. Bill approached me, Bible in hand.
"Good morning, Elleni! It's a beautiful day, isn't it?"
"Yes, it is. Alex and I were just talking about that."
"Alex?"
"He ran off right before you came over to me."
"Right. I'm glad to hear you're making new friends; that is one of the best things about camp. Would you like to help me throw in some firewood for tonight?"
"Sure."
Bill and I worked in silence for a while as campers trudged up the small hill to take their seats.
"Tracy and I were just saying last night how glad we are that you are here. So much has changed in the past several years, but having you around has been like having Monica again." For the first time since I arrived, I

picked up on underlying grief in his tone. "Did you ever learn how to play the guitar?" he asked.

From the corner of my eye, I caught a glimpse of Julian coming up the hill. His hair looked damp like he'd just showered, and he was wearing a white T-shirt and black basketball shorts. I could smell his body wash from where I stood, the scent carried by the wind. He caught me looking at him, and for a split second, I wanted to run into his arms, breathe in his scent and beg him not to walk out of my life. He broke eye contact and found his seat.

"Elleni? Did you hear me?"

I looked at Bill with a start.

"I'm sorry, what was the question?"

Bill studied me for a moment. "I asked if you learned to play guitar."

"Oh." I looked down sheepishly. "Yes, I did."

"That's fantastic. I hope you'll grace us with a song this week."

"Maybe."

Once everyone was gathered, Bill opened up with a word of prayer before handing the devotional time over to Dakota, who took to the front and opened up scripture to John 3:16. Usually a joker with his brother at his side, he seemed a little out of his element. We turned to the key verse with him.

"For God so loved the world that He gave His only begotten Son, that whoever believes in Him should not perish but have everlasting life."

When Dakota finished reading, he squared his shoulders, shaking out his arms as if preparing for a UFC match.

"We've heard this verse all of our lives, right?"

I looked over at Julian who, instead of participating in the scattered response, sat quietly, looking straight ahead.

"*We* have, but not everyone has. *Most* people in the world have never even heard of John 3:16." He ran a hand through his blonde hair, a faraway look coming over his face. "Everyone should go on a mission trip. My family and I have been all over the world. We've been to countries where people worship statues on every corner. Places where people are demonically possessed, many of them roaming the streets without clothes. Did you know that the Bible is illegal to own in over fifty countries? We've met teenagers and children who..." his voice trailed off. Up until this point, the activity among Dakota's audience hadn't ceased fully. Each word out of his mouth had been met with pages rustling, the scribbling of pens against the paper

Dreamer

and a bit of side chatter. But as Dakota paused, the words and actions of my campmates died.

We watched as Dakota buried his face in his hand, his shoulders shaking slightly. The silence that followed was uncomfortable at best. Mark stood up and placed a hand on his brother's shoulder. Dakota sat down, his face still in his hands. Mark squared his shoulders, much like his twin had done, and stood in the same spot he had just occupied.

"We heard word last night that some of our friends abroad were recently taken captive in Pakistan. We believe their captors are the same people who burned a house church to the ground last week."

Selah gasped, her hand flying to her mouth. Daniel, who up to this point had been throwing sideways glances at Annie, now fixed his eyes on Mark, his face twisted into a scowl.

"Dakota's penpal, Haris, was among the people taken. He's only fourteen. His oldest sister, Daisha, is believed to have been taken too. Their mother is in intensive care after a gunshot wound that barely missed her heart. Unfortunately, their father is dead. It was the middle sister, Aiza, who got in contact with us. She witnessed the whole thing but managed to get away."

There were times I didn't understand what God was doing. He loved Haris and Daisha, I was sure of it, so why would he let this happen to them?

Bill took to the front and placed his hand on Mark's shoulder. "Todd, Amanda, Tracy, would you and the counselors join me up here for prayer? Let's all take a moment to lift Haris and Daisha before the Lord and ask Him for His protection over them."

As I crouched on the dirt, the sound of praise and prayer floating up from all around me, the presence of God fell over Campfire Hill.

It was then that an image appeared in my mind of a slender young woman on her knees, her back to me, long black hair poking out from under the veil which draped over her head. Her feet were bare, and she seemed to be among ruins, but despite the chaos surrounding her, she prayed. It was then that my mind's eye traveled upward, as if through an aerial view, and beneath, I made out the girl, kneeling. From this perspective, I could also make out a young boy, his hands clasped with hers in prayer. As my view widened, I saw a host of angels surrounding them on every side. I looked to my left and right, only to realize that even here, filling the skies around me, were multitudes of heavenly beings with radiant faces, garments whiter than snow, and swords drawn.

The vision ended, and I hit the ground on my knees.

To my left, Josh was sprawled near my feet, face down, not unlike me. Leah, who up to a minute ago had been sitting at his side, now knelt, her arms up, and her face radiant as she cried tears of joy.

By the time our prayers came to an end, something had changed in all of us, and we knew that no matter what happened, God was in control. And *that* was enough.

Lunch

Ever since the morning's devotional time on Campfire Hill, a buzz had generated among the campers and counselors. Workers who'd started to look worn out by the week's activities now seemed to walk with an extra skip in their step, and each time I came across Bill, he was blubbering into a red bandana and praising God.

I wondered what had taken place in everyone's heart on Campfire Hill. At first, I thought they'd all seen the vision of Daisha and Haris, but as I asked around, everyone had similar accounts of the peace they felt come over the camp, but not one of them mentioned a vision.

I caught sight of Dakota, sitting quietly by Daniel. I sat on the space beside him. "Hey Kota," I said.

He looked over at me, his eyebrows slightly raised. "Hey."

"I was wondering if you happened to have a picture of Haris and Daisha."

Dakota dug his hand in his pocket and retrieved a red wallet. From it, he produced a photograph the size of a credit card. It was of him, a couple of years younger than he now was, in a group picture with his brother, a younger black-haired boy, and a girl with long black hair and smiling eyes. And I knew, without a shadow of a doubt, the girl from my vision was Daisha. I felt a peace come over me, and at that moment, I felt an overwhelming prompting to tell him:

"They're alive."

Dakota took the picture back from my hands, with a puzzled look. "How do you know?"

"I saw her, praying with her brother, right after Mark got done speaking."

Dakota swallowed, his eyes full of hope. "Are you sure it was them?"

"Yes. And God's protecting her and Haris. He loves them much more than we ever could." As another feeling of peace and warmth came over us, we broke into a grin.

After Dakota and I got done talking, he picked up his tray of food and went to join his brother at another table. I looked around, wondering where Julian had gone. I hadn't seen him since that morning before the prayer time.

"She blew me away. She *absolutely* blew me away," Daniel was saying now, his voice interrupting my thoughts. He was hunched over his untouched *sloppy Joe*, for once completely uninterested in his food.

"Do you think you might be overreacting a little?" I asked, finally turning my attention to him. Shaking his head, he lowered his voice as if letting me in on a secret.

"Leni, she's incredible! Yesterday during archery, she hit the bullseye twice! Do you have any idea how much hand-eye coordination it takes to pull something like that off? Not to mention her manhunt skills today!" He looked up to where Annie was standing at the salad bar, completely unaware of my brother's adoring smile. I tried not to laugh out loud.

"Did you hear about Annie after the prayer meeting?" Leah whispered from beside me.

Daniel leaned over the table. "What happened?"

"She got saved."

Daniel's eyes froze on her face for a full ten seconds. I recognized the look. It was the one he got right before challenging someone from an opposing team to a match: the face of someone about to do something either incredibly heroic or fantastically idiotic.

"Take it easy," I warned, watching in horror as he slammed his hands down on the table, drawing the attention of a few people nearby.

"*Daniel.*"

It was no use. He puffed out his chest, squared his shoulders, and turned his full attention to Annie, who by now had caught wind of the silence that suddenly fell over the dining cabin, all eyes on Daniel.

"Annie!"

She jumped, the salad on her plate spilling over the edges. "Yes?"

He swaggered toward her, commanding her attention with each purposeful stride before stopping just inches from her. "I *like* you. A lot."

The intimidation in her face was replaced by surprise, and slowly, delight. She moved her bangs out of her eyes, a small smile making its way across her face.

"I like you too."

"Really!?!"

"Yes."

"Will you be my girlfriend?"

"Yes!"

Leah gave her biggest, most wistful *"awww!"*

That's when we caught a glimpse of Todd, walking over to Daniel from across the room, his face formed into a scowl.

Leah's *aww* slowly turned to an *ooh*. Daniel's smile was now plastered on.

"Nice show, Dani boy, but you forgot one thing," Todd said, crossing his arms over his chest.

Daniel gulped. "What's that?"

"My permission. To date my *niece*." Daniel tried in vain to keep a squeak from making its way into his voice. "That was my bad, sir."

"So, tell me, what are your intentions with my sweet Annie?"

"To treat her like a princess... no, a queen! With the utmost respect. I promise to make sure she focuses on her studies."

"That all sounds very nice, but I've yet to hear if you'll be getting her to come to church." The two turned to Annie who beamed back at them.

"Absolutely. I'll be there." Todd raised his eyebrows as my brother broke into a grin. "Well then, I guess that's that! Oh, and Daniel?"

"Yes?"

"You saw what I did with that throwing knife yesterday?"

Daniel's smile dissipated.

"Good. You two have a nice lunch."

Todd turned toward the door, a mischievous grin on his face. That's when I caught sight of the clock hanging above the exit. It was time to go.

*

I waited outside the dining cabin as instructed. A few minutes later, I heard tires crunching along the road and followed the sound to find Tracy waving at me from a golf cart. I waved back.

She pulled up next to me dressed in jeans, a flowy blouse and sandals. Her hair was down and just past her shoulders in blonde curls. "Climb aboard, Leni girl!" she said.

"Wow, Tracy. You look beautiful. Was I supposed to dress up too?" I looked down at my faded T-shirt and leggings. My hair, though up in a ponytail, was undoubtedly frizzy. Tracy laughed. "Oh hush, silly. You are a beautiful girl no matter what you wear. Come on, we don't want our lunch to get cold."

We made our way past Campfire Hill and took a right down a little road I'd never noticed before. After a while of rumbling down the dusty path, a charming little cottage came into view.

"Is this it?" I asked in awe. The cottage was painted a light blue with white shutters and had a porch with a white veranda. The yellow door matched the large sunflowers poking out of the ground beneath the windows.

"This is home," Tracy replied. "Have you met Juliet? This cottage used to belong to her grandparents. All we did was repaint it." We parked in front and made our way up the steps. To the far right of the porch was a swinging bench with yellow and blue throw pillows. Tracy opened the front door, and we made our way inside.

The first thing to hit me was the smell; it was enough to knock me back a few steps. I hadn't expected the Josephs' home to still smell like their home in Florida. Most of all, the smell of their home reminded me of *her.* The next thing I noticed was the decor: seahorses, shells, starfish, and so on.

"Come on into the dining room, Elleni!" called Tracy from the kitchen. I followed the sound of her voice and took a seat at the white dining table. Each place was set with yellow plates and blue cups. In the center of the table, there was a vase with yellow daisies.

Tracy appeared in the doorway holding a tray.

"Can I help you carry anything in?" I asked.

"No, thank you, love," she said, sliding an appetizing piece of lasagna onto my plate. She paired it with a piece of homemade garlic bread. She then set down a pitcher of lemonade, the ice cubes and slices of lemon floating inside.

"Think you can drink this?" she asked.

"Did you add mint leaves?"

She smiled. "Of course. I'm so glad you remember."

D.S. Fisichella

I took a sip but was almost unable to get it past the lump that had begun to form in my throat. The familiarity of the drink, plus the smells and the Florida décor, were almost too much to handle, but it was lovely nonetheless.

We ate until we were stuffed and talked about our lives in the past four years. Tracy told me how before they started to build the cabins, when it was just her and Bill, she'd caught him fishing for their lunch in his tighty-whities. Before we knew it, a couple of hours had come and gone and we'd run out of things to talk about. I suspired happily and sat back in my chair, wishing for the millionth time that Monica could be here.

"She would have loved this place," I said.

Tracy smiled. "I think so too."

"I'm just so sorry. For everything."

"Oh, honey. I know it was hard for you to be *so young* and to lose your best friend so suddenly, but nobody blames you for anything."

"I never got to tell her goodbye."

"Monica loved you. She understood how hard it was for you to say goodbye to her. You don't need to apologize. In fact, the reason I brought you here today is that *I* need to apologize to *you*."

"What could *you* possibly have to apologize for?"

Tracy looked at me sadly for a moment before retrieving a well-worn envelope from behind the flower vase. She put it into my hands, closing her own fingers around mine.

"Forgive me for keeping this from you," she said, letting go.

I looked down at the envelope I held, the name 'Elleni' written across the front and framed by doodles of hearts and smiley faces. Just beneath was the number 13.

"I found it on her bed the next morning. It was her last words to you, honey." My jaw dropped open, and I began to shake uncontrollably. "I'm sorry I kept it all these years. I hoped it might bring some explanation for why she was gone out of our lives, but in my heart, I knew that this letter was only for your eyes, so I never opened it."

I turned the envelope over in my hands where, sure enough, the envelope didn't look tampered with.

"I was selfish. I didn't realize that in keeping this letter from you, I kept you from closure. To my horror, just months after we'd moved here, I received a call from your mother saying that you had made an attempt against your own life." Her voice cracked, tears spilling from her eyes. "I've carried around so much guilt because of that. If only you had received closure, maybe I could have prevented that from happening."

"Oh, mama," I said, throwing my arms around her. She dabbed her eyes with a napkin, straightening back up. "Leni, Papa Bill and I are sharing our testimony about Monica tomorrow night. It would mean so much to us if you would be there."

I fidgeted with my bracelet. "I'll be there." She leaned down and planted a kiss on my head before clearing out our dishes.

We rode back to the cabins in silence. All the campers were enjoying free time now, and I knew that if I went down for a nap, I'd have the afternoon to myself. Upon entering the girls' cabin and confirming there was nobody there, I shut the door and climbed up the ladder to the loft.

I tried in vain to sleep, but after ten minutes of zero progress, I began to pace across the floor, holding the envelope in my hands. After a few failed attempts to open it, I stuffed it under my pillow and continued to pace.

"God, I can't go back there again. Please don't make me."

Silence.

"Lord, that was the worst thing I've ever done, and you know I'm not strong enough to do this."

Nothing.

"GOD!" I screamed. "Don't leave me!" I threw myself on the bed in a fit of fear and fury, not wanting to remember, completely willing to forget.

Chapter 23

"For the wages of sin is death, but the free gift of God is eternal life in Christ Jesus our Lord."
Romans 3:23

Four Years Earlier

"Mami, please don't do this," I said under my breath, a smile pasted on my face. I looked over at Papi, who only shrugged, and at Daniel, who thought it was hilarious for our mother to be gesturing grandly with her arms and asking everyone at Solar Polar Ice Cream to sing the birthday song with her. We were turning thirteen… not *three*. How mortifying.

"Ready, everyone? Happy birthday to you…" She turned to us, a big smile on her face, and much to my discomfort, a lot of finger-pointing.

This isn't happening.

"Happy birthday to you,"

Everyone looks embarrassed for me!

"Happy birthday, Daniel and Elleni,"

It's almost over. Just hang in there.

"Happy birthday to you! How old are you now…"

NOOO!

As soon as we blew out our candles, Daniel made a dent in the cake to trace out his half, before plunging his spoon right in. Papi and Mami stared at him, halfway fascinated, and halfway disgusted by the display.

I shared my half with them.

Once we'd eaten so much ice cream that it felt like sprinkles would come out of our ears, we got in the car and went straight to Monica's house. I was looking forward to spending the next twenty-four hours with her before the big ugly move. I'd packed my overnight clothes and my sleeping bag into the back of Papi's car earlier in the day.

Even going back to the house to grab my belongings seemed like an unnecessary waste of time when we were just days away from getting torn apart until who knew when. I'd even been wearing my bathing suit under my outfit all day long, just so that when we made it to her house, we could go straight into the pool as planned.

SLUMBER PARTY

"You're here!" Monica was saying over the phone. My parents had bought me a cell phone for my birthday, and from the moment we left the ice cream shop, we'd been chatting about all of our plans for the night. Daniel didn't understand why we couldn't just wait until I got there to talk about it all. Ugh. Brothers.

Monica was running out the front door when we finally parked, and as soon as I'd thrown the car door open, I was met by a big hug, followed by a lot of dancing in place. Mami and Daniel got out of the car. Daniel plunged his hands into his pockets.

"Hey Monica," he said. "Happy birthday."

Monica turned to him with a big smile and threw her arms around his neck. "Happy birthday to you too, little brother." After a few seconds of uncertainty, Daniel returned the hug. When they pulled away, there were tears in his eyes. Monica put a hand to her mouth, "Oh goodness. Why are you crying, Dani?"

Daniel wiped his eyes with the back of his hand. "I just… wish you didn't have to go. You're like family."

Mami patted his back before pulling Monica into her arms as well. "Hi, princess."

"Hi, Mami. I'll miss you," she said, burying her face in my mother's neck.

"I'll miss you too, my other daughter."

Papi put down my overnight luggage and made his way over to Monica, extending one arm out for a side hug. Monica took it gratefully, resting her head on his shoulder. Papi leaned his cheek against her head, the sweetest thing I'd ever known my dad to do. "Cuidate, Chiquita." *Take care of yourself, little one.*

I wasn't ready for her to leave. I hated goodbyes, but I was willing to try to make the best of our last day together. After a dip in the pool and some of Mama Tracy's minty lemonade, we headed inside to change into our pajamas. Two bags of popcorn, one princess movie, and a jar of candy later, we finally broke out our presents for the other to admire. Monica *oohed* and *aahed* over my new smartphone as I strummed my fingers on the strings of her new acoustic guitar. I rubbed the strap between my thumb and forefinger; it had a piano key pattern. Her gift was perfect for her. We were both so happy.

"When are you getting a cell phone? I don't have anyone to text," I said, tearing open a *Twinkie* wrapper.

"Mom and Dad said we could get a family plan in a couple of weeks when we get situated. But don't worry. In the meantime, I can just write you letters."

"Leni, Monica, dinner's here!" Bill called from the living room. Monica and I met eyes and smiled. *Pizza.* Mo's favorite.

I preferred Mama Tracy's homemade lasagna, but when she didn't feel like cooking, we went for pizza instead. Monica and I raced to the living room where we usually plopped down on a dining chair, ready to eat, but this time, we found Papa Bill and Mama Tracy sitting cross-legged on the carpet in front of two pizza boxes and a two-liter bottle of soda. Mama Tracy smiled widely at me and patted the space beside her. I sat down. Monica sat by Papa Bill, who engulfed her in a bear hug before handing her a plate. Sometimes, I wished Papi was as affectionate as Bill. As always, I forgot to pray before taking a big bite of our dinner, and as always, Bill asked God to bless the food already in my belly.

*

Dreamer

I woke up to the sound of someone opening the back door of a moving van. Monica was leaning against the wall, one hand holding open a gap in the shutters. She hadn't noticed me stirring awake.

Once I'd blinked the sleepiness from my eyes, I saw something unfamiliar in her features. Her usual pale legs were tan and seemed longer in airy white shorts. Her blonde hair seemed lighter in color and almost angelic. She'd yet to twist it into a braid, so it cascaded freely down the back of her strappy pajama top, longer than I remembered it before. Everything about her seemed older, more graceful.

Monica didn't dress like the girls in the magazines. She didn't wear makeup or talk about boys. She was content being herself. I envied that about her. She held one delicate finger to her lips, a moment later running the back of her hand across her cheek.

"Are you crying?" I asked, startling her.

She turned her emerald eyes on me, and for a moment, I saw something there. Fear? Grief? It appeared for only a second, then it was gone, replaced by her natural smile, so convincing that I thought I'd imagined it all.

We dressed slowly, wanting to drag out our last day together for as long as we could. I slipped on a pair of denim shorts and a T-shirt, piling my hair up into a high ponytail. Monica wore capris and a tank top, her hair fixed into a French braid. Immediately, I felt self-conscious. Her outfit was far from extravagant, but she wore it like a supermodel. I looked at the full-length mirror still on her wall, my thick legs and wide hips hard to miss. Next to Monica's long, graceful features, I felt pudgy and out of place. Sometimes, I wished I could hide my curves a little better.

We got on our bicycles and rode to the flea market. It was there that we intended to buy gifts for one another with money we'd saved up from babysitting jobs throughout the summer. We walked through the stands, ogling the displays of everything from ceramic cats to custom-made T-shirts. It was then that Monica grabbed my arm, pulling me toward a row of tables.

"Look, Leni!" I did, and there on the tablecloth were bracelets surrounded by hundreds of trinkets and charms.

"Custom Made Jewelry," said the sign. *"You design it, we make it!"*

Monica smiled at me. "What do you think? Should we make some bracelets?" I surveyed the options laid out on the table before looking over at the middle-aged woman beside the cash register. She had long curly blonde hair with hints of white and grey. Her eyes were the color of the ocean on a stormy day. From her neck hung a large opal pendant on a silver chain, and her ears were adorned by silver swirls.

I waved her over. "Excuse me, how do we know these bracelets aren't going to break?"

"Oh, well that's a very good question," she replied, taking out a display. She had a ring on each finger. "We have several metals I assure you will not break or rust over time."

"Good," I said, "because we need these bracelets to last."

Monica winked at me. "What do you say we design each other's bracelets?"

"Good idea. You start."

She picked out the turquoise beads for me. "I always loved the way this color looked with your skin tone," she said. For Mo, I picked out the jade beads. "To match your eyes," I told her. The lady got to work on our bracelets, adding some additional flair with silver beads to match the color of the chain.

"Okay, ladies. Any charms?" the lady asked. Monica and I pointed at two charms laying side by side. One said 'Best Friends' and the other said 'Forever.'

"Which one of you wants the one that says 'Best Friends'?"

Monica looked over at me. "You pick first. I like them both."

I thought for a second and decided that I wanted the one that said *'Forever.'* It was a promise I wanted to cling to now more than ever. I pointed at the charm. Monica nodded, "I'll take the one that says 'Best Friends.'"

The lady finished our bracelets, assuring us that a screw clasp would be unlikely to break. It was shaped like a round bead with a pretty design. We took turns fastening our new bracelets on each other's wrists before paying and thanking the lady. We strolled through the stands of food, looking for the perfect pizza slice for lunch. It was then that my mental boy-radar sounded an alarm as I caught sight of a familiar perfect head of hair.

"*Monica*," I squealed, "look!"

I'd had a crush on him ever since I watched him skateboard past my street one day after school. He had long hair he constantly had to flip out of his gray eyes and just about the most perfect smile I had ever seen. Monica followed my line of vision before letting out a groan.

Dreamer

"Elleni, I don't know why you bother with that guy," she said. "He's had five girlfriends since you first started to like him. I really don't see the appeal."

"Uh. Only because he's absolutely—"

"Hey girls."

I stopped mid-sentence, turning abruptly to find Cal standing two feet in front of us, a cocky smile perched on his perfect face. He flipped his hair to the side.

"How's it going?"

"Hello," said Monica drily.

"You two live near Oak Drive, right?" he asked.

"What's it to you?" she replied. I elbowed her, finding my words at last.

"We're nearby," I said.

At first, Cal seemed amused by Monica's standoffish demeanor, but when she didn't break her glare to answer any more of his questions, he turned his charm on me instead.

"My brother is throwing a little party at my house tonight with some of his high school friends, and he said that I could invite some people over. Would you be interested in coming?"

"Yes," I said, a little too quickly. Monica turned a warning look in my direction. "I'd love to," I finished.

Cal grinned again. "Okay. I'll see you tonight. Party starts at nine."

I watched him walk away. As soon as he was out of earshot, I turned to look at Mo. "Can you believe it?"

Monica crossed her arms across her chest. "No, Elleni. I can't believe you."

I laughed it off. "Come on, Mo. It's our last night together. You should see this as a rite of passage: our first high school party."

"We'd never get permission from our parents."

I thought about this for a moment. "They don't have to know."

Monica narrowed her eyes at me. "Are you suggesting we *sneak out?*" I shrugged. Monica scoffed. "I'm not going, and neither are you."

"Don't talk to me like I'm a kid," I snapped.

"Then stop acting like a child!"

Her words felt like a slap to the face, but I wasn't about to let her see that. "I'm a teenager now. You don't get to act like my mom just because you're one year older than me."

"Leni, you just *turned* thirteen."

"So what!?"

"So, what if he tries something? He doesn't have the best reputation, you know. Do you know the kind of girls he goes after?"

"What kind of girls *does* he go after? Please, Monica, enlighten me."

"Gullible, insecure, foolish girls!" I felt my face drain of color as I stood there, fists clenched at my sides, on the verge of tears. Monica realized her mistake a moment too late, the anger melting away. "No, Leni—I didn't mean *you*..."

"Why do you care, anyway?" I shot back. "You're beautiful and thin. You've never had a shortage of boys looking at you." I felt myself getting louder, drawing the attention of people nearby, but I didn't care. "Look at me! What kind of chance does a fat girl have with a gorgeous boy like him? This might be my only chance to have a boyfriend!"

"You're beautiful, Leni. You don't need any boy to complete you."

My bottom lip quivered. "You don't get it," I said. "You're *leaving me*." Monica opened her mouth, but nothing came out. I pressed on. "When you're gone, that's it. No more friends. No one to share my secrets with. No one to tell me I'm pretty or to believe in me or dream with me about the future. How could you go? How could you not stand up to your parents and ask them if you could stay? You *know* I miss my family and my old friends in Costa Rica, and now, you're leaving, too."

Monica wiped her cheek. "I know, Leni. I don't want to leave you, but there's nothing I can do about it. I'm sorry."

I huffed. "Fine, but don't you see what I'm saying? Things could be different if I had a boyfriend."

"Cal is not interested in being your boyfriend!"

"Why not? Why is it so hard to believe that a boy like him could like me?"

"That's not what I said."

"You're just jealous!" I cried. "You won't have me following you around like a puppy dog anymore. God forbid someone takes your place. You know if I was dating I wouldn't idolize you anymore, and you can't stand it. You like being the prettiest, the smartest, the best one of the two of us. Well, when will it ever be *my* turn?" I ran for my bicycle.

I could hear her calling after me, but I pedaled away as fast as I could. I weaved through the neighborhoods, cutting across yards and speeding through back alleys until I reached my house, dumping my bike on the driveway.

Upon entering my house, I burst through my bedroom door and began rummaging through my clothes. I pulled out my best pair of jeans and a black glittery sleeveless blouse with a plunging neckline. When my mom bought it for me, she had made me promise to always wear a camisole underneath and a jacket or cover-up to keep me from showing too much. I ignored my mother's rule as I only grabbed the blouse and the jeans to hide under my pillow.

My new cell phone began to buzz from my bed, the screen lighting up. A text from Mama Tracy's phone:

"Leni, please call mom's phone. I would've come to your place, but she insisted on us visiting my grandparents and going out to dinner as a family. I'll wait for your call. Mo."

I had been so excited to talk to Monica when my dad surprised me with my first cell phone, but not anymore. I managed to fill the rest of my afternoon with TV time and bickering with my brother. I made my parents think I was ready for bed at eight o'clock, using the excuse that Monica and I stayed up all night the night before. I kissed them both before heading back to my bedroom, closing the door behind me and locking it shut.

I waited under the covers for my parents to retreat to their bedroom and for their conversation to cease. In the other room, I could hear my brother playing the new video game he got for his birthday. When I was sure no one was coming to check on me, I got to work with what little makeup I owned and a flat iron hair straightener. An hour later, I was slipping into my jeans and blouse. With my outfit, push-up bra, and full hair and make-up, I convinced myself I could pass for fifteen.

I turned off my desk lamp before unlatching my window, slipping the bottom upward and sticking my leg out to find with my bare foot the paint can I had placed there earlier in the day. I'd never snuck out before, but going through a window was nothing new for me since I often forgot my keys when I walked home from my bus stop.

I felt my phone buzzing in my pocket as I pulled my other leg through the window, reaching back in for my wedge heels before sliding the window quietly shut. It wasn't hard to guess that Monica was still trying to reach me. She was the only person besides my parents that had my number.

It was only two blocks to Oak Drive, and I made the trip easily, cutting through an alley and somebody's backyard. My bare feet sunk in the cool grass, damp from an earlier shower. My heart pounded harder as I got closer to Cal's house. It was easy to spot, as it was the only house on the block blaring loud music.

Through the front window of the house, I could see Cal from across the street. He was sitting on the couch looking bored with a can in his hand, surrounded by high school kids passing cigarettes around and some couples exchanging saliva. I balanced on each foot by turn, slipping into my wedges before taking a final breath and urging myself forward, across the dark street.

BEEP!

I jumped at the sound to my right.

"Move it, loser!" someone yelled from inside the car. I heard laughter as I hurried to get out of the way. Embarrassed, I looked back up at Cal's house, hoping nobody had seen. Luckily, no one seemed concerned with what was happening outside. Once I reached the open door, I stepped in with one final deep breath.

I looked around uneasily, squinting through a cloud of smoke. I had been around smokers before, but this pungent sweet smell was a different kind of smoke. I didn't know much about drugs, but I held my breath as I moved forward, just in case. No one paid any attention to me, until…

"Hey!" I looked over to my left where Cal stood, beer still in hand. "Aren't you the girl from the flea market?" he asked, a flirtatious smile across his face.

"Yeah, I'm Elleni," I said, feeling a little taken aback that he hadn't used my name. But now that I thought about it, I realized he had never asked for it.

I'm sure it just slipped his mind.

"Right, right, Ellen," he said, plopping down on the couch. I began to correct him, but then he motioned for me to sit next to him.

I stepped over some styrofoam plates and dusted off some chip crumbs from the couch cushion before taking my seat. He slipped his arm around me. I smelled sweat, beer, and body spray as he looked me up and down, more specifically as he looked down my shirt. I didn't know whether I should feel uncomfortable or thrilled that my crush was sizing me up. I pushed my panic aside, thinking I didn't want to seem childish.

"Here, have some of this," he said, passing me the can in his hand. I took a sip. Ugh. It tasted bitter. I started to give it back to him but he had already retrieved a fresh can from a cooler by the couch. I turned back to my drink and decided to down it. Cal looked at me from over the rim of his can and handed me another. Before I knew it, I was almost finished with that one too. Cal gestured at someone behind him, who handed him what was unmistakably a blunt. I watched as he took a long, slow hit.

"Here," he said, smoke expelling from between his lips, "it will relax you." He passed it to me. Already feeling fuzzy, I followed his instructions, mimicking his movements. My throat burned, and I coughed repeatedly, wishing I had water instead of alcohol. Cal threw his head back laughing. I started to giggle, the toxins going to my head. Everything felt surreal.

An hour later, I was feeling sick. I'd managed to eat an entire pack of *Oreos* by myself and felt it festering in the pit of my stomach. I turned to Cal to ask where the bathroom was and was met with his sticky mouth on mine. I didn't know what to do. I began to turn away but then I felt his hot breath in my ear.

"...my room. Come on, don't be a wimp." He was pulling me off the couch. I didn't want to go, but I couldn't get my lips to say what I wanted. As I stumbled forward, my head felt very heavy. I slurred, "no—" but the music was loud, and it was really hot in there. He pulled me harder. I wobbled, tripping over the trash on the floor. I started to pull away again, but he was too strong.

That's when we heard the deafening screech of tires coming from the open front door.

Everything stopped, and someone turned off the music.

"Call 9-1-1!" a girl screamed from the doorway. Phones were being pulled out, and beer cans hurriedly picked up as, for a moment, I lost Cal in the crowd that was pouring out onto the yard. I moved with them, relieved when the night air hit my face, bringing with it a gust of clarity.

"Did anyone see who hit her?" someone was asking. "I didn't get a good look at the plates!" I weaved my way to the front of the group and stopped, unable to register what I was seeing.

There, in the middle of the street, lay a body. From her wrist, hung a familiar charm bracelet.

"Monica!" I screamed, falling on my knees beside her. I placed my ear to her chest. Silence. "Wake up, please!" I cradled her face in my hands, willing her to open her eyes for me. "Please," I whispered, tears blurring my vision. "I'm sorry, Mo. Don't go," I cried.

But she already had.

I peered down at my hands which were covered in her blood and scrambled to my feet, falling on the grass across the street. I puked until there was nothing left. The sound of sirens was heard in the distance. Panicked, I kicked my shoes off and scooped them up, running blindly and sobbing all the way home.

I was awakened by the sound of knocking. My heart was pounding in my ears, and I couldn't remember how I had gotten into my bed. Mami's muffled voice came from the outside of my bedroom.

"The door is locked, *Mi Amor.*"

I slowly sat up, looking down at my clothes. I wore pajamas, my hair damp. *I don't remember taking a shower,* I thought while I unlocked the door.

Mami stood in my doorway with a tear-stricken face. "Leni, I need to tell you something," she said, making her way to my bed. I sat next to her, looking at the ground. "Your dad is at the hospital with the Josephs. It's Monica, she was hit by a car." When I said nothing, Mami continued, "She is with the Lord."

Chapter 24

"For I am sure that neither death nor life, nor angels nor rulers, nor things present nor things to come, nor powers, nor height nor depth, nor anything else in all creation, will be able to separate us from the love of God in Christ Jesus our Lord."
Romans 8:38-39

Thursday Night

"What's wrong with Elleni?"

"Man, I don't know! I found her like this. She hasn't even touched her food."

"Shh."

Julian cleared his throat and took the seat across from me, waving his hand in front of my face. I blinked.

"Elleni, are you okay?"

I didn't respond.

"Are you sick?"

I shook my head.

"*Okay*, well we are headed to the Chapel now. Wanna come with us?"

Finally, I focused on him.

"You guys go ahead. I'll meet you there," I replied robotically. He seemed unsure, but seeing that I wouldn't budge, he gave up.

"Okay guys, let's go."

The dream from the night before had been the worst dream of them all. I'd spent the whole night in and out of sleep, haunted by the scenes from my last day with Monica, unable to stay awake long enough to avoid dreaming altogether. When Amanda came to check on the girls in the morning, she found me with bags under my eyes, bloodshot from crying. Startled by my condition, she ran to get her first aid kit, taking my vitals as the rest of our group headed down for morning devotions and breakfast.

"I think it's best if you stay in this morning, okay? I'll have Selah bring you your breakfast."

Selah left my tray by the bed, followed a few hours later by Annie, who brought me my lunch, taking away my untouched breakfast tray. By dinner, Amanda was back, taking one look at the once-bitten sandwich from my lunch before turning her worried face on me. "Okay girl, if you're not going to eat in here, I'm going to make sure you come to dinner and eat with the rest of us. Plus, you can't miss Chapel again." She waited downstairs as I got dressed for dinner. Not knowing why, I reached under my pillow, retrieving the envelope Tracy had given me, and stuffed it into my back pocket before I could change my mind.

Back in the dining hall, I picked up my tray of untouched food, dumping its contents into the trash bin by the door. *So much for making sure I ate dinner.* I made my way outside, taking one final look around the campground before sprinting past the Chapel in a last-minute effort to disappear off the face of the planet.

My hair flew behind me like a black flag of defiance, my chest on fire as I turned the corner into the nearest tree line. Ten meters in, my foot caught on a root, sending me crumbling to the ground. I hugged my legs to my chest and shut my eyes as hard as I could before transforming myself into a tight, hyperventilating ball. *Now all I need is for someone to kick me into outer space.*

"Hello?"

Perfect.

Footsteps crunched on the ground nearby, a flashlight shining through the trees until the beam fell over me.

"Elleni!" Alex ran to me, kneeling by my side. "Breathe, breathe, *easy*—"

I mimicked Alex's breathing motions until my heart rate began to settle down.

Dreamer

"You had me worried I wouldn't find you! It's a good thing I was running late to Chapel, otherwise I wouldn't have seen you run over here."

"Alex, please don't make me go to Chapel. I promise that nothing good can come from it."

"Woah, slow down. What's going on?" I shook my head, rocking back and forth. "Whatever it is," he said, "God has *not* given you the spirit of fear, but of power and of love and of a sound mind."

I glared at the ground, my heart still racing, but my breathing finally under control. "I asked for His help this week, Alex, but He's been very quiet. It's almost like... like He's watching me with his arms crossed. Where is He? I need Him, Alex. Where *is* He!?!"

Alex dropped his head and gave out a heavy sigh.

"God doesn't work according to our timeline, Elleni. He has His perfect timing, and He doesn't need *our* permission to carry out His plans. Sometimes He lets people *feel* like they're alone to teach them that it's not *about* feelings. He doesn't change based on *anyone's* circumstances. He's always the same." I sat, sulking, knowing he was right and hating the fact. Begrudgingly, I took his outstretched hand and let him help me to my feet.

As soon as we made it into the Chapel building, we found Julian waiting by the door. Alex nodded to him before slipping back out into the shadows. Julian and I made our way over to two seats in the back as the music portion of the service was ending.

I gripped my bracelet for dear life as Bill and Tracy made their way up to a couple of stools on the stage. Bill opened up in prayer before asking us all to turn to Psalm 23:4.

"Even though I walk through the valley of the shadow of death,
I will fear no evil, for you are with me;
your rod and your staff, they comfort me."

"Eighteen years ago, my wife and I put our dream of starting this camp on hold to pursue an even greater dream: the dream to start a family. To this day, we don't regret that decision because every moment we dedicated to raising our daughter, Monica Grace Josephs, is a moment that has fueled our passion to serve the Lord in a greater way here and now."

Grace. How had I never known her middle name was Grace?

Tracy put her hand on her husband's knee, picking up where he left off. "Our daughter was our most prized possession. She was our perfect gift

D.S. Fisichella

from Heaven. By that, we don't mean to say she was actually perfect but that God, in His perfect will, gave her to us for a little while to mold us into the people that we are today."

Mold? Like clay in the hands of a potter? I didn't feel like God was molding me at all. All I felt was Him breaking me, but why? Why would He want me broken? Didn't He want me to *have* something to give? Didn't He want me to get better so I could *do* something for Him?

I don't need you, Elleni.

What?

I've broken you to teach you that I don't need you to do anything for me… but I do WANT you. I CHOSE you because I LOVE you.

"Four years ago this July, our daughter died in a terrible car accident."

I held my breath, bracing myself for what was coming next.

"To this day, we remain unsure about everything that happened before the accident, but these things we know to be true: on the night of our daughter's birthday, she snuck out of the house and headed to a high school party where drugs and alcohol were present. Clearly, somewhere along the way, our daughter was influenced by the wrong kind of people."

That's not true.

Tell them.

"Her father and I have no one to blame but ourselves."

How could they think that?

They don't know any better.

"We should have paid better attention to our daughter's needs."

God, I can't.

My grace is sufficient for you.

"We are here today, sharing our story because we want to warn teens of the dangers of following a path that leads to destruction."

I'm not strong enough.

My strength is made perfect in weakness.

"Sometimes, we think we stand strong in the faith, but unfortunately, our beloved daughter is proof that even the strongest Christian can fall prisoner to the enemy's tactics."

I started to get up to leave, but Julian put a hand on mine, a question in his eyes. 'Are you okay?' No. I wasn't.

In the mountain or in the valley, I will never leave you nor forsake you.

Prove it.

Dreamer

"STOP!" I shouted, rising to my full height.

I wasn't sure who I was talking to. The Josephs? Julian and his prying eyes? The Holy Spirit? It didn't matter. I just wanted everything and everyone to stop. Bill and Tracy were watching me, startled, as was everyone else in the room. Daniel and Annie had turned around in their seats, Daniel mouthing, 'what are you doing?' Leah was staring at me, wide-eyed, biting her nails. Josh, beside her, had turned his video camera on me. I'd forgotten the Josephs had asked him to take video footage for their promotional video.

I tried to take a deep breath but was finding it hard to breathe past the hollowness in my chest. "Please... Bill, Tracy, you don't know what you're saying. Monica didn't do anything wrong. I—" I bit my lip, it was now or never. "It was my fault! I AM THE ONE RESPONSIBLE FOR THE DEATH OF YOUR DAUGHTER!"

Tracy put a hand to her heart. "What—what are you talking about?"

I buried my face in my hands, trying to collect my thoughts. "The reason Monica was at that party was that she was trying to get to *me*. She'd tried to keep me from going, but *I* snuck out that night, *I* drank and smoked that night, and I was almost *raped* that night... but it was Monica, *your daughter,* that died trying to get me safely home." I didn't care that my words were coming out jumbled together or that my face was a mess of tears and snot. I couldn't hold in the truth any longer. "It should have been *me. I* should have died that night, not *her*!"

I watched as the Josephs stared at me, wide-eyed and speechless. Unable to stand there any longer, I dodged my way out of Julian's grasp, darting towards the door.

I ran blindly, downhill, faster and faster until I reached the tree line furthest away from the Chapel. I didn't care that every few feet I was stumbling over another large branch. I didn't care if I fell; I'd simply pick myself up and start again. I ran until I stopped hearing everyone's voices behind me. I ran until I lost all track of time and direction. I ran from my past, I ran from the truth, I ran from reality, I ran from responsibility and blame. I ran and ran until I'd run from everything and everyone but God.

Breaking through the brush, I found myself on the edge of the small waterfall, the large shape of an X marking the Spot #2. Through the spooky canopy over my head, the moonlight shone over the pool beneath. I reached frantically for my bracelet, unclasping it and casting it as far from me as I

D.S. Fisichella

could, into the water below. I heard it land with a splash. I paced back and forth across the grass, crying.

"Father, I know she can't hear me, and I don't know if I can ask this of you, but there are so many things I wish that I could say. So, if there is any way that you could let her know that I am sorry, I pray you will grant me that request. Please, tell her I am so sorry and that I miss her and love her so much!"

Overwhelmed with grief, I sat down on the ground, feeling a crinkle coming from my back pocket as I did so. Reaching for the source of the noise, I retrieved the envelope Tracy had given me. I opened it without further hesitation.

Dear Elleni,

You've reached the big 1-3 and, amazingly, after all this time, God has given me the privilege to be here to see it. *sigh* Today we fought at the flea market right after you gave me this beautiful jade friendship bracelet. I'm really sorry for what I said. I know you'd love to have a boyfriend to start off the seventh grade... but when I said that Cal wasn't the one, I didn't mean to make you feel like you weren't good enough for him. Rather, he could never deserve you, Leni. I mean that.

I know we've been talking about this move for a while now and we've talked about all the cool things we are going to do while we're away from each other. Like, how I'm going to learn to play guitar and you're going to learn to play piano, and one day we're going to tour the world with our awesome girl band. Haha. And although my parents gave me this beautiful guitar for my birthday, I STILL want you to learn to play guitar too someday... remember that it's a lot easier to carry than a piano!

But seriously, I know this is really hard on you. I mean, it stinks for me, but I know that for you it's even worse because you already feel like everyone you love keeps disappearing on you.

Since I got saved, I learned a scripture about love that goes like this:

"For I am convinced that neither death, nor life, nor angels, nor principalities, nor things present, nor things to come, nor powers, nor height, nor depth, nor any other created thing, will be able to separate us from the love of God, which is in Christ Jesus our Lord."

Romans 8:38 & 39

Dreamer

Did you read that? NOTHING can separate us from the love of God... not even death! I've been learning that Jesus wants us to love others and to love God. I love you, Leni. And if I love you with the love of God, don't you think maybe His love can keep us together, no matter what?

In case I don't get to say all of this to you in person or on the phone before I leave, I wanted to make sure that I wrote this down:

I know you said things you didn't mean and it's okay. You were upset and I forgive you. I just hope you can forgive me too. I'm sure we will work this all out and I want you to know it's in the past.

I'm going away for a little while and I'm not sure how long it's going to be for. But this I DO know: When I see you again, it will be like we just saw each other yesterday. You are my favorite person in the world. Thank you again for my bracelet. I will never take it off, after all, we are best friends forever, right? That will never change.

See you soon!

Love,
Monica.

I read it three times. With each reading, it was like a piece of the puzzle fell into place, and along with it, a piece of my heart revived. I rose to my feet, hastening to the place where earlier I'd thrown my bracelet. I couldn't see it from where I stood, and suddenly, I wanted to cry. But then, as I closed my eyes, I saw the bracelet in my mind, floating downstream to a place I may never be able to find it. Yet, in the eye of my mind, the moonlight glinted off a single charm which read:

Forever.

Suddenly, the image of the bracelet was replaced by a vision of a young woman in white, her smiling jade eyes unmistakable, her blonde hair blowing freely, and her hand raised in greeting. Her wrist, bare.

That's when I understood.

The bracelet, which was meant to signify our friendship, had become a shackle for my wrist, forever connecting me to the dead, and the guilt and shame brought on by her memory.

God never meant for me to be imprisoned by my past. Rather, He'd come to set us both free.

It was because of His Grace that people like Monica and I could come to know a love that defied human understanding, a love that knew no limits and no death. Monica and I were indeed friends forever because even though she was no longer *here,* I knew that I would see her once again as a result of putting my trust in Jesus Christ, just as *she* had.

Chapter 25

"Brothers, I do not consider that I have made it my own. But one thing I do: forgetting what lies behind and straining forward to what lies ahead, I press on toward the goal for the prize of the upward call of God in Christ Jesus."
Philippians 3:13-14

"I am so sorry," I said to the backs of the Josephs. They turned around, breathing a huge sigh of relief.

Back at the Spot #2, I'd had a moment of panic as I realized I wasn't sure how to get back to the Chapel, but after pacing around for a bit, I was met by the welcome sound of Juliet's sing-song voice calling out my name.

"I'm here!" I called back.

There was some rustling through the brush before she appeared, a flashlight in her hand. When she finally saw me, she suspired, wordlessly running to pull me into a hug. We walked arm in arm all the way back to the Chapel, where I now stood apologizing to Bill and Tracy.

"You had us *so* worried!" Tracy threw her arms around me as Bill wrapped us both in his enormous embrace. Juliet stood off to the side, a small smile on her lips.

Bill raised his head for a moment. "Juliet, get in here, girl."

Juliet put up her hands to refuse. "That's okay."

D.S. Fisichella

The Josephs and I exchanged a glance that said 'nice try' and together, we scooched over to where she was and engulfed her into our little love nest. She broke free after a few seconds and made a run for it, leaving us rolling in laughter. Something changed in the air, an unusual chill coming over the campground. I hugged myself, surveying the landscape. It was somewhat deserted, everyone already in their cabins getting ready for bed. A sudden pang of embarrassment came over me as I thought about facing the campers after the show I put on at Chapel.

"I know *that* look," Tracy said, coming closer. "Elleni Salgado, don't you dare let the enemy take away from the freedom you've experienced tonight."

"How did you know?" I asked. "Is that what they call women's intuition?"

Tracy's eyes didn't leave my face as she said, "No, honey. It's the Lord's prompting." She studied me for another moment. "He speaks to your heart too, doesn't He?"

"Y—yes, He does. But how come He didn't tell me what He told you just now? About the enemy trying to get in my head?"

Tracy smiled. "Maybe it's because He wants you to know that He's surrounded you with people who will help you hear His voice, even when your heart is clouded by doubt and fear."

"And on that note," said Bill, "we need to tell you something." He leaned down to my eye level. "We would *never* in a *million years* put the blame of our daughter's death on the shoulders of a little girl."

"That's right," said Tracy, "you had *no idea* what was going to happen that night, and Monica's death was *not* your fault."

"Or *yours*," I interrupted.

Tracy let out a sob as Bill slid one arm over her shoulders securely. "I think we are beginning to see that too," he said quietly.

Tracy reached for my hand. "We feel just *terrible* that you carried around that weight all these years. You *do* know that you are forgiven, right?"

"Yes, mama. I know that now."

"Good. You should head back to your cabin and get ready for bed, okay? Everyone needs to be well-rested to pack up in the morning."

"Actually," I said, another feeling extinguishing any sleepiness completely, "I was wondering if I could stay up for a bit to work on something for tomorrow morning's devotional."

Dreamer

The Josephs agreed to allow me to use the Chapel to do what I needed to do to prepare. I gave them one final goodbye before heading back to my cabin to retrieve my guitar.

Friday Morning

On the way to Campfire Hill the next morning, my guitar strapped to my back, I ran into Alex, who was wandering the campgrounds.

"Alex, wait up!"

He turned at the sound of my voice, a grin spreading across his face. "Good morning, Elleni. I am glad to see you looking so well."

"All thanks to you."

"Me?"

"You encouraged me to go ahead and face my fears last night," I said. He brushed it off with a wave of his hand and pointed a finger to Heaven.

"All glory belongs to God." We walked toward Campfire Hill together. "So tell me, Elleni. What will become of your friendship with Julian?" His question took me by surprise.

"I don't know. On the one hand, I really like him, you know? But on the other hand, he's not a Christian."

"God's ways are above our ways. The Lord was with Monica, even on the night she died. Do you believe that?"

"Yes, I do."

"In the same way, God has been there with both you *and* Julian from the very start. From the moment you were conceived to the moment you saved his life on that bridge... all the way up to now."

I nodded, temporarily distracted by the sound of footsteps and chatter coming from the cabins. That's when it hit me: *I never mentioned the bridge!*

"Wait, how did you—" I turned to Alex, but he was no longer there. I scanned the campgrounds, spinning a full 360 degrees, but he was gone. The events of that day on the bridge flooded back into my memory.

I remembered the sensation of someone's strong grip on my shoulder, pulling me back to keep me from falling over the edge of the bridge as I tried to save Julian's life. When I turned around, there was nobody there.

Could it be?

His mouth was full of scriptures. He seemed to keep to himself, conveniently appearing every time I needed guidance. And each time I had an encounter with the Lord, he always seemed to just *know*.

Julian walked up to me. "Did you lose something?"

I scoffed in happy bewilderment. "Julian, did you tell Alex about the bridge?"

"No. Why?"

"Good morning you two!" called Bill, passing by us.

"Bill! Do you have any idea where Alex is this morning?"

"Alex? Your friend you were talking to the other day?"

"Yes, the counselor."

"Honey, we don't have any counselors *here* by that name."

Julian opened his mouth, ready to protest, but I put my hand on his arm to stop him.

"Oh, *my mistake*!" I called back.

He shrugged. "Oh, Elleni, before you give your devotion, do you mind if someone else says a few words?"

"Not at all!"

"Wait," Julian said, shaking his head as Bill walked away, "what was *that* about?"

I smiled. "I'll tell you later."

Todd had spent the week as a main counselor for the boys. It was weird not seeing him at the front of the group like he was in the Youth Group, but between fishing, knife throwing, archery, kickball, manhunt, and every other testosterone-ridden activity the boys decided to participate in, he'd had his hands full. As he stood at the top of Campfire Hill ready to introduce the opening speaker, he looked happier and more at ease than he had for as long as I could remember.

"We have a special treat, everyone. I've asked one of our new family members in Christ to come up here and share his testimony. Now, he's been working on it since yesterday morning, and he tells me that he's never done anything like this before. Please be kind and attentive as he comes up here, and turn your Bibles to Second Corinthians chapter five."

I reached for my Bible and turned there with everyone else. That's when I caught my first glimpse of the upcoming speaker. He looked up and met my eyes, smiling his perfect single-dimple smile.

"Let's start on verse seventeen," he said. *"Therefore, if anyone is in Christ, he is a new creation; old things have passed away; behold, all things have become new."*

Tears stung my eyes as I heard him recite my life verse.

"My name is Julian Rossi," he began, reading from his notebook. "I am seventeen. Just a few months ago, I was dealing drugs, getting drunk with my so-called friends and hating my life. I had just broken up with my girlfriend, who I had caught cheating on me with my best friend, when I decided my life was not worth living anymore. That's when I attempted suicide. I almost succeeded, but a Jesus Freak stepped into the picture, and against my will, saved my life."

I remembered the first time I shared my heart with him at the hospital. The bandages on his arms, the anger in his eyes, the mocking in his voice. He looked at me again, this time keeping his hazel eyes locked on mine.

"She was persistent. I didn't know it *then,* but she was there on that day with a purpose. She was patient and faithful, and she didn't leave my side. Not when I made fun of her, not when I told her to go away. Eventually, I found out that she wasn't being phony or religious. She was different because against all logic and all odds, she loved me."

My breath caught. I knew it was true, but not just in the way he was referring to.

"I hurt her. I let her down—but somehow, nothing I did made her stop loving me. That's when I learned that it wasn't *her* pursuing me, but God pursuing me *through* her." His voice broke. "I'd heard about Jesus before, but I'd never seen Him being lived out the way that I saw it through her life. The more I got to know her world, the more I started to meet other people that held to the same faith."

The peace in him was unmistakable. The joy. The pure, unadulterated love.

"I didn't understand it, and there were times I did everything in my power to run from it."

I remembered.

"I knew God was calling to me. I wanted what she had, what the people at the Church had, but I felt so undeserving, that is until I learned that it was never *about* me." He closed his notebook and took a step forward. "It's all about *Him* and what *He* did on the cross for sinners just like me."

"Amen!" shouted Bill.

"He drew me to him. He gave me the desire to know Him and the ability to believe in Him, and it's because of those facts that I finally called on Him. Once I did, God gave me eternal life through Jesus Christ, His Son."

I watched as Leah and Selah rose to their feet, followed by Jake and Josh. Daniel and Annie followed suit, as did Mark and Dakota. Todd, Amanda, Bill, and Tracy exchanged hugs, and even those campers whose names I hadn't learned stood to their feet and clapped. I was among them, praising God in my heart for the work He had done in Julian's life not just this week, but his whole life, leading him to this place.

I thought about Miss Josie praying for Julian, hinting this could happen. I thought about Alex asking about what would become of my friendship with him. He must have known. He must have been one of the angels rejoicing over this sinner repenting. I laughed, wishing Monica was here to see this.

Julian approached me with a smile and simply said, "Thank you," before sliding his arms around me. I returned the embrace, burying my face in his chest, my ear to his heart. There was no music sweeter.

He looked after me as I let go and situated myself at the front, turning in my Bible to Philippians 3:13 and 14 and instructing everyone else to do the same.

"*...Forgetting those things which are behind and reaching forward to those things which are ahead, I press toward the goal for the prize of the upward call of God in Christ Jesus.*"

Looking around Campfire Hill, I took in the faces of the people that I had learned to love so much. I'd spent the last four years trying to hide from their friendships, afraid to get too close, but in less than a week, I could confidently say that I had a large family surrounding me once again. They may not be from Costa Rica, but we were related by blood, nevertheless. The blood of Christ.

"There have been few times in my life when I felt truly *triumphant*. In my mind, the triumph was all about winning the gold, but in holding that kind of mindset, I missed the most important part of the race: *The Journey*. Paul encourages us to run our race with patience in the book of Hebrews, and I think this is because he understood that the victory was not just in getting to the finish line. The victory is also in the method by which we get there. We are called to leave the past behind and press forward toward the prize, our calling in Christ Jesus."

I looked at my brother, his arm draped around Annie's shoulders, tears in his eyes.

"For years, I carried a burden that I should have left at the foot of the cross the moment He saved my soul. Last night, I *finally* laid that burden down, and today, I want to finish out this morning's devotions by encouraging you to do the same."

Bill and Tracy looked at each other lovingly.

"Whatever burden you brought to camp with you this week, lay it down at the feet of Jesus. It is only when you lay your burden down that you can truly fix your eyes on the finish line and appreciate every step along the way."

I turned my back on the crowd to retrieve Monica's last earthly possession.

"I would like to share with you a song that I wrote in memory of my best friend, Monica Grace Josephs."

After struggling the entire summer to write the hardest song I'd ever had to write, I finally did it, surprised at how easily it came, like a well-rehearsed dance, once the truth was out in the open for everyone to see.

I held Monica's guitar in my arms, knowing there was no better way to remember my friend than in song, a song as effortless and free as she now was.

Someday
Words failed me for years, this much was true
You had no way to know how God was using you
I wish you were here, 'cause I have things to say
I miss you, my friend, but I'll see you someday

Someday, when the water as clear as the sky
Will crash on the shoreline, a sweet lullaby
A paradise, holy, the place you now live
Beholding the Father, all praises to give

A family reunion, with brothers and friends
Fellowship music where love never ends
Where children and angels all dance as they meet

D.S. Fisichella

To sing their Hosannas at our Savior's Feet

Someday, when the water as clear as the sky
Will crash on the shoreline, a sweet lullaby
A paradise, holy, the place you now live
Beholding the Father, all praises to give.

*

"Hey slackers! Where have you been?" My brother and Julian approached Annie and me after devotions.

"Who are you calling a slacker?" Annie challenged. My brother broke into a grin as he put his arm around her.

"Woah, cool it with the sappiness," Julian joked. I laughed as Daniel made a mocking face at us, leading a giggling Annie away to the dining hall for breakfast.

"Hello," I said to Julian. He smiled sweetly at me, plunging his hands in his pockets.

"Shall we walk together?" he asked.

"Okay."

We walked quietly, waving at fellow campers as they passed us, and enjoying the fresh air and the closeness we shared. It seemed that for the first time since we met, there was no tension between us: All was well with Julian and Elleni.

We approached the dining cabin. Going up the ramp, Julian let me get in line in front of him. After we received our meals, we sat down across from Daniel, Annie, and the rest of our friends, where we spent our last Grace Place meal praising God together.

These are my new truths:
I am fully loved, forgiven, and accepted by God.
Someday, I will see my best friend again, and
I love a boy, a boy who now loves the Lord.

Whether or not being with Julian is ultimately God's will for our friendship, I don't know for certain, but I am at ease, knowing our story isn't over and Jesus can be trusted to finish what He has so perfectly started.

As for me?

I will live for the Lord, free of shame, anxiety, and the pain that once plagued my past, because I am a new creation.

Dreamer

With the Holy Spirit's help, and a new song in my heart, I have the rest of my life to discover my true identity:

That of a dreamer...

In every sense of the word.

THE END

"For all have sinned and fall short of the glory of God."
Romans 3:23

Dear Reader,

Have you ever done or said something you wish you could take back? When we do something that goes against God and is offensive to Him, that is called sin. I sin every day, how about you? Maybe you consider yourself to be a pretty good person. Most of us would agree that we're not as bad as____ (fill in the blank). By our own standards we're usually okay people, but what would you do if God judged you by His standards and not yours?

Let's take a little quiz to see if you are 'good' enough to get to Heaven.

1. Have you ever cared about anyone or anything more than God?
2. Have you ever worshipped someone else other than God? Maybe yourself?
3. Have you ever used His name as a cuss word?
4. Have you ever neglected to keep the Sabbath Day holy, or to go to Church?
5. Have you ever dishonored your mom and dad?
6. Have you ever killed someone? If not, have you ever hated someone or been angry at them for no good reason? Jesus said it's the same thing!
7. Have you ever cheated on your spouse or even lusted after someone by the way they look?
8. Have you ever stolen something?
9. Have you lied?
10. Have you been jealous that someone had something you didn't?

D.S. Fisichella

If God was to judge you by the ten commandments would you be innocent or guilty?

'Well, guilty. But, D.S. my God would never send someone to Hell'

Maybe your God wouldn't, but there is only One True God, the God of the Bible, and by His standards, if you even break ONE commandment, you deserve to go to Hell.

> *"For whoever keeps the whole law but fails in one point has become guilty of all of it." James 2:10*

God's standard is PERFECTION.

God is a Judge, His commandments are the law, and you have a guilty verdict and are on your way to death row (Hell). That's the bad news. But here's the best news:

The Judge's son has come into the courtroom and said, "I'll do it, Dad. I'll take their place."

Jesus is the Way, the Truth, and the Life and NO ONE comes to the Father but by Him! He died on that cross and was placed in a tomb, but three days later He rose again and is at this very moment seated at the right hand of the Father in Heaven!

Jesus Christ is victorious over death and Hell and He is willing and able to give you Eternal Life if you let go of thinking you can do it on your own, and place your faith in Him instead.

When you do that, not only does God not give you what you deserve (Hell), and pardon you. He goes as far as to adopt you into His family.

Dreamer

Are you ready to give your life to Christ?

If so:

1. Repent: that means change your mind about your sin and agree with God that you are in need of His grace and forgiveness, and

2. Believe and CALL upon the name of the Lord Jesus and ask Him to be YOUR Lord and Savior. He will wash away your sins with His blood, and your heart will be made white as snow.

Holy Father,

I pray for this dear one today. I ask that you meet them where they are at this very moment. Lord, you know their needs even before they voice them, but most importantly, you know the state of their hearts and whether or not they are in right standing with you. I ask you, Lord Jesus, to draw them to yourself. I ask that you will call them by their name and that they may be adopted into Your family. Father, bring hope and healing into their lives as a consequence of them putting their Trust in You. May it have been an act of mercy that you have placed this message into their hands today. Your will be done, Holy One. It's in Jesus' name that I pray, Amen.

> For "everyone who calls on the name of the
> Lord will be saved." Romans 10:13

If you have any questions or you want to share your story with me, please don't hesitate to contact me through social media or my website.

With Love,

D.S. Fisichella

Printed in Great Britain
by Amazon